"Meredith's ex-hu...
    Max said softly.

He spoke as though two-year-old Caleb might hear and understand what Max was saying.

"He brutalized her," Max went on. "And got away with it because of the power his position gave him. I gather he had a pretty impressive record with the Las Vegas police. I know he was older than her. Her family—both parents and a brother—were killed in a car accident when Meri was a kid. She was alone in the world. She married him at eighteen, and the first time he hit her was less than a year later. She stayed with him nine years."

He would've felt disloyal telling Meri's secrets if Chantel had been just a friend. But she was a cop. And would help him find Meri.

"It took Steve less than three months to track her down the first time she left. He was still a Las Vegas detective back then. She got away almost immediately and managed to elude him for about a year that second time."

"This guy's determined." Chantel sounded serious. All cop. And Max took his first easy breath in more than twenty-four hours.

Hold on, Meri.

Help is on the way.

Dear Reader,

Sometimes circumstances trap us in situations that defy logical solutions. The "right" things have all been tried. They've all failed. And the human spirit—hope—suffers.

But, always, there is a force that's stronger than logic. Stronger than anything the human mind can conjure up. That force resides in the human spirit; it's there, waiting to spring into action. All it needs is for us to let it go—to set it free to work.

And, always, one of the hardest things to do is give in to the intangible, the often illogical *something* inside us—to trust it and follow its dictates. Sometimes we lose hope and settle for a situation that isn't ideal.

Sometimes, though, trusting that far-too-quiet inner voice is the only way we'll survive.

Husband by Choice is the story of one such situation. And the woman who thought herself weak, but who's actually strong enough to listen to her heart, to act on the instinct inside her even though it drives her straight into danger. This story is fiction. I don't recommend that any woman face violence on her own. I do, however, fully embrace every woman's right to live by her heart. To fight for that right. And to know ultimate joy.

May we all be a part of the sisterhood shared by the special women who come and go at The Lemonade Stand!

I love to hear from my readers. Please connect with me on Facebook, Twitter, Pinterest and Instagram, visit me at www.tarataylorquinn.com or write to staff@tarataylorquinn.com.

Tara Taylor Quinn

TARA TAYLOR QUINN

—

Husband by Choice

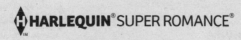
HARLEQUIN® SUPER ROMANCE®

Recycling programs
for this product may
not exist in your area.

ISBN-13: 978-0-373-60872-0

HUSBAND BY CHOICE

Printed in U.S.A.

www.Harlequin.com

ABOUT THE AUTHOR

With sixty-eight original novels, published in more than twenty languages, Tara Taylor Quinn is a *USA TODAY* bestselling author. She is a winner of the 2008 National Reader's Choice Award, four-time finalist for an RWA RITA® Award, a finalist for the Reviewer's Choice Award, the Bookseller's Best Award and the Holt Medallion, and appears regularly on Amazon bestseller lists. Tara Taylor Quinn is a past president of Romance Writers of America and served for eight years on its board of directors. She is in demand as a public speaker and has appeared on television and radio shows across the country, including *CBS Sunday Morning*. Tara is a spokesperson for the National Domestic Violence Hotline, and she and her husband, Tim, sponsor an annual in-line skating race in Phoenix to benefit the fight against domestic violence.

When she's not at home in Arizona with Tim and their canine owners, Jerry Lee and Taylor Marie, or fulfilling speaking engagements, Tara spends her time traveling and in-line skating.

Books by Tara Taylor Quinn

HARLEQUIN SUPERROMANCE

SINGLE TITLE

EVERLASTING LOVE

HARLEQUIN MIRA

*Shelter Valley Stories
‡Chapman Files
^It Happened in
 Comfort Cove
+Where Secrets are Safe

Other titles by this author available in ebook format.

For Adam. I pray that you are, now and forever, my daughter's "Max."

CHAPTER ONE

"SHA SHA, MAMA. Sha sha! Geen, Go! Geen, Go!"

Easing her foot slowly off the brake as the traffic signal turned from red to green, Meredith Smith Bennet tuned out Caleb's chatter because she had to.

And took comfort from it at the same time. The blond-haired toddler, strapped into his car seat behind her, kicked his feet repeatedly with glee. *Sha sha*—French fries. That was all it took for him to be happy. The anticipation of a French fry.

With a glance in the rearview mirror, keeping the small green car four vehicles back in the other lane in sight, she turned left at the familiar Santa Raquel corner.

"Sha sha, Mama! Sha sha!"

She'd promised Caleb French fries at his favorite fast food place—a treat on the one day a week he had to spend an afternoon at day care—and he'd had his eye on the Golden Arches where they'd been heading before she'd been forced to turn off the main drag.

"Sha shaaaaa!"

Instead of excitement, she heard the beginning of tears in his voice as the arches disappeared from view. The green car had made an illegal right turn, cutting off another vehicle to cross over two lanes.

"I know, Caleb," she said. Her son was not going to suffer. Or know fear. Not by her hand. "In a minute," she said, keeping her voice light and cheerful—her husband's description of her "mommy" voice. A voice he was certain he'd never tire of hearing.

But he'd also been certain that Steve was in the past.

"Mama's going a different way," she continued, changing lanes without a signal and making a quick left turn the second she saw the chance.

As luck would have it, she was able to cross three lanes and make a right and then another left turn before the not new, not old, not big and not particularly small green car with the black-haired man behind the wheel could follow.

She'd lost him.

For now.

PEDIATRICIAN MAX BENNET was finishing up his afternoon's charting, listening to the chatter of the front office staff in the clinic he shared with several other family physicians. His private cell phone buzzed at his hip.

Last he'd spoken to his wife, she'd been leaving to take Caleb for French fries on his way to day care. But Meri knew his last patient, a four-year-old needing a well-check, had been at three. She probably needed him to stop for milk on the way home. Or vanilla wafers. Caleb was addicted to them. And since they were the only sweets the little guy was allowed....

The caller wasn't his wife of three years. It was Caleb's day care.

"I'm sorry to bother you, Dr. Bennet, but Mrs. Bennet isn't here yet and Caleb's not happy. He's been upset since she dropped him off, but it's gotten steadily worse. He's crying so hard he just threw up."

He and Meredith had disagreed on the whole day care thing. He'd thought it was important that Max be integrated. She'd wanted to keep the toddler with her or a private sitter.

She was paranoid about safety. With good reason.

But Caleb had grown too attached to them—the separation anxiety he was experiencing was, in part, their fault.

They couldn't let Meri's fears paralyze their son.

"It's three-forty-five," he said, glancing at the clock on his wall—a Seth Thomas he and Meri had purchased together at a little shop in Carmel. "What time did she say she'd be back?"

"Technically she's not due until four but when he was so upset at her leaving, she said she'd be back by three."

It got earlier every week. "What time did she drop him off?"

"One."

They'd gone from one full day a week to one half day. And now it was down to two hours?

Still, it wasn't like Meri to be late collecting their son. Ever.

"Mrs. Bennet had a client this afternoon," he told the woman on the phone. "I suspect she ran over. I'll be done here in another fifteen minutes or so and will stop by there on my way home. If she shows up in the meantime, have her wait for me, will you?"

They'd have to talk about increasing Caleb's time at day care again. Later. Maybe over a glass of wine. When Meri was relaxed.

"Yes, sir. What do you want me to do with him in the meantime?"

"Tell him to go play," Max said. He supposed he sounded harsh. But his son had to learn to cope away from his mother's watchful eye.

At two years of age, Caleb was showing no signs of asserting his own independence.

Clicking to end his call, Max dropped his phone to his desk. And closed the file on his laptop. He wasn't going to get any more work done. Might as well pack up and get Caleb.

But first, he put in a call to his wife. She wouldn't answer if she was still in session with the little boy who had Down syndrome. His parents had hired her for private therapy one day a week in addition to the speech pathology work she did with him at the elementary school where she worked part-time.

Not surprised when she didn't pick up—if she was out of session, she'd be getting Caleb—he put his cell phone in the breast pocket of his lab coat and headed out to the minivan he'd purchased when they'd found out they were expecting Caleb.

He pretended that he was as relaxed as he knew he should be. Meri was fine. There was nothing to worry about.

Trouble was he'd told himself that once before—in another lifetime. About another woman. His first wife.

And he'd been wrong.

She hadn't been fine at all.

She'd been dead.

WAVING GOODBYE TO DEVON, who stood with his mother in the doorway to their home, Meredith hurried to her white minivan, a much less posh version of the one Max drove—her choice because she didn't like to stand out or attract attention. With the remote entry device in the palm of her hand, her finger poised over the panic button, she waited until she was in front of the car, with a view of both sides of the vehicle, ensuring there was no one there waiting to jump in one door as she climbed in the other, and then, pushed the unlock button.

Ten seconds later she was safely inside with the

doors locked. Mrs. Wright, Devon's mother, was just closing their front door.

Adjusting her rearview mirror, she stole a panoramic glance of the road behind her. No green vehicles. No vehicles in the street at all.

And no one sitting in a car in a driveway that she could see.

No one loitering in the yards or on the sidewalks or the street.

Nothing suspicious looking at all.

Unless the absence of human life outside was suspicious....

Starting the van, she slowly pulled away from the curb. She was late. She'd told the day care she'd be there to pick Caleb up at three. But technically, based on the agreement she'd made with Max, she was supposed to leave Caleb at Let's Pal Around until four.

She'd told her husband she'd try to leave him that long but hadn't expected to succeed. Today, thanks to the new at-home client and the many questions his mother had asked, she just might make it. She just might manage to leave Caleb at day care for the full three hours.

The important thing to do right then was act as if everything was normal. Get Caleb. Go home. Have a normal evening.

And find a way to disappear. Before Max figured out that something was wrong and called in his cop friends to save the day and put himself and Caleb in danger in the process. Before Steve got tired of the little cat-and-mouse game he was playing—had possibly been playing for days if he was the one who'd left that note on her van three days before.

A note with no signature and no number, only a demand to call. She'd tried to convince herself it was a mistake, that it had been meant for some other vehicle. She'd heard Max's calm voice in her mind, telling her that the past was just that, the past. That Steve hadn't been around in years and she was letting him win by living in fear.

Keeping a watch behind her as she entered the main thoroughfare on the outskirts of Santa Raquel, Meredith made a mental plan of the route she would take back to her son. A route that wove in and out of various neighborhoods, seemingly going nowhere fast, until she could be certain that no one was following her.

Her rendition of Max's voice in her head had been telling her to calm down. To stop worrying. To smile.

She'd tried to smile.

And had seen that car following her that afternoon. She couldn't pretend any longer. The note, this car—they added up to only one thing. Steve knew where she lived. He knew her routine.

Caleb had had a particularly hard time being left at day care. Her sweet little man had probably picked up on her tension. It had gone against every maternal instinct she had to leave him there today.

And yet, she *had* been grateful to turn him over and walk out that door. He'd be safe there.

Safer than he'd be anywhere with her?

There was a green car behind her. Two cars back. It had been behind her since she'd turned out of Devon's neighborhood. Staying back in traffic. Not always in the same lane. But there.

The same green car that had been following her earlier. It was a message to say that he was on to her. That if she was driving he knew. That she belonged to him. Was a part of him. Would always be a part of him. They were both parts of the same body. The same soul.

She knew the words. Could hear his voice in her head, too. Louder than Max's.

Just as she heard her own—telling her to get as far from Caleb's day care as she could. As quickly as she could.

Her plan wasn't fully formed yet. She wasn't ready.

But her time was up.

HIS JOB WAS not to panic. When he'd married Meredith Smith, alias Cassandra White, alias Lori Wade, alias Pamela Casey, he'd promised not only to love and to cherish, to be faithful and kind until death did them part, but he'd promised to be the keeper of their calm. The one in charge of making certain that fear didn't rule their lives.

He'd promised her he could live with a woman whose life could possibly someday be in danger.

And in the three years since they'd made those vows, he'd been able to keep every single one of them.

But unlike Jill, the cop who'd made him a widower four years after they'd married, and who'd driven him crazy with worry countless days and nights before that, Meredith's entire life revolved around keeping herself and her loved ones safe. Not putting herself in danger to keep the world safe.

Jill's job, and her penchant for leaping into the middle of any situation if she thought she could help, had made living without fear impossible.

Meredith made keeping fear under wraps easy.

The woman was a walking safety course in action.

So she was a few minutes late. Today had been her first private session with Devon Wright, the eight-year-old with Down syndrome. She'd been working with him for more than a year through his school. The at-home session had probably run longer than she'd expected. And that was all.

He could hear Caleb's cries as he entered the deserted front lobby of the Let's Pal Around day care, chosen because of its proximity to the elementary school, their home, and his clinic, as well as its distance from the beach. And because of the superior instructors as well, but he wasn't kidding himself. As soon as Meri had seen the security systems in place at Let's Pal Around, he'd known she'd made her choice.

"Dr. Bennet," Alice something-or-other, looking slightly harried with her graying hair falling out of the twist on the back of her head, and a bit of something white spilled on the front of her shirt, greeted him when he walked through the door. "Caleb will be very glad to see you."

A sentiment, no doubt shared by the Let's Pal Around staff.

"No word from my wife?" Why was he asking? Clearly, if Meri were there, he'd see her.

"No, sir." Alice swiped a card and disappeared behind the half door leading to the children he could hear, but not see. The top half of the door closed and latched as well, but remained open during business hours. He knew from his tour that there was another door, a locked security screen door, behind which the children played.

Hands in his pockets, he rocked back and forth on his tennis shoes and told himself there was nothing to worry about. Meri was fine. He was not going to check his watch.

When Meri hadn't answered her phone, he'd left a message. And sent her a text, too. She'd be in touch as soon as she finished with Devon.

In the meantime, he'd take Caleb home and start dinner. They'd moved chicken from the freezer to the refrigerator that morning. Talked about doing it on the grill with some of the fresh corn on the cob they'd picked up at an outdoor market that weekend. Maybe he'd best put the poultry back in the freezer. Might be too late to grill outside by the time she got home.

They could eat one of the ready-to-go meals in the freezer.

Meredith wasn't even an hour late yet. And she'd warned him that today's session might take longer than usual since she'd never been to Devon's home and would need to prepare the working environment once she saw what she had to work with.

Turning, he couldn't help but see the little analog clock on the screen of the computer by the receptionist's window. See, it was only four o'clock... four-oh-one.

Meredith was officially late.

But he wasn't going to worry.

His job was too stave off the paranoia that threatened their well-being.

Meredith was a speech pathologist. Not a cop. And her past, while dangerous to her at the time, was no longer a threat.

They'd had four peaceful years together, including the year they'd met and dated.

Meri was fine. And had even managed to leave Caleb at the day care for their agreed upon duration.

He should be celebrating.

At the very least, he was going to keep his fears in check.

Their happy life together depended upon his doing so.

CHAPTER TWO

STEVE WAS GETTING SLOPPY. She'd managed to give him the slip two times in one day. With shaking hands, Meredith gripped the steering wheel, gritting her teeth as her sweaty palms slipped on the smooth leather.

More likely he was playing with her. Taunting her. Letting her know he had her on his hook and could pull her in at any time.

She couldn't go home. She'd lost Steve again, for the moment, but he was moving in on her. As long as she stayed away, Max and Caleb would be safe. Steve didn't want them. He wanted her.

As far as her ex-husband was concerned, Max and any child she'd borne him didn't exist because the marriage didn't exist. It couldn't when she was still married to him.

He'd refused her pleas for divorce. Hadn't signed the papers when they'd been sent to him. The judge had finally granted the divorce, signing it into law without Steve's agreement, after Steve had failed to show up for court.

In Steve's world, if he didn't acknowledge it, it didn't exist.

It was simple, really, if you could accept his version of reality and breathe at the same time.

But she knew him. He'd have shown up for court and fought the divorce if he hadn't been afraid she'd expose his abuse of her. She'd finally found the strength to fight him—to file for divorce—he couldn't be sure what else she might do. He'd have denied any allegations. And she'd had no physical proof. But the perfect Las Vegas detective hadn't wanted the hint of scandal on his record.

She had to get off the road. He could be around any corner. Probably had some kind of GPS device planted on her van.

Which was fine. She had that much of her plan ready. She'd always worried that this might happen, and much as she'd tried to dismiss the note left on her vehicle the other day, it had ignited her fears.

She'd lead him out of town. Ditch the van. And her cell phone, just in case. Just because he was no longer a member of the Las Vegas police force, didn't mean he'd divested himself of all his tracking devices.

Or the knowledge he'd gained during his ten years as a cop.

He'd know where to find illegal means of keeping tabs on her.

Clearly.

And he wouldn't hesitate to use them. He lived

by the "law according to Steve." Neither the divorce, nor the restraining order she'd been granted against him in the state of Arizona—and reinstated in the state of California—had fazed him.

Eight years, four states, and four aliases hadn't stopped him from finding her.

Nothing would.

She knew that now.

Just as she knew that she couldn't run anymore.

There was no point.

THERE WAS A benefit to being a widower of a cop killed in the line of duty. A single phone call and you had a group of trained men and women at your disposal, offering to help in any way they could.

His "group," the Las Sendas Police Department just north of San Diego, was smaller than some, but when Max hadn't heard from Meredith by five o'clock that Wednesday evening, he placed his call. He'd moved from Las Sendas to Santa Raquel shortly after Jill's death. Was no longer within the jurisdiction of anyone who'd known her. But cops helped cops—and the families of cops. It was a statute written in some kind of cop blood code.

He knew it well. Knew it would serve him.

Because that code—that cops stood up for cops—had gotten his wife killed.

MAX FED CALEB. He wiped the toddler's face and hands, and when his son asked for his mama, he assured him she'd be right back. He was calm. Moved with ease around the kitchen. And when he dropped Caleb's Melmac *ABC* plate, splattering the remains of Meredith's pre-made ground beef stew all over the floor and lower cupboards, he carefully cleaned up every drop.

He had a follow-up call from his Las Sendas police contact. And when Caleb cried for a cookie, and Max remembered that they were out of the little vanilla wafers that were the only treat the boy was allowed, he lifted Caleb out of his chair, grabbed his keys, strapped the toddler into his car seat and went to the store.

He wheeled the cart around the store without hurry, going up and down every aisle, aware that Caleb attempted to touch things he couldn't reach, and focused on the displays in the aisles and the wares on the shelves. Considering them all with utmost concentration so that he didn't miss something else they might need, or were out of.

Meredith had been missing for a couple of hours. She'd left Devon's house late. He'd had confirmation on that point. But she should have been at the day care by the time Max had arrived.

There'd been no reported accidents anywhere in the area involving her. She wasn't in a hospital emergency room.

And they didn't need toilet paper. He'd had to replace the roll before dinner and there'd been a twelve-pack in the closet.

Ditto on the paper towels. He'd used half a roll on stew cleanup. And had found a bulk pack in the pantry.

Meredith was a firm believer in being prepared.

Tissue, he couldn't remember. He hadn't used any. But if Caleb's nose started to run, he'd need a lot of them. Certain that Meri had extra tissue at home, too, he threw in an extra three-pack anyway. It didn't spoil. They'd use it eventually.

Better safe than sorry.

Wherever Meri was, it probably wasn't good. She'd have called or texted if she could and since she hadn't....

She'd put on her stiff-chin face, get through it, and fall apart when she got home. She'd deal with whatever challenge she was facing with enough strength to move mountains. And be too weak to climb the stairs when it was all over.

In the safety and security of his arms she'd tell him what had held her up. Like the time she'd passed an old woman waiting at a bus stop and given her a ride. Or the time she'd helped a friend get a deadbeat ex-son-in-law out of her home. She'd survive. And then she might fall apart, depending on the situation.

The tears, when they came, could last a while.

Tissues were good.

Still, in both of those instances, and various others, she'd always called or texted him. Meri didn't want him to worry. Because he had a past, too.

"Mama!"

With a force that hurt his neck, Max swung around in the paper product aisle, expecting to see Meredith walking toward them. But he and Caleb were the only ones there.

"Mama!" Caleb said again, kicking his feet against the grocery cart.

The boy was staring at Max. Obviously expecting him to produce.

"Mama's busy, son, I told you that, remember? She's helping someone and she'll be back very soon." He didn't lie to Caleb. And the words calmed him as much as they appeared to calm the boy.

Meri didn't risk her life. Or the safety of her family. It was the golden rule by which she lived.

So different from Jill's call to serve—with a gun at her side, a Taser and a club hooked on her belt and a knife strapped to her ankle.

But like Jill, Meri had enough compassion to fill an ocean. And couldn't bear to let someone suffer.

Opening the box of vanilla cookies, he gave one to Caleb, and pushed on, navigating his cart through aisle after aisle.

He would not let Meri's panic infuse him. It was the golden rule by which *he* lived. He'd promised her he'd be the keeper of her panic. His job was to make certain that old fears didn't live in their home, lest fear rob them of the second chance at happiness life had afforded them. Steve Smith, former

Vegas police detective and abusive ex-husband, was in her past.

Caleb needed a bath. And it was coming close to bedtime. But he wasn't leaving the store. Not until his phone rang and he knew that Meredith would be at home waiting for them. Or, at the very least, knew where she was and that she was safe.

Of course she was safe. His phone would ring any minute now.

CALEB TOOK AN extra-long bath. Happy to splash in the water, poking at bubbles and pushing his plastic boat up the sides of the ceramic tub, he asked for his mother a few times, but then went back to his play.

Max sat on the travertine floor, leaning against the wall, one arm on the side of the tub, ready to grab his son if he slipped or tried to stand. He stared at his tennis shoes—purple high-tops that day—and tried to remain calm.

Purple was a spiritual color according to Meri. She'd told him about color associations and some of that had infiltrated his thoughts, as well. But he'd chosen to wear his purple shoes that day because they were the pair closest to the front of the closet. Not because he'd felt in any need of spiritual protection.

Chantel Harris, Jill's best friend and fellow police officer, had told him to go home when she'd called and found out he was at the grocery store.

Someone needed to be at the house in case Meri returned. Or someone else tried to contact them. He'd given her a list of places Meri frequented, from their dry cleaner and grocery store, to clients' addresses and schools where she worked. Other than Caleb and him, she didn't have any close friends.

But there were several people, all women, whom she'd helped out of tight spots during the four years she'd been in Santa Raquel.

Chantel had assured him that local police were checking out every place on his list. As a precaution. Meri was only a few hours late. No one was really alarmed. There wasn't any need for panic.

But in the four years he'd known her, Max had never known Meri to go anywhere or do anything on the spur of the moment. And she'd never once failed to be where she'd said she'd be without a phone call or text to alert him first.

Chantel was checking into Steve Smith's last known whereabouts, too. Just to assure Max that he was right not to let Meri's natural inclination to believe the man would find her someday take over rational thought.

Maybe his shoe laces were too long. They looked like the floppy bunny ears on the wallpaper in exam room four. Not his favorite room.

Caleb splashed.

And Max's phone rang.

The toddler turned, staring at him as he lifted the

device he'd been holding in his hand and glanced at the caller ID. It was almost as if Caleb knew they were waiting.

As if he wanted to know where his mother was as desperately as Max needed to find his wife.

And like Max, was man enough to remain in control while he waited.

Chantel.

"Did you find her?" Watching his son, he kept his tone easy.

"Not exactly."

Hearts couldn't actually drop. He was a doctor. He knew how the pumping vessel was attached. And knew what stress could do to it, too.

Chantel's tone made him want to hang up. To watch his boy play in bubbles and know that tomorrow was another day. That the sun would shine again and....

"They found her van, Max."

Caleb made a motor sound with his mouth. Seemingly unaware that darkness had descended in their bright and cheery bathroom.

"I can't do it again."

"Hold on."

Of course. That was what he'd do. His fingers gripped the side of the tub, slipped and gripped again, bruising the pads and turning his knuckles white. Pressure stopped the blood flow.

With no blood flow there was no pain.

Was there blood in the van? Jill had bled out on the street. And the clean-up crew hadn't been fast enough. A vision of the empty street with a pool of his wife's ended life—a photo that had been all over the news for days after she'd saved the life of a fellow officer—sprang to mind.

Caleb splashed. Laughed out loud. And looked to him for a response. Max smiled. His lips trembled and his cheeks hurt, but he kept that grin plastered on his face.

"Tell me," he said into the phone, careful to keep his tone neutral. He'd promised himself he'd never again be at risk of a phone call like this.

He'd promised.

And then he'd met Meri. Safety conscious, paranoid, locked-in-fear Meri. Who'd found the heart and soul in him that he'd thought dead and gone, awoken it. And given him a son.

"There's no sign of struggle," Chantel's voice held a note of sympathy, but not alarm. "The van was parked nine rows down in front of Chloe's at the Sun Oaks shopping center."

An upscale shopping development in the next town over. A maze of stores and parking that covered a square city block.

Meri liked to shop there.

Max's thoughts calmed. And he rumbled inside. His stomach. His blood pressure. Every nerve on alert.

"Her cell phone was inside," the thirty-year-old

police officer continued. "That's how they found the van, by tracking her cell. She'd left it on the console."

Meri's phone was a lifeline to her—her safety net. One push of a button and she could be connected to law enforcement. To Max. Or to The Lighthouse—a women's shelter she'd been volunteering at since he'd known her. The shelter she'd lived at when she'd first come to Southern California.

She didn't go from one room to the next without that cell phone. Wore it in a holster that clipped to any waistband. Showered with it on a shelf she'd had him install above the tile in the stall....

"There was a note, Max." Another drop in Chantel's tone. Another splash from the tub. Another rumble inside. "She said that she just couldn't do it anymore. That she was too worried about Caleb all the time. That she couldn't even leave him at day care for an afternoon, so how would she ever cope when he went to school? She was afraid that her paranoia would rub off on him. She said she had to go before he was old enough to remember and be traumatized. She left the phone because it was in your name."

She'd have told him if she was leaving him. She would never have left Caleb. It didn't make sense. He wasn't going to panic.

"Were the keys in the car?" If she was ever in trouble and had to run—if she ever thought Steve was after her—she'd leave the car parked with the keys under the driver's seat. It was one of the many precepts she'd laid out when she'd agreed to marry him.

Precautions, she'd called them.

They had to be prepared, she'd said.

"They were in the closed cup holder. Just like she said they'd be in the note."

Who left a note in a car telling whoever looked that the keys were in the cup holder?

He sank down a little farther against the tub. She'd very clearly told him she'd leave them under the driver's seat.

"She left you, Max. I'm so sorry...."

Another rumble. Another splash. And Dr. Max Bennet started to panic.

CHAPTER THREE

JENNA MCDONALD SAT at the white faux antique desk, a diary opened in front of her, and picked up a pen.

DAY ONE.

Pausing, pen suspended over the page, she read what she'd written.

Not her usual handwriting. There was some familiarity to it, but it was too shaky. It would improve. With time.

Everything did.

Until a time came that it didn't? Did one have warning when that time had come? Did one know?

The wall in front of her was off-white. Her gaze following the color upward, she studied the soft gold-painted wood trim at the top. To remind her that a pot of gold awaited her, she'd been told. Different rooms had different messages. She'd chosen the pot-of-gold room. Jenna liked gold.

Something good to know. To hang on to.

Turning, she took in the generously sized room. Off-white metal furniture, including a queen-size bed, nightstand, and two dressers, fit with room to spare. The floor was carpeted, a light plush beige.

Nice. Peaceful.

The adjoining bathroom had a granite vanity, extra deep tub and walk-in shower. All donations, she'd been told. And lovely.

The closet was small. But too big for the couple of outfits hanging there—chosen from the impressive collection on-site—more donations. They'd told her to take as many as she'd like or thought she could use.

Taking things one day at a time suited her best. Until she figured out what was to come.

It had been said that clothing choice spoke of personality. Jenna's personality wasn't clear to her yet.

Somewhere in the folder of paperwork she'd amassed over the previous couple of hours, there was a coupon for a makeover, too, if she wanted one. Though her lack of need for one had been stressed ten-fold, lest she think she wasn't good enough just as she was.

Lovely surroundings. And the price of admittance was higher than money could ever pay.

With a sigh, Jenna turned back to the diary she'd found still wrapped in its package, along with a new pen in the drawer of the desk at which she sat.

DAY ONE. She read again.

She might do the makeover. Just for the fun of

it. Having someone fuss over her might be nice. As long as she didn't get used to it.

Jenna McDonald was going to live an independent life.

At least she wasn't financially dependent. She'd grabbed the few hundred dollars she'd had hidden behind the glove box closure. And always kept a few hundred hidden in her purse, too. She had her checkbook for the personal account Max had insisted she have, just so she'd feel safe. There was enough money in there for her to be fine for a while—not that she wanted to use it. The checking account could be traced....

She glanced at the diary. It was something she had to deal with. The woman who appeared on that page.

DAY ONE. Jenna touched the pen to the page.

I'm bereft. So much so it hurts to draw breath. The pen faltered as her fingers grew weak. She paused. Read the written words. And resumed writing.

The future looms before me. Frightening. I feel today that my life will be short. I won't grow to be an old woman. I won't live another year.

I want to live. I want to be the wife and mother I tried to be. More than anything.

Pen clutched in her sweaty grasp, Jenna gritted her teeth, closed her eyes. And breathed. She was fine. She'd been here before. Oh, not the room, here. Or even the building here. But she'd been at this point.

And being here again…this she could do.

Opening her eyes, she picked up the pen again. She couldn't turn her back on the woman on the page.

How does a woman leave the man who is her whole world? Who cherishes her and loves her as much as she loves him? How does she leave a good man?

And how does she leave her baby?

Jenna's pen flew across the page so quickly now her hand cramped up.

How did her heart continue to beat? Her blood to flow and her stomach to feel hunger pangs?

How could it be that she'd woken that morning as one woman and would go to bed that night a totally different person? Not just a woman with a different name, but a woman who was irrevocably, permanently changed?

But I did the right thing. The only thing. I am putting action to the greatest gift life has to offer. The gift of love. I, of all people, know the value of unconditional love. I was given a chance to know it in its truest sense. And now I must honor that love by loving selflessly back.

I can live the rest of my life, however long or short, knowing that I loved my men enough to put their well-being before my own. I can leave this world in peace knowing that.

Peace. I need it. For them, first. And for me, too.

The pen paused and eyes closed, Jenna tried to clear the mind that raged inside of her. The mind of a woman who'd been so many people. In so many places.

I am absolutely certain that I am not going to run again. I don't know yet how I'm going to do what I'm going to do, but I am in a place where I will be safe while I figure out exactly how I am going to stand up to the man who's determined to keep me down, to hold me locked in an embrace that stifles everything that is good inside of me.

As soon as I have figured out how to beat Steve Smith at his own game, as I know now that that is the only way to beat him, I will present myself for battle. To his death or my own. I must either be free to live with my husband and son, or die fighting for that freedom. There is no other life for me. I am not the same powerless woman he once knew. Love gives me the strength to fight the demon....

Jenna jumped as a knock sounded on her door and quickly closed the diary, sliding it inside the desk drawer without making a sound. She moved just as quietly to the bed, lying down with her back to the door.

"Come in."

"Jenna?" She recognized the voice. Lila McDaniels had introduced herself earlier that evening as the managing director of The Lemonade Stand—Jenna's current abode.

"Yes?" Hoping that the older woman would respect her need for solitude and go away, Jenna didn't turn over.

"We missed you at dinner."

She'd smiled when they'd rattled off the cafeteria hours. And smiled a second time when Lila and Sara had invited her to join them.

"I had some fruit in my bag," she said. And still did. Left over from another place and time. It had been meant for another. A little boy. She'd get rid of it before it rotted. Just not that night.

The bed depressed and knowing that she wasn't going to get her way, which was to be left alone, Jenna rolled over. And welcomed the calm that descended over her as she met the other woman's gaze.

"You're sure there's no one we can contact on your behalf?" Lila asked.

"No, ma'am, but thank you."

She was an adult. Free to travel from place to place as she chose.

"No one who will be worried about you?"

"No."

"Someone knows you're here then?"

"Someone knows I'm gone. No one knows I'm here." The point was critical.

Lila nodded, a sad smile on her face, looking as if she wanted to say more.

"That's fine, then," she said. "Your secrets are safe here."

"I appreciate that so much."

"When you're ready, I hope you'll talk with one of us, Sara or myself or any of the other counselors. We're here to help. And anything that's said within these walls stays here."

"Thank you." She'd met Sara. Had liked her. But Jenna could probably facilitate any counseling session these good women had to give. There was nothing they could tell her, in terms of battered-wife recovery, that she didn't already know.

And sometimes all the knowing in the world, all the protection in the world, wasn't enough.

Sometimes a woman had to be enough all on her own. No matter the consequences.

"You're sure you don't want us to notify the police?"

"No!" She almost sat up at that. And calmed herself. "Please, no," she said. This point was not negotiable. "It does you no good to do so behind my back, right?" she felt compelled to point out. To reassure herself. "There's nothing to report if I don't speak up."

"That's correct. But we wouldn't go behind your back in any case, Jenna. Not unless you were a minor or had a minor with you. In that case, we have no choice but to involve the police."

She nodded. Understanding. And concentrated on relaxing her muscles. One at a time.

The diary in the desk was bothering her. Burning at the edges of her concentration. She was going to have to hide it. Or have it on her person at all times.

"Do you have my cell phone?" she asked now. Lila had mentioned a prepaid device that she could have if she wanted it.

"I do." Reaching into the pocket of her suit jacket, she pulled out an old-fashioned looking flip phone.

It would do nicely.

"You can't text or get email, but you can make calls...."

"That's fine," she said, sitting up to take the phone and liking the way she could clutch the thing securely in one hand. "I don't have anything to text or email to anyone."

And she wouldn't send either if she did have something to say. Data could be traced.

She had a phone. An untraceable phone. The air in the room lifted. Being without a phone had not been good for her. Making a mental note to have an extra prepaid cell phone on hand at all times, she waited for Lila to stand and go.

"I know that there's nothing I can say that will help you trust me, Jenna," the woman said instead. And frowned. "Very few of our residents trust any of us at first. I understand that. Trust has to be earned...."

And sometimes trust came too late to do any good.

"But you...you're different."

Yes, she was. Oh, she'd been a battered wife like everyone else staying in the bungalows at The Lemonade Stand. But the physical beatings she'd taken had been the easiest part. "I get the feeling that you've been here," Lila said, unsettling Jenna with the uncanny resemblance to her own thoughts just minutes before. "I've been at The Lemonade Stand since day one and I know I've never seen you before." Lila shook her head. "And yet, I feel as though you know this place. Or one like it."

Four like it. The shelters had been the only places Steve had never been able to breach. Most often, the general public knew of them, but didn't know the exact location of the buildings where the women stayed. At The Lemonade Stand they were sprawled across several acres hidden behind a two-block strip of shops also owned and run by the Stand.

Others had had a known home office, with housing buildings situated in various and changing locations around the city in which they were located.

In each shelter, in different cities, she'd become reacquainted with the self she'd been before he'd found her again. She'd found a way to believe once more. To venture out...

Not this time. Her stay at The Lemonade Stand was for one specific purpose only. To have a safe place to formulate her plan. She needed a little time to research the psychology of abuse, to get so deeply inside Steve's head that she could figure out how best to manipulate him. Undercover work at its best. Ironic that she'd take what she'd learned while living with an abusive detective to finally be free of him. She'd do the necessary research at the on-site library, or from a computer there. Figure out where and how to meet up with him. Practice until she could act in her sleep.

And then, as quietly as she'd arrived, she'd leave this place.

"You can trust me, Jenna." Lila's expression was genuine, the compassion Jenna read there wrenching at emotions she couldn't afford. Or allow. "I…I…just, please, know that no matter what, you can come to me. Any time of the day or night. All rules and regulations aside. Don't let anyone stop you. Not staff, not security. Not anyone. If you need me, you get to me."

The speech wasn't normal. Didn't resemble any of the other first night welcome talks, or any other talk she'd ever had at any of the other shelters where she'd sought solace.

And Jenna instinctively knew, as she sat there on the bed with the gray-haired woman, that Lila had never said those words before.

Not to anyone.

"Yes, ma'am." She swallowed. Knew that she needed to rest. Sleep would ease the need to cry.

Lila sat with her for several more minutes. A silent companion. And then without any fuss she stood and left.

Waiting until she heard the door click shut, Jenna slid off the bed, retrieved the diary from the desk, and tucked it into the waistband of the pair of dress slacks she was no longer going to need. Then, without turning off the light or visiting her adjoining private bathroom, she lay back down on the bed, cell phone still held securely in her palm, and went to sleep.

In the morning, things would look different.

In the morning, she'd know the next step to take.

In the morning....

CHAPTER FOUR

MAX PUT HIS son to bed right on time. Routine was important. Keeping Caleb's boundaries the same would give him a sense of security.

Max needed the toddler asleep so he'd quit asking for his mother.

The boy complied with relative ease. Almost convincing Max that he was overreacting—panicking too soon.

She'd left the keys in the car. Not under the seat, which she'd stipulated would be her sign if she was running from Steve, but in the cup holder. That had to mean something.

He wandered through the rooms of their home. Hearing her laughter at the bottom of the stairs. In the living room it was her assertion that one maroon wall would give the place more life—she'd been right.

Because he'd insisted that Meri would have talked to him if she'd truly wanted out of their marriage, or maybe because she'd felt sorry for him, Chantel had agreed to use her off-duty time to continue looking for Meri, following up on all leads, making calls, attempting to locate Steve Smith who'd left detective work and had fallen off the grid....

The kitchen reverberated with the echo of excitement in his wife's voice as she rattled off the money she'd saved with her shoppers card and coupons—money that they both provided in excess of their needs.

Eventually he wound up in their bedroom. And turned right around and headed back out again. Caleb was still sleeping in a crib. He wouldn't be up wandering in the night, looking for his parents to be in their bed. No risk of him finding it empty and being frightened.

The guest bedroom wasn't finished yet. A bedframe, mattress and bedding. An empty nightstand that Meri had seen at a sale and had to have because it reminded her of her childhood, back before the car accident that had taken her family from her—both parents and her younger brother.

Without turning on the lamp, he sank down onto the edge of the bed. And because it was the most sensible thing to do, he slowly lowered his head to the pillow.

He hadn't brushed his teeth. Was still wearing scrubs minus the lab coat and purple tennis shoes. But sleep was wise.

Hands behind his head, he closed his eyes. Opened them again. And found himself staring at the ceiling, looking for a pattern in the circle of plaster he could see illuminated from the small night-light in the hall.

Ah, Meri, you didn't have to do this.

The thought was followed by another that had him sitting straight up in bed. Maybe she'd thought she *did* have to do it.

Meri was always paranoid, but she knew that and took her overreactions into account before acting on anything.

She'd meant what she said in her note. Clearly he'd believed her, the way he'd been slogging around all evening feeling sorry for himself.

And Caleb.

Feeling lonely as hell and wondering how he was going to live through the loss of another wife.

What a jerk he'd been, thinking about himself, his own heartache, instead of putting Meri's first.

She'd meant the note, but she wouldn't have left *just* because she was feeling paranoid. She'd at least have talked to him first. Looked for other options. She loved them too much to just walk away out of fear that her paranoia would hurt their son in the future. They still had three years before Caleb started school. And there were other options to help her deal with her fears.

Anything could happen between now and then. Which was why she took one step at a time.

A motto she lived by. Had taught him to live by.

And all of that meant there was something else going on.

Swinging his feet to the floor, Max sat on the side of the bed in the dark. Why would she just up and leave? Their mail hadn't arrived until four—long after she'd left the house. It had still been in the box when he got home.

No unusual calls showed up on her cell phone records—he'd checked their usage online himself.

She hadn't logged into her email account—all of the messages had still been on the server, unread.

And that left physical confrontation.

There'd been no sign of a struggle.

So she'd gone willingly. To avoid physical harm? To herself or to him and Caleb?

Meri would give her life to protect Max or their son. But they hadn't been threatened.

Would an abductor have waited for her to write a goodbye letter and leave her keys in the cup holder?

He would if her abductor was a determined ex-husband who would want to make certain that Max knew that she was leaving him of her own accord. Steve could have made her write the note.

But why put the keys in the cup holder instead of under the seat? If Steve didn't know she'd hidden them, or even if he did, what could it have mattered to him whether they were in a cup holder or under a seat?

No one but he and Meri knew about the hiding place.

Which was why they'd had the predetermined keys-under-the-seat agreement. An overkill safety measure agreement, in his opinion, but one Meri had insisted on having so that they'd have a way to signal each other if the other was being taken against their will.

Leave the keys under the driver's seat if you needed help.

She'd left her keys in the cup holder. She hadn't taken them with her, or disposed of them, so he could imagine that she'd been unable to leave them. They'd been in the cup holder. Where she'd deliberately left them. Not under the seat.

Her message to him was clear.

She didn't need his help.

The Meri he knew would never have left such a message.

It had to be Steve. He'd found her and she'd reverted back to the terrified woman who did as he demanded so he didn't beat her senseless. The woman who believed that the former detective, with all of his underground contacts, was more powerful than the laws that were there to protect her. Who believed, deep down, that she'd never be free of him.

She hadn't wanted to talk about Steve. Seeing how much it upset her—and honestly believing, after years of no sign of the ex-cop, that he posed them no danger—he hadn't pushed her for more information.

Lying there in the dark, Max feared that in not doing so, he might have made one of the biggest mistakes of his life.

DAY TWO.

Sometimes the part of me that takes on different names scares me. She's so capable, but like an automaton. She goes through the day, doing what is expected of her, even watching for and trying to help others when opportunity or necessity presents itself.

She adapts to the situation in spite of her own needs.

And she doesn't cry. Ever. It's as if she can't and that worries me. She is me and if I'm reaching the point where I can turn off so completely, I fear that my heart is really and truly dying.

Pen suspended over the page, Jenna read what she'd written. And shook her head. Sitting at the antique desk in her room just after dinner that Thursday night, she bent over her diary once again.

I just need to trust, like Max tells me so often. Jenna is impressive. She's the part of me that holds all of my strength. And dispenses it as I need it. Today, she agreed to a group counseling session that I'll be attending once a day for at least the next week, when all I really wanted to do, when the invitation had been offered, was shake my head and run.

I don't need any more counseling. But I do need this time here, to mentally prepare myself to get into the psyche of a man with no moral boundaries, and to figure out when and how to meet him to somehow end his reign of terror. And if I must do counseling to keep up appearances, to maintain my cover of an abused woman seeking help, to satisfy those around me that I am getting the help I need, then so be it. After a full day here I am completely committed to my course of action and know from within the deepest chambers of my heart that I am doing what I have to do. Steve's torment has to stop. And if I can't find a way to make that happen—legally and for good—then I am willing to die trying.

Because if I don't, if I live, and don't live with Steve, Max and Caleb are at risk. Steve knows how much I love them. He knows I'd do anything for them. And he wouldn't hesitate to use that knowledge as power against me.

Only if Steve is gone, or I am, will Max and Caleb be safe. Unless I go back to Steve. The third possibility isn't even an option.

I choose death over life with Steve. Better to watch my boys from above (after all, what better place to watch over and protect them?) than to bring Steve's rage into their physical space. Because I know my Max. He thinks he has all the protection we need in that small police force of his.

If I'm with Steve, Max would come charging in to rescue me. And get himself killed...

Jenna's hand came to a halt as a tear splashed onto the page. Meredith was hurting. Understandably so. And Jenna had to keep a firm hand on those emotions right now. She would be steady on her course. Reach her goal. For Max. And Caleb.

If there was an opportunity to deal with her heart and soul later, then she could cry buckets.

With her emotions once again firmly in check, Jenna glanced at her watch. She'd told Lila that she'd meet with her later that evening. Over a cup of hot tea with milk in the woman's private on-site suite.

She'd never had hot tea with milk. And she had a sense that Lila didn't generally invite residents into her private quarters after hours, either.

The upcoming event would consume part of the long evening ahead. But she wasn't due in the older woman's suite for another half an hour.

Caleb will have finished his supper by now. I picture him in his booster seat at the table with tomato soup smeared over his chin and the corners of his lips.

I can smell the soup. And see his sweet little face, those precious big brown eyes crinkled almost shut, as he lifts his mouth up to be wiped.

I can't think about him missing me.

I also can't picture his father's identical eyes at the moment.

Maybe in time.

As another tear dripped onto the page, Jenna set down the pen and shut the book.

MAX HAD JUST deposited his cranky son in his crib Thursday night, turned on the monitor, the night-light, and shut the door when the doorbell rang.

Meri. Heart racing, he descended the stairs two at a time, his black canvas high-tops hardly touching the ground at all, before he realized that if his wife had returned she'd use her key, not ring the bell.

And before the thought slowed his feet, he countered it with the realization that Meri had left her keys in the cup holder of her car. He was supposed to have picked them up at the police station that afternoon but he'd had a late walk-in, a little boy with swollen adenoids and a panicky first-time mother, and the day care had been calling about Caleb's distress and....

He was pulling open the door before it occurred to him that Meri wouldn't have left her house key in her car for anyone to find. If someone stole her old van, oh well...but she wouldn't take a chance on a stranger happening along and getting access to their home.

A woman stood on his front step. Her uniform, the blond hair, caught at his heart and he took a step back before he realized that she wasn't Jill.

"Chantel," he said, sounding as surprised as he

felt. He wasn't at his best. Had none of the infamous Bennet bedside manner.

"You look like you were on the losing end of a water fight," she said, standing on his front porch as though it hadn't been years since they'd seen each other.

The last time had been....

Jill's funeral. She'd stood next to him. Squeezed his arm once. And too choked up to speak, had walked off into the sunset.

"Caleb wasn't happy to take a bath tonight. Kept insisting that Mama do it."

Her expression didn't change much, but he was used to reading a female cop's eyes. The way they'd glisten almost imperceptibly, focus a bit more, when the woman was moved.

"You decided to go with superhero today," she said, remarking on his black, white and red superhero imprinted scrubs, that were wetter than not at the moment. The shoes matched because Meri liked it when he bothered to find the right color, which he did about half the time.

"You're a long way from home," he replied.

"Three hours." She shrugged. "And I'm here on business." Holding up her left hand, he recognized Meri's key ring dangling there.

He snatched the ring. Not wanting anyone to wipe away what was left of Meri on those keys. Resisting the urge to raise them to his lips, he studied them for the couple of seconds it took him to get himself under control. He'd have to go get her van.

He'd gone to work that day because he hadn't known what else to do. Chantel, people she'd called, were making some follow-up queries, but as far as they were concerned, Meri had left of her own free will.

She'd left a note. There'd been no sign of a struggle.

Didn't matter that he *knew* better. Husbands always thought that.

Still, he'd referred most of his patients to another doctor at the clinic that day—a pediatrician in private practice like himself who traded duties with him whenever one or the other of them was sick or going to be gone.

He'd seen a couple of minor cases. And tried to get caught up on his reading. And on a paper he was writing for the pediatric journal, whose editors had sought him out.

"Her house key is missing."

"It looked like it to the officers here, we just needed your confirmation that a house key had been on there in the first place. I'm guessing she kept it." Chantel's tone was soft, filled with a nurturing that he knew she didn't often express. "It's further proof that she left of her own accord, Max. An abductor isn't going to wait for her to take a key off her ring. Just like he wouldn't wait for her to write a note."

"Any news on Steve Smith? Surely the man didn't just disappear into thin air."

Chantel's hair bounced around her shoulders as she shook her head. "He's not coming up in any databases," she said, leaving Max with the feeling that their attempts to find the man had been cursory—a matter of professional courtesy only.

"Can I come in?"

He was facing another sleepless night. Alone with a panic he'd promised not to feel. He had to get her to understand that Meri was in danger.

"Sure," he said.

And tried to pretend he didn't notice when her hand brushed his arm as she passed.

CHAPTER FIVE

ONE OF THE things Meredith Bennet never failed to marvel at in her life with Max was being able to crawl into bed beside him every night. Like magic, she could cuddle up to the warmth of his body, rest her hand atop the springy dark hair on his chest, and sleep without fear.

Without nightmare.

Meredith's alter ego, Jenna, who'd awoken alone no fewer than four times with cold sweats the night before, was just as happy to be sitting on the antique chintz sofa in Lila's sitting room, even if it meant giving more of herself than she wanted to give.

If this plan—to put an end to Steve's presence in her life—was going to work, she had to be flexible. To go with the flow. At least until she'd had enough time to get ready....

And the plan was going to work. One way or another....

She was out of choices. Out of the will to run, to invent yet another life. She'd found the life she was meant to live—the only life she wanted.

She'd found a love that was real and true and as deep as it got and the only way to honor that love, to keep it in its purest form, was to love unconditionally. Selflessly.

There was no way Max would let her confront Steve on her own, and no other way to make the man go away. Max trusted his cop friends. Jenna was dealing with a man who could think like the cops and stay ahead of them at every step.

A man who didn't respect the jurisdiction of any law but his own.

She knew. She'd seen him in action.

If Max knew that Steve was after her, he'd call the cops and end up getting hurt. Cornered, Steve was the devil himself. He very well might snatch Caleb, hurt an innocent little boy, just to get her to do what he wanted.

Which was why she had to let him know she'd left her family, rather than chance going home again. She'd left her cell phone so he'd find the van, the note she'd left. He'd read that note and think she left Max just like she'd left him. She hoped she was buying time by making him look for her again.

To keep him in the game of finding her.

"Did you go to college?" Lila, sitting in a wing-backed armchair opposite Jenna, asked her. She held her cup of tea with both hands, and looked as though she was settled in for a long chat.

"Yes," Jenna said. She'd tried the tea. Didn't

like it all that much. The milk made it too heavy. But she'd sip it. Slowly. Because she could tolerate pretty much anything as long as she didn't focus on it going down.

For now, her cup sat in its delicate china saucer on the walnut claw-footed table beside her.

"What did you study?"

"Various things. How about you, do you have a degree?"

"Yes."

She'd been at the Stand a little over twenty-four hours and it hadn't taken her that long to realize that no one knew much about the managing director. After Lila's visit to her room the night before, she'd done a bit of quiet asking around.

"What did you do before coming to The Lemonade Stand?"

Lila's gaze was pointed as Jenna's question lay between them. Jenna expected a prevarication. Just as she wasn't being completely honest with her. Such a contrast to the day she'd had, sharing lunch with women who told their stories openly. Dams bursting and releasing the hell of terror they'd experienced in one form or another.

"I was a school teacher," Lila said conversationally.

From school teaching to managing a shelter for battered women?

"Do you miss it?"

"No."

Because Lila was satisfied with the life she was leading? Fulfilled by it?

Meredith Bennet knew about living a fulfilling life. And so Jenna knew. But that wasn't for her to dwell on. Not on that or anything else that would take away focus and strength from the task at hand.

She'd been called to Lila's suite for a chat. So she chatted. "You didn't like teaching?"

"Yes. I liked it very much. But it was time for a change."

Lila's gaze wasn't piercing anymore. It was... assessing. And warm. In a motherly sort of way.

Jenna took a sip of tea. Admired the rose silk flower arrangement on a side table.

"What about you?" Lila asked. "Do you have a career?"

"I'm a speech pathologist."

Lila's brows rose and she asked, "What's your specialty?"

"Pediatrics."

"Are you willing to donate some time while you're here?"

A slippery slope if ever there was one. They wouldn't find a license for Jenna McDonald. But, if she could have even a small piece of her real life back, just enough to remind her how great it had been, to keep her strong while she prepared to face down the evil spirit in her life....

If she could help others while she was protecting Max and Caleb....

Lila's stare was intense. It was as if the woman could read her mind. And her mind was the one thing no one got close to unless she invited them in. Max and Caleb were her only guests. Ever.

She'd fought too hard, for too long, regaining control of her mind from Steve, to give it up again.

"I'm willing to help out anyplace I can." Innocuous words. She'd see where they took her.

"I'm assuming you have certification? A state license to practice?"

"Yes." Under her married name. The only legal name she'd had since she left Steve Smith seven years before.

"Can I have a copy of it?"

A vision of Devon Wright's effusive smile as he'd said goodbye to her the day before flashed across her mind. A picture of little Olivia, the three-year-old who was having surgery in another couple of weeks and would need help learning to swallow again. She'd spent six weeks with the little girl already, earning her trust, preparing her....

Jenna had a job to do. Meredith had a life to live.

But she couldn't live it until Jenna did her job. And only if Jenna was successful....

She'd been at this crossroads before. Three other times. And each and every time she'd given up not only the life, but the goals. The joy. She'd allowed Steve to take away more than just her freedom. He'd taken away vital parts of her....

"Your secrets are safe here." Lila's soft tone was

like a buzzer in the cacophony rumbling through her mind.

"It's not my secrets I'm concerned about."

"You are safe here."

She wasn't concerned about herself, either. But knew better than to say so out loud. At least in this atmosphere.

She wasn't here to recover from domestic violence. She had a mate who treated her with decency and respect. Who was fully a partner and companion.

She'd sought the life she wanted and obtained it, just as she had every right to do. She'd stood up, pressed forward. She'd dared to reach for her dreams.

She'd succeeded.

Steve hadn't gotten the message.

She'd looked fear in the eye and her ex-husband was looking right back at her.

So she was going to stare him down. And the first one who looked away would lose.

This was it. Her stare down.

She wasn't turning her back again until Steve was out of her life for good.

Because there was no way in hell Steve's evil was going to touch Max or Caleb. At least not on a daily basis. Not as a way of life....

"You don't have to take this journey alone."

Jenna's gaze focused outwardly again. Lila was watching her, and judging by her compassionate, almost knowing expression, she'd been doing so for quite some time.

The older woman had asked for her certification. For Meredith Bennet's certification. And unlike the other personas she'd left behind each time Steve had resurfaced in her life, Meredith was not going to fade away.

Meredith had a husband. And a son. Both of whom she loved more than she loved herself. She couldn't turn her back on them. Even if she never saw them again.

And that was something else she couldn't think about. Because in order for them to be safe, Max had to believe that she'd left him. He had to move on. She had to let him.

And if she succeeded? If she lived to see herself free of Steve? Was it right or fair for her to hope that somehow Max would be available to take up where they left off?

"I can show you my certification." She had a scanned copy on the tablet she kept in her purse. "But if I do so, I put someone I love at risk."

"How so?"

Something told her Lila was different. More than a counselor. Or a paid helper. More than a crusader for the cause.

And maybe Meredith had grown soft. Maybe Jenna's skin wasn't as hard as it needed to be.

"Jenna McDonald is not my real name, but it is the only name anyone here can know me by."

"And if someone here knows you by your legal name, who would be hurt?"

Jenna couldn't think of a thing to say.

Lila sipped tea. Jenna wanted out. It was past Caleb's bedtime.

Not a Lemonade Stand thought.

"Okay." The older woman's voice broke the silence again. Broke through the emptiness inside of Jenna. "Block the name out. Show me the certification and I can put you to work immediately. We have a seven-year-old boy whose speech has become practically paralyzed with stutters...."

"You can look up my license number and know who I am."

"I didn't say give me a copy, I said show it to me."

"Okay."

"Okay."

"You want it now?" Jenna reached for her purse.

"Yes."

She pulled out her tablet. Turned it on.

The certification was legible, but small. Holding the tablet with her thumb over her identifying information, she carried it over to show Lila.

The woman lifted her glasses. Read.

"Thank you."

Jenna returned the tablet to her purse.

"When you're ready, you bring me the rest of that and whatever I see there will remain between you and me. You have my word on it."

"It's not you, Lila, I just…"

Holding up her hand, Lila stood. "When you're ready," she said. "Just remember that I am here. That's all I ask. When you need me, you do whatever you have to do to find me." The woman repeated what she'd said the night before.

Jenna nodded, more because it was expected of her than because she could foresee any circumstance where she might do as the woman asked.

"And when you have something to say, there is space, right here, between you and me, to put the truth, no questions asked."

Emotion rose inside of her, tightening her throat. Jenna picked up her tie-dyed cloth bag and slipped away.

CHAPTER SIX

"DID YOU WORK TODAY?" Max returned to the living room after exchanging wet scrubs for a pair of red basketball shorts and a gray T-shirt with a faded FBI emblem. It was left over from a trip he and Jill had taken to Washington, D.C., a decade before. As he walked in, he found Chantel standing at the mantel over the fireplace, looking at pictures.

Mostly they were of Caleb, taken in the different stages of growing from newborn to two. The center photo was of him and Meri, taken on their wedding day.

In one corner was an old photograph of a much younger Meri with her parents and little brother.

And in the other, Max's favorite photo of Jill—in a sundress, not a uniform, taken on the day he'd passed his residency. There'd been a party. And she'd been wholly his wife that day. For the entire day.

It had been nice.

"Yeah, I worked and then headed up here as soon as I was off shift," Chantel said, her back to the photos now as she watched him.

"Shouldn't you be getting back?"

She'd asked to come in.

"I'm off tomorrow." She was watching him. Chantel ran her finger along the edge of the frame that held Jill's photo. "You remember that night?" Chantel asked. She'd been at the party, too. Everyone who'd played a part in their lives had been there.

"Of course I remember."

"I got drunk and told you I thought you were great."

Actually what she had said was that no other guy added up to him and if Jill hadn't snatched him first, she'd have done so. He'd just completed his residency. Had already had an invitation to share a well-established pediatric practice. Everyone was telling him how great he was that night.

"I've been embarrassed about that ever since," Chantel said now, while Max felt the computer in the other room drawing him.

Meri was "out there" somewhere. Facing a second night without him. As he faced a second night without her. Their first two nights apart since they got married. Even the night she'd had Caleb, they'd been together. She'd spent the night in the hospital and he'd stayed with her.

"I didn't want you to think that I was coming on to you while you were married to my best friend," Chantel said, turning back to face him, her hands on her hips.

She was a pretty woman. Slender. Blonde. Brown eyes. A little tall for his tastes. A little hard around the edges. But still, damned attractive. Especially when she smiled. And let her hair down out of its ponytail as it was now.

She wasn't smiling though. "I loved Jill," she said. "I would never have done anything to hurt her."

"I know that."

"She was such a fool, you know?"

No, he didn't know. Jill had been larger than life. A true warrior. Everyone thought she was amazing.

And the way her life had ended, saving the life of a fellow officer, she'd died as she'd lived—a heroine.

"She didn't get what she had in you," Chantel said now. "If I'd been lucky enough to find a guy as great as you, I'd damn sure have thought twice about strapping on the gun and going out to fight crime."

"It's what she was born to do. Why should she be less than herself just because she was married?"

Okay, so maybe he'd have liked it a hell of a lot better if Jill could have been happy with a desk job. Making detective and tracking criminals with a little bit of distance. Or teaching at the academy.

But it hadn't been what she'd wanted. Wouldn't have made her happy....

"You could have had any number of great guys," he said now, remembering the flock of admirers that always seemed to be trailing behind the attractive cop.

"I guess."

"You seeing anyone?" he asked. Because he wanted to ask her to take him seriously and help him find Meri's ex-husband. He was growing more and more certain that Steve was somehow behind this.

"I was seeing someone. A captain of another squad. It didn't work out."

"I'm sorry."

"I'm not. And I didn't come here to talk about my love life," she said, moving away from the mantel. "I came to see what I could do to help you," she said. "I heard the concern in your voice last night, Max. And while, officially, I'm pretty convinced that Meri left of her own accord and is fine, I'm also your friend. I've got the next couple of days off, and I wanted to make a personal appearance at the station here, which I did tonight, to talk to the guys and see what I could find out about where Meredith might be. You know…in case you want to talk to her, to maybe patch things up…."

It was a wonderful, selfless thing to do. A friend thing to do.

"I just…you called and asked for help and…it's what Jill would want me to do, to help you. It's… she made me promise, the night before you two married, that if anything ever happened to her, and you needed help, I'd be there. I just wanted to, you know, clear the air, first, in case you—" she tipped her head from side to side "—got the wrong idea about that…night." With her thumb she gestured to the photos behind them.

He might have wondered a time or two about Chantel's interest in him…but everyone knew that he and Jill had a good marriage. And Chantel was Jill's very best friend. From grade school. It was understood that he and Chantel would grow to have a genuine fondness for each other. Hell, they'd spent every holiday of his marriage to Jill together.

And hadn't spoken more than half a dozen times since his first wife's death.

"You're fine," he said now, crossing his arms as he stood there in his bare feet eager to get to the business at hand. "No wrong ideas about that night. So what did you find out?"

"Nothing," she said. "They aren't looking for her. They hadn't yet opened a missing person's case when her van was spotted and they didn't need to do so once they found her note. There was nothing suspicious, nothing that warranted expenditure of already limited manpower. Let's face it, Max, an abductor isn't going to stand around and wait while she writes a note."

"He would if he was her ex-husband forcing her to write it."

"I know. You mentioned that concern last night and in light of the fact that he's an ex-cop, and that he was abusive to Meredith, I got someone to pull the parking lot surveillance tape where she ditched her van. Meredith was alone, Max. She pulled in. Parked. Sat in the car and wrote the note and then got out. There was no one there, forcing her to do anything."

"Just because you didn't see anyone doesn't mean he wasn't there."

"What are you saying?"

"I know my wife. If she was going to leave me, she'd tell me to my face." Kindly, no less. Meri was not only hot as hell, incredibly sexy, the mother of his child and the love of his life, she was also the nicest person he'd ever known.

"She did leave you." There was no pity on Chantel's face. But her concerned expression held more than just a cop's distanced compassion. "That's what I'm telling you."

And he knew differently. Appearances could be deceiving.

"Meredith's ex-husband was a fiend," he said softly, as though Caleb might hear and understand what Max was saying. "He brutalized her, not only physically, but mentally, too. And got away with it because of the power his position gave him. I wish I knew more about him, but I gather he had a pretty impressive record with the Las Vegas police. I know he was older than she. Her family, both parents and a brother, were killed in a car accident when Meri was a kid. She was alone in the world. She grew up in a foster home. Met Steve through her foster parents. She married him at eighteen, and the first time he hit her was less than a year later. She stayed with him nine years."

He'd have felt disloyal, telling Meri's secrets, if Chantel had been just a friend. But she was a cop. And would help him find Meri.

Chantel and Max had spent four Christmases together. He trusted her. And had told Meri all about her.

"It took Steve less than three months to find her the first time she left. He was still a Las Vegas detective at that time. She got away almost immediately and managed to elude him almost a year that second time."

Chantel's eyes narrowed. "And you think this is the third time?"

He shook his head. "The third time was in Arizona. Five years ago."

"This guy's determined." She sounded serious. All cop. And Max took his first easy breath in more than twenty-four hours.

Hold on, Meri.

Help is on the way.

Day Three.

It is night again. Friday night. Carly went to bed two hours ago. I heard Latoya turn off the television in the living room an hour later and then her door shut, too. It's just the three of us in this bungalow. The three of us and the darkness.

It occurred to me last night that since my folks were killed when I was twelve, I've never had a room to myself. Ever. There were foster homes shared with other foster kids. And then there was Steve. And later, the other shelters, they were dorm room–style. As was the one dorm I was in between shelter one and shelter two. Between two and three was a one-room apartment shared with a shelter sister, and between three and four, a two-bedroom apartment shared with four sisters. After four, it was the YWCA. I'd wised up by then. I knew not to room with shelter sisters. Steve always knew how to find me. He might not find the exact shelter house I was in, or if he had, hadn't been stupid enough to breach them. Much easier to be patient and wait for me to be out on my own. But he'd find the home office instead. And watch it. I'd leave the shelter when I was ready, get an apartment and by then, he'd already know of and be following women who came and went from the home office. By my continued association, he'd eventually find me. Took a lot of time. A lot of tedious waiting and watching.

Apparently I was worth the effort to him.

I actually thought changing my habit, going back to my legal name—something he'd never suspect— moving into a YWCA instead of an apartment—had finally won me my freedom. Or rather, I wanted so badly to believe....

I feel kind of silly writing this down. I know all

of this stuff. But if I don't make it through this attempt to stand up to him rather than run, to face him head on and somehow threaten or trick him into leaving me alone, I'd like to think that my journey might be of some benefit to someone else who is a victim of domestic violence.

Today's group counseling session got me thinking about that. I guess because there were so many of us who are new here—including my two bungalow mates. Carly—she's twenty-seven and was abused and then stalked by her boyfriend—has been here for a couple of weeks. Latoya just arrived yesterday. She's in her forties, escaping her husband of twenty-four years, and I'm pretty sure this is the first time she's ever sought help. Her youngest just left for college.

Carly's external bruises have healed. The left side of Latoya's face is still too swollen for us to know what she really looks like.

In counseling today Sara told us that it's not just the few of us in shelters who feel so isolated—so cast apart. It's one in four of those hundreds of women dropping their kids off at school every day, getting their nails done or walking the aisles in the grocery store.

I know this stuff.

And yet, today, I could feel the shock of the facts reverberate all the way through me. It was as though I'd heard them for the first time.

Or rather, I felt them for the first time. And I

knew I had to do what I could to help. I will make my life matter. Even if I am at the end of my life.

I will share this, my attempt to fight back, with my sisters. In this diary. And maybe…someday…if Caleb wants to know more about his mama, someone will make these writings available to him.

What a comfort that thought is to me. I am writing to help Caleb understand me someday. To understand the challenge I faced and the choice I made. I am not deserting you, Caleb. I am not walking out on you.

You are not being abandoned! You are so loved, my little man. More than you will probably ever know. I need you to know that if I don't make it through this, I am okay with that. I will die at peace because I died for you and your daddy. I died protecting you from a fiend I should never have brought into your lives.

I undertake this job with the assurance that if I leave this earthly life, I will be watching over both of you from above. I will always be around, loving you, protecting you. I need you to know that….

Tears dropped onto the pages and Jenna knew she had to stop. But although it was late, she still had many hours of darkness to endure. Her housemates were both in their rooms for the night. And if allowing Meredith to pour out her deepest heart, and some tears along with it, would help her—Jenna—to make it through the days, then so be it.

She was only human.

And so, with eyes blurring the script, she wrote long into the night. Completely sober, yet scribbling drunken-seeming avowals of the undying love she might never be able to express again. She wrote because she couldn't sleep. She wrote to keep her sanity.

She wrote because she missed her men so much she wasn't sure that she could stay on top of the pain.

WHEN MAX GOT home from work Friday night, Chantel was there. She'd spent the night in his home more times than he could count during his marriage to Jill. His and Jill's spare room had been dubbed Chantel's room. She'd kept a toothbrush and change of clothes there.

Her staying Thursday night had seemed a bit odd—and yet logical, too. There was no way he was going to send her out to find a hotel in Santa Raquel at midnight and it was even less acceptable to let her drive the three hours back to Las Sendas after spending the evening helping him try to track down Meri's ex-husband. The guy had spent some time as an undercover cop. If he didn't want to be found, finding him wasn't going to be easy.

Chantel was offering him professional expertise on her own time. Because it was what Jill would have wanted.

She'd also cooked dinner for him and Caleb, as Max had discovered when he'd come into the house through the garage, his son on his hip, expecting to find a cold and deserted house, and finding, instead, a casserole in the oven and a plain-clothed cop poring over pages of reports on the laptop computer she'd set up at his kitchen table.

Meri would never have put a computer on the dinner table.

Dining came before business—always. Family before business—always. But now the business was finding Meri.

Which was why, at ten o'clock Friday night, he and Chantel were still sitting at the kitchen table.

She'd used her password-protected account to search crime databases and found seven Steve Smiths in the Las Vegas area who'd been charged with counts of domestic violence during the years Meri would have lived there.

And was trying to connect any of them to the Steve Smith on Meri's Las Vegas marriage and divorce records.

There were one hundred and twenty Steve Smiths just in the North Las Vegas area.

"None of the seven charged Smiths match up," she said as soon as he finally got Caleb asleep two hours past his bedtime.

It was the first they'd been able to speak freely since he'd arrived home. Caleb might not understand the significance of words, but he could very well remember them, and he wasn't going to risk his son being adversely affected. Caleb was already showing signs of anxiety, just having Meri gone, without a bunch of adult-type talk involving police searches confusing him further. It wasn't so much the words, Max knew, but the serious tone of their voices that would alarm him.

"Two are in jail. One is dead. Three are still married to their spouses and living and working in Las Vegas. And a seventh moved to Massachusetts and is remarried. None of them were cops. Do you have any idea how old Meri's ex is?"

"Six years older than she, which would make him thirty-eight."

"None of these guys are thirty-eight."

Then they weren't looking in the right place.

"Are you sure she pressed charges against him?"

Was he? He'd assumed she had. But had she actually said so? "She said that turning him in hadn't helped," he said, trying to remember her exact words. It wasn't as though he and Meri sat around and discussed the abusive past that she was trying to leave behind.

She'd been through counseling. And said that her best course was just to move forward. If she ever hoped to have a normal life she had to move on from being a victim.

Or something like that. Those conversations had been more than four years ago. He'd taken away the pertinent facts and left the rest.

Chantel changed screens. Typed.

"I'm looking up restraining orders with any of

her names on them." He'd given her Meri's aliases
the night before. "If she filed something we can
make an educated guess that the man she filed it
against is Steve." Chantel's screen went blank before lists of green writing popped up. "I'm assuming she only had one abuser?"

"That's correct." No doubt in his mind about that
one. "And she did file a restraining order," he said,
remembering. "More than four years ago." Steve
Smith had been a curse in Meri's life. And a threat
to his life with Meri from the very beginning.

One thing was certain, when they found the guy,
he was going to pay.

Even if he wasn't immediately responsible for
Meri's disappearance, and he hoped to God he
wasn't, he was most definitely peripherally to
blame. If not for Steve's years of abuse and later
hunting her down like an animal, Meri wouldn't
suffer from such paralyzing paranoia.

"I've got it." Highlighting a record, Chantel
opened it up. Clicked to bring up an official looking document. "It was filed almost five years ago
and was granted for one year," she said slowly,
reading. He tried to see by leaning over from where
he was sitting, but couldn't make out the fine print
on the PDF form.

"Five years ago he was working as a P.I."

He hadn't known that.

"Steve had written to her via the last shelter she'd

been in, using her newest assumed name. The letter was the basis for the order...."

He was trying desperately to remember things he'd only wanted to forget.

"Private investigators have to be fingerprinted to get a license to practice in Nevada," she said. "So I ran a search, matching the Steve Smith named on Meri's restraining order with a Steve Smith in the fingerprint database under the same address. It came up a positive match."

"So he was a private investigator." Not great news, but not the end of the world either. "I'm guessing Meri didn't think that was nearly as frightening or noteworthy as him having been a cop. It was his police connections that scared her. And he had to do something when he left the force."

"Do you know why he left?"

"Meri was certain he left so he could pursue her exclusively."

Frustrated at his lack of knowledge, Max waited while Chantel continued to type and read. Steve Smith had been a ghost in their lives—one who'd left a lot of fear.

"The restraining order was reinstated in California when she moved here. It's good for five years."

He'd known it was good in California. He hadn't known about the reinstatement part.

"Steve was a detective with the Las Vegas police for ten years."

"I told you he was a cop."

Chantel continued to read whatever private database she had access to. "I didn't realize he was this decorated. The man would have contacts, Max. And there are a lot of loyal men on the force...."

He'd heard stories from Jill about how fellow officers overlooked claims of domestic violence against their own, understanding that a bit of aggression came with the territory.

Believing, too, that a man who risked his life every day to save others wouldn't cross the line and hit a member of his own family.

If there were allegations, the force recommended counseling. They watched over him. Made sure there were support facilities available to him and to the members of his family.

"He retired from the force without a blemish. I find it hard to believe this is the same man that would behave as Meredith told you he had."

Chantel knew police work. She knew Jill. She didn't know Meri.

"Talking about Steve upset Meri," he said with confidence while, inside, he was running scared as hell. "He hadn't been around since she left Arizona and I was certain he'd moved on. He didn't follow her to California. Either he got the message to leave her alone, met someone else and let Meri go, or was in jail. Didn't much matter which it was as long as he stayed out of our lives.

"I assumed Meri didn't know and didn't want to

know what he was doing. I honestly didn't think he was still a threat, because of the order and because he'd gone so long without bothering her. In my mind, the problem wasn't so much his showing up again, as it was the effect his years of abuse had had on her. I tried to play down her past to help her move on."

"Restraining orders are enforceable in all states. And she could have filed for one in California, had her hearing, without him ever having to attend. He would've known that."

Chantel continued to scroll. And he needed her to understand.

"When I first met Meri she was always looking over her shoulder. Not afraid of her shadow so much as being in constant preparation for a hit from behind. It was as if she didn't think she was allowed to live a normal life and be happy."

"Sounds like a woman used to keeping secrets."

Her words seemed to be a direct threat to his marriage.

"I'm not saying that she'd betray your trust or anything, but that maybe keeping secrets had become a matter of survival to her."

Chantel's big brown eyes were filled with compassion.

Max focused on his own computer, where he was searching social networks for Steve Smith. There were lots of them.

Lots of Steve Smiths. Ordinary-looking guys with ordinary families. And jobs.

"I'm just… I guess what I'm trying to say is that someone like this, someone who's had to hide to this extent…it's understandable that you might not know her as well as you thought you did. In terms of you being so certain that she wouldn't leave you."

Chantel was talking about a woman she didn't know. Making her sound like someone he didn't know.

His job was to stay calm.

CHAPTER SEVEN

AT A COMPUTER in a private cubicle at the library in the main building of the Stand on Saturday, Jenna studied various domestic violence websites, reading about the abusive personality, fantasy bonds, dependent relationships. All things she knew about, but only from the victim perspective. She had to get into the mind-set, to imagine the feelings so deeply that she could predict reactions to stimulus. The goal was to figure out what stimulus to use on Steve to get the reaction she needed—him to choose to set her free.

She read statistics and psychological data. On victims. And abusers—who'd often been victims themselves. She read victims' stories. There was Emma, who'd left an unfaithful husband for a wonderful man, Robert, she'd met online, a man who was a friend to her for a couple of years before she finally divorced her cheating husband and moved in with him, only to end up bruised and broken a couple of years later.

There was Lottie, a teenager abused by her boyfriend. Belinda, who'd suffered abuse since childhood at the hands of her father. The list, the stories, went on and on.

She felt as if she knew each and every one of the women she read about, wanted to give each of them a hug and a promise of emotional support from now through eternity.

Jenna acknowledged the feeling, understood it as a consequence of identifying with them so completely. And she moved on.

She wasn't here to read about her sisters. She had to know everything she could find out about abusers. Not how to identify them. She knew those lists all too well—could remember the first sickening time she'd been on a website, reading a list, and finding Steve in every single characteristic she read.

But what made a man do what he did? She had to know how to get him where he hurt. To find the humanity in him and appeal to it somehow. Not verbally of course. That would just feed his sense of control—hearing her beg. Experience had taught her that during her first year of marriage.

She read for hours. Unaware of fatigue. Or hunger.

And then she found James.

His mother had died when he was two and he'd been raised by a paternal aunt who had no children of her own. And didn't want any. She resented her brother, a long-haul truck driver, leaving James with her, but took him in because it was her godly duty to do so.

She went to church on Sunday morning and Sunday night and Wednesday night and took him with her every single time. And for every sound he made that interrupted her spiritual oneness she would burn him with the tip of her cigarette when they got home. Not enough to blister, or leave scars. Just enough to remind him of the dangers of hell's fires.

The little boy did everything he could to please his aunt and when she took sick while he was in his teens, he kept her home, caring for her with patience and kindness until the day she died. Some thought he'd done so for the money he'd inherit when she was gone. But he'd known they were paupers. He'd cared for her himself because he'd known what kind of state facility she'd have ended up in if he hadn't kept her home.

She'd opened her home to him. It was his duty to keep her there. God—and his aunt—had taught him well.

Shortly after his aunt died, he met a girl who'd lost her family tragically young. They hit it off from the very beginning because they had in common that sense of not really belonging, of having been denied the core foundation of a stable home life. And they married as soon as she was out of high school.

He was good and patient and kind to his wife, understanding her tender heart. He just did not tolerate any actions from her of which he did not approve. He was boss of the house now. And with that responsibility came the right to make those in his home follow his rules. By whatever means.

He provided. So he got to rule. And sometimes ruling meant that you had to teach those in your care about the dangers of hell's fires.

He didn't burn anyone. Remembering the burn-related nightmares of his youth he would never do that. He just used his words, and later his hands, to save his wife from falling down the devil's hole.

He did so with God's blessing. Using scripture to manipulate and control. To instill fear. Using hard work and dedication to family as proof of his own good heart.

And...

"Are you okay, dear?" Jenna jumped in her seat at the sound of a voice just over her shoulder.

"Yes!" she said, quickly minimizing the screen. "I'm fine, why?" Still lost in the story she'd been reading, she wasn't sure if the sixtyish woman was the same one who'd been behind the desk when she came in, if she even worked there at all, or was a resident like herself.

"You were trembling so hard I could feel you," she said, pointing to an adjoining cubicle perpendicular to the one at which she sat.

The woman had presumably been on a computer as well, and since the computers were reserved for residents, that would make her one.

"I'm sorry," Jenna said now. "I guess I'm a little cold. They've got the air conditioner blowing pretty hard in here."

It was. But she hadn't noticed that either, not until then.

"I'm Renee," the woman said, nodding.

"I'm Jenna."

"I know. I saw you at dinner last night. You hardly touched a thing."

"I wasn't very hungry."

"You also don't act like this is your first dance. You aren't looking lost, or trying to figure out the way things work."

She shrugged.

"It's not mine, either."

If the woman needed to talk, she'd listen. There were others milling around. A woman a few tables over, with an opened encyclopedia and a pad of paper and pen in front of her. Another sitting in an armchair reading a magazine. And someone else reading from a tablet. There were a couple of women huddled together across the room, too.

Women seeking solace through conversation with other women was part of the healing process.

"You've been here before?" she asked Renee, as the other woman pulled her chair around and sat down.

"A few years ago. I'd just put my husband of forty years, Gary, in the hospital with a shove that ended up paralyzing him."

Renee couldn't have been more than a hundred pounds. "You hurt him?"

"The police said it was self-defense. So actually did Gary when he realized that he could lose me if he lied about it. He'd been about to throw me down the stairs. I shoved against him, purely a terrified reaction on my part, and it caught him off guard at just the right moment and he went down instead."

It wasn't a story she'd heard before. She could only imagine the guilt mixed with fear and confusion that one would carry in such a situation. She'd gone through years where she'd believed Steve's anger was her fault. If she didn't nag as much, ask so many questions, if she didn't need so badly to be loved, if she hadn't pissed him off at just the wrong moment, if she'd been more understanding of the very real pressures of his dangerous job....

Renee shifted and it dawned on her that she wasn't meeting the woman on the "outside." Renee was back in a shelter for abused women.

"You said your husband was paralyzed. Was it only temporary, then?"

"No."

"But he hurt you again?" They were sisters, in a place where secrets were safe.

"No, he didn't. He went through counseling, and once he saw what he'd been, he was truly sorry. He met with his group every week, long after he'd completed the program, just to make sure he never slipped back. He said that since he hadn't seen the abusiveness in himself to begin with—you know the lies they tell you, they sometimes believe them, too—he wasn't going to take a chance on having that happen again. He really did love me...."

Renee's eyes filled with tears. And Jenna was at a loss. Hearing about an abuser who was also one's true love wasn't...something she'd ever been privy to before. Or even considered.

"But...you're here...."

"Gary died last year, just after Christmas. Our son, Brian, who'd gone through a divorce shortly before his father was hurt, had moved home to help me take care of Gary these last few years. He... It was hard for him, to see his father so helpless...."

Uh-oh. Jenna's heart lurched.

"...the counseling, he was all for it at first. I mean, he'd known the back of his father's hand a few dozen times himself. But later...he said the weekly meetings, they turned his dad into a wuss...."

Wanting to stop what was coming so Renee wouldn't have to relive something she shouldn't have had to endure the first time, Jenna held herself back with effort.

Renee wouldn't be talking to her if she didn't need to do so. And sometimes, worse than having to tell your story when you didn't want to, was having someone tell you to stop when you did. "Brian's ex-wife, at the time of the divorce, had claimed that he was too much like his father. Brian said she was crazy, that she was just trying to make his life miserable, to make him pay, because he couldn't put up with her lying anymore. He'd caught her with another man. We believed him at the time. I knew my son. He's the assistant pastor of our church...."

Renee stopped and her chin trembled. So did her lips. But her eyes didn't waver as she looked at Jenna and continued, as softly as before, "The first time he raised a hand to me, I died a bit inside."

A mother shouldn't ever have to face such an atrocity. No woman should ever have to face abuse period, most particularly from a trusted loved one, but from your own child? From the human that you grew and bore and raised with unconditional love? Your own flesh and blood?

In the moment, Jenna felt incredibly lucky.

"You're here because Brian's been abusing you?"

"That's right. It's been... I've been here for six weeks, and really, I should be ready to go, but...."

"Are they pressuring you to move on?" Most places had to. With money constraints and regulations that didn't allow them to house residents long-term; shelters could only do so much.

"No! They don't do that here. Not unless you aren't trying to help yourself. But even then, they help find alternate housing. The Stand isn't funded principally with government money. There's some, but it's primarily funded by investments and private donations and a lot of the work is done by volunteers, so they aren't as tied to generic regulations as most places."

"So you can stay until you're ready to go...."

She nodded. "I just... He's still a pastor at the church where he grew up. At the church where his father and I grew up. I'm just... I..." She glanced at Jenna's computer screen.

"I was standing behind you for a bit before I called attention to myself. I... You were shaking and seemed upset, but you were engrossed and I... The article you were reading... I..."

Understanding dawned. She'd been reading about the abuser who used religion to keep his victim under his control. "You want to help your son."

With tears in her eyes, Renee nodded.

"You realize you can't help him if he's not willing to help himself."

"Are you telling yourself the same thing?"

"I'm... My situation is different." She couldn't let the other woman assume...she couldn't be responsible for setting an erroneous example. She was willing to die in this quest. She couldn't be responsible for another woman doing so. "I'm not trying to help anyone else." The words finally came to her. "I'm trying to help myself by gaining an understanding of...the other side."

Renee studied her for a long minute. And then, standing, she nodded.

"Please." Jenna reached out to her and was surprised when Renee took hold of her hand. "I'll...

We can study together, if you like. We can learn together. I just…promise me one thing…."

"What's that?"

"That you won't put yourself in a position that will allow your son to hurt you again."

"I can promise you that I won't have false hopes where he, or my ability to help him, is concerned. But he's my only child, Jenna. I can't promise never to be alone with him again."

It wasn't what she'd asked. But she understood that it was all the other woman could give.

And that made it enough.

For now.

CHAPTER EIGHT

CHANTEL HAD TO leave on Saturday. She was on shift that evening. Max didn't want her to go. While she was there, working with him, he felt as though he was actively on the way to finding his wife. He was actually doing something to bring her back home to him.

He'd continue his online searching—people were more open on social networks. They showed their true colors. And as Chantel had said, abusers with ego problems could be drawn by a social network's platform to brag about oneself.

Cops, she'd warned, were less likely to use online social networks, however, because they were so aware of their traceability.

She'd promised to continue investigating from her end, though she was treading carefully until she found out how the Las Vegas Metropolitan Police Department viewed Steve Smith—as one of their own that they would protect, or as one who'd betrayed them all by making a mockery of the badge.

From what she'd been able to determine so far, it was the former.

"What about that list of contacts I gave you?" he asked her while Caleb sat on the living room floor engrossed in a kids' show on TV. He and Meri didn't let the television babysit Caleb. But Meri had walked out on them and now he had to make do the best he could.

Ashamed of the thought he moved a little closer to the front door, while still keeping his young son in sight.

"Dead ends."

Chantel was doing what she could. So was he.

And so, he was certain, was Meri.

It would all work out. They were going to be fine.

"I'll stay on this, Max," she told him. "Between the two of us we've spoken with anyone she had contact with recently. I'll continue making calls."

"Thank you." But... "Something made her run."

"I agree. I'm just not convinced it was the dangerous threat you assume it was. She might just be a runner, Max." Chantel's voice was soft. "You married a woman with serious issues. They aren't her fault. I'm not saying they are. Based on the little bit we've been able to put together this weekend— her aloneness in the world, her marriage to an allegedly abusive detective from LVMPD, a man who is now a private investigator and has hunted her down on four different occasions—she couldn't help but have issues. Some women, when they start to feel emotionally pressured, or to feel as if they're going to fail, run. It's their way of avoiding the pain of disappointing those they love."

He wanted to push her out the door and close it behind her. Permanently. "You're saying they're motivated by their fear of retribution to get out before they disappoint," he guessed, because the rational part of him knew there was some truth to her statement.

Just not with Meri. She'd never be afraid of him.

"Sometimes. Or maybe it's like she said, leaving Caleb at day care was too much for her. You said that she'd fought you on that issue, that the amount of time she left him each week was getting less and less. And she knew you weren't going to allow her to get away with it."

This wasn't about their son's day care. He and Meri had talked about that issue. And he gave in to her whenever she was at the point of panic.

Because he really did understand.

Just as she understood that he had a bit of a sensitivity where losing his wife was concerned. She wouldn't just up and leave him.

"If your relationship was exactly as you say it was, if Meri is all you believe her to be, then why would anything make her run?" The question came quietly, but also with grave seriousness. Chantel, a couple of inches shorter than he was, somehow made it difficult for him to look away. "If she trusts you as much as you think she does, why didn't she come to you with whatever was bothering her? Why not talk to you about it before she took off?"

"Because Steve wouldn't let her," he said, engulfed with tension anew. "It's what I've been telling you for three and a half days. He was there even though you didn't see him on the tape. He's got her, Chantel. I'm certain of it. For the reasons you just stated."

And what if Meri wasn't running because of fear for her own life? What if another part of the letter she'd written was the truth? The part about protecting Caleb? What if she was somehow protecting her son from Steve Smith?

It didn't really make sense. She'd call the police if that was case. She knew he had an "in" here, just like Steve used to have in Las Vegas.

But what if Meri was in the grip of irrational fear, if she wasn't being logical? Then there might be truth to the idea that she believed she had to run to protect *them*. "We have to find him."

The brown eyes gazing up at him shadowed, and Chantel grasped his arm, holding on tight. "We will, Max. Even though I'm not sure you're right about Steve, or Meri's reasons for leaving, your conviction makes me think you might be. I'm going to keep looking for him. I'm going to find her. For you. I'm not going to desert you. I promise."

He nodded. And, choked up with too much emotion for one calm guy to handle, held on a little too long when she leaned in and hugged him goodbye.

Day Four.

I have the bungalow to myself tonight. They're having Saturday night at the movies up at the main building and both Carly and Latoya went. They wanted me to go with them. I just couldn't. I can't be a part of their temporary family unit. I have a family.

Whether we ever see each other again, whether Max would ever forgive me for leaving like I did, with no warning, whether I'm successful in my attempt to have the threat of Steve permanently gone from my life or not, able to return to Max and Caleb or not, they are and will always be my family.

Jenna stopped writing, read the words on the page. And stared at the wall in front of her desk. On it hung a picture of an elegant, old-fashioned boudoir—a woman's place with upholstered eyelet furniture and soft roses in a vase.

And it occurred to her that she liked her room. Felt safe there. And couldn't remember a time when she'd really felt safe.

They said that secrets were safe at The Lemonade Stand. Maybe some were. Some probably weren't.

She was a secret.

And needed desperately to be a safe one.

I made a decision today. I know that my purpose, to keep my boys safe from Steve's ugliness, to keep them apart from the sense of being hunted like animals, from the fear of being hounded, gives me strength. Meredith Bennet gives me strength. She is the me I was born to be.

And while I was talking to Renee it occurred to me that if I am to succeed in my mission, I must keep alive the parts of myself that drive me. I must keep Meredith alive.

Jenna is a necessary part of me. And Meredith is even more so. Beyond this journal. Beyond my own mind.

I, Meredith, am a three-dimensional human being with a full life. And if I am going to keep her spirit alive, I have to be allowed to fly. At least a little bit.

Renee is a mother. Her selfless love for her son touched a chord in me and I know that it was no mistake that she found me today. She needs me. I got that right away. But I needed her, too.

I must stop Steve's stalking, put an end to the threat he poses to me and my family. But I must also keep Meredith's life alive where I can. It is the life that I am willing to die to preserve.

Tomorrow, I am going to make a phone call to the mother of the three-year-old patient I've been working with. Someone I can still help, someone from Meredith's daily life who can coexist in Jenna's. Olivia's mother, Yvonne, is a survivor. She will settle for as little as I can give her.

And then, maybe later, if I can figure out a way

*to do so undetected, I will check in on Max and
Caleb. I will watch over my men.*

For now.

And for eternity.

This I promise them.

And I promise me, too.

Goodnight.

"MAMA! MAMA!" The childish cry rent the air and
Max flew out of bed and into the hallway before
he was even fully awake.

"Mamaaaaa!" Caleb was crying, screaming, and
his father stubbed his toe on the way into the nurs-
ery to find the toddler standing up in his crib, arms
stretched over the bars that contained him.

"It's okay, boy," he said, hardly aware of the
throbbing in his little toe as he pulled the toddler
from his crib. "Daddy's here."

"Mama!" Caleb's voice broke on a hiccup, but
the crying had stopped. Throwing his arms around
Max's neck, Caleb held on tightly and laid his head
against Max's shoulder.

"It was just a bad dream," he said, hoping the
words were true, but not willing to settle for hope.
He took his son into his room, laid the little boy
down on his bed and proceeded to look him over
for any signs of illness. He checked his belly for
rash, his skin for hives, his fingernails for coloring, his eyes for dilation, his pulse and adenoids

while the boy lay there, tears on his lashes, staring up at him.

"Mama?" Caleb's voice was tiny as he lay in the middle of the big bed.

"Mama's not back yet," Max said over the lump in his own throat. *Oh, God, Meri, would you be here if you could?*

Or did you really choose to leave us? For whatever reason....

Are you still alive, my love?

Everyone was so sure she'd left him of her own accord. The facts pretty much proved that she had. Chantel, the local police, they all seemed to think she was safely out there somewhere starting a new life for herself.

He just couldn't believe that.

So much so that he still hadn't told anyone she'd left. They'd made calls, asking if anyone had seen her, heard from her, but as far as his work was concerned, no one knew the truth.

He'd made calls to the clients she'd had on her calendar for the coming week, saying that she was under the weather. He'd called the school to let them know she wouldn't be in.

He was doing what he had to do to take care of his family.

If Smith had Meri, would he kill her for having married another man?

"Mama home." Caleb lay still, watching him.

"She'll be home soon, son," Max said, scooting

the little body up and over so that his head lay on Max's pillow. He flipped off the light he'd turned on upon coming into the room, and climbed into bed beside his son.

Chantel was using her police skills and resources to look for Meri. She'd promised him that she'd find her. They'd talk again in the morning, just as they had every day since Meri's disappearance.

Tonight, he would do what Meri would do if she were there. He'd cuddle their son for her.

And find strength and solace in sleep.

But as Caleb snuggled into Max's chest and the little boy's breathing evened out, Max lay wide-awake in bed beside him.

Caleb had just had his first nightmare.

And his mother had not only missed it, she'd caused it.

JENNA DIDN'T ATTEND Sunday morning service. She went to the library instead to do more reading. To get into the mind-set of the abuser so she'd know how to approach Steve.

She had to convince him that it was in his best interest to let her go. The question was, how did she do that without getting herself killed?

If it were easy, or clear, she'd already have done it. She knew the risk she was taking. Had a pretty good idea the chances of her getting out alive weren't in her favor.

But he'd pushed her as far as she could go. This wasn't just about her and Steve anymore.

When the hour grew decent enough for a phone call, she went for a walk on the property—acres and acres of lushly landscaped colorful gardens and perfectly manicured lawns—pulled her untraceable pay-by-minute cell phone from the edge of her bra where she was now storing it, and dialed a number she knew by heart, waited for the machine to answer and said, "Yvonne?"

Olivia's mother wouldn't pick up an unknown number. "This is Meredith. I'm going to call back in a couple of minutes. Talk soon."

She walked, head down, not wanting to engage in conversation with anyone. She waited a few minutes and then called back. Yvonne's three-year-old daughter was going to be having surgery and would need to learn how to swallow again. Jenna had already started the little girl on exercises that would facilitate that learning.

"Meredith?" The woman sounded breathless as she picked up on the first ring.

"Yes."

"I... Someone came to the house the other day, a policeman. He was asking about you. I've been worried sick."

"I wouldn't let you and Olivia down," Jenna said, walking, turning her head as someone passed, staying in constant motion so that she wouldn't be overheard.

"I was worried about you!"

"I'm fine, Yvonne. No need to worry." Yvonne had enough problems of her own—she was still being hounded by an abusive ex who had already violated his restraining order once, in addition to dealing with her little girl's medical issues—and Jenna didn't want to add to them.

Or set a wrong example, as she'd almost done with Renee the day before. She was going to have to be very careful. Sisters in victimhood watched each other, watched out for each other, learned from each other—all part of that which made recovery possible.

She couldn't betray that sisterhood. Couldn't have one of the other women following in her footsteps as she headed out to confront her abuser on her own.

And still, she knew she was on her own right course. "Is Olivia still on for surgery next week?" she asked, nervous about being on the phone at all. She couldn't be traced. She knew that. But still…

"Yes, Tuesday at nine a.m. I just got confirmation on Friday morning. Are you home?"

"No, I'm not. And…I'm not going to be. Listen, Yvonne, I want to help you, as I promised I would." Olivia was due to have reconstructive surgery to repair a bone in her jaw that was broken when her father shoved her mother while Yvonne was holding Olivia. "I want to do Olivia's throat therapy after surgery. She trusts me and we've worked through the exercises so while someone else could certainly take over, I think I'll be the most effective at getting the quickest results and giving her the best chance for complete recovery."

"So you'll be back home then?"

"No. And here's the thing. I will help you but I have to do so on my terms."

"Of course. You know I'll do anything I can to accommodate you. You've helped me so much. Without you—"

She'd first met Yvonne in a therapy session at The Lighthouse women's shelter—where she'd been a resident when she'd first moved to California, and then later, a volunteer.

"I'm…in hiding," Jenna said, surveying her surroundings as she reached the Garden of Renewal, an exquisite piece of natural art set apart from the rest of the Stand's property by a forest of trees. She'd never been inside the Garden. And didn't go now, as there were sure to be other residents inside, sitting on the benches, enjoying the waterfall she could hear from the edge of the trees.

"From Max?" Yvonne sounded horrified.

"No! Of course not from Max. But he doesn't know where I am and he can't know," she said. "This is nonnegotiable, Yvonne. You said someone has already been there asking about me. You won't know where I am or have a way to contact me. I'm not going to put you in the position of lying about that part. I will keep in touch with you. We'll have to find someplace safe for Olivia's therapy, someplace no one would think to look. It's vitally important that I can trust you not to tell anyone when or where that happens."

"Of course, I'll do whatever you need me to do, you know that."

Making arrangements to be in touch with the other woman after surgery, Jenna finished with, "I'm sorry it has to be this way...."

"Don't you dare be sorry. This isn't your fault. And the fact that you're still willing to help us..."

"I...thank you."

"You're in danger from your abuser aren't you?"

She'd known there would be questions. Yvonne wouldn't let a fellow survivor hide without support.

"I... Max and Caleb... I'm not good for them. I need them to be free to pursue a life without me." It was what she'd written in the note she'd left. She had to stick to her story.

But as she said the words, as she ended the call, Jenna was bereft. Each step she took was a step further from Max. She'd left him free to pursue a life without her.

Which opened the door for another relationship. She'd only been gone a few days, but there was no end in sight at this point. And what woman wouldn't want to step into her shoes?

Max was not only a financially solid, kind and decent man, he was also deliciously sexy. And a doctor to boot.

Thoughts tumbled one on top of the other.

Max didn't like to be alone. Women rarely left him alone.

He also had a son to raise. One who needed a mother.

As she once again contemplated the dangerous possibility that Max could replace her before she had a chance to complete her mission, Jenna faltered.

If he did find someone else, she'd have to find a way to be happy for him.

Jenna put one foot in front of the other and walked on.

CHAPTER NINE

CHANTEL CALLED SUNDAY morning just like Max had known she would. He'd just settled Caleb in his chair with breakfast.

"Things were busy here last night," she said, "but I wanted you to know I'm making enquiries, trying to find someone I know who knows someone in Las Vegas."

"Whatever the cost, if you need to hire someone…I realize you can't just drop everything for this," he said, pacing the living room while his son sat at the kitchen table with a glass of milk and a pile of vanilla wafers in front of him.

Not the best breakfast, but not the worst, either. At least Caleb was eating. And watching a cartoon on the tablet that was propped up on the kitchen table.

His parenting skills sucked at the moment. He got that. But a guy had to do what a guy had to do.

And right now he had to find his wife.

"I'll keep that in mind," she said. "But as it turns out I know one of the guys on the force in Santa Raquel. That's one of the reasons I'm calling. I found out last night that he'd transferred up there and I wanted you to know. He was in the academy with me and owes me a favor. While we were in training I helped him reconcile with his wife after he screwed up in a bar one night...."

Max wondered about her life. About what she'd been doing in the years since Jill's death—other than the captain who hadn't worked out. About what was important to her. But that question wasn't a priority just then....

"You think this guy will help?" he asked.

"I know he'll do what he can, but because there's no crime here, it could take a few days, Max."

"I'll do anything I can from my end, too," he said. They'd already called anyone he could think of whom Meri might have inadvertently mentioned something to. Anyone who might have noticed something. He'd even called The Lighthouse— a women's shelter where she'd been volunteering since he'd known her. "I'll keep doing my internet research, but I can also drive around, canvas neighborhoods. You let me know what to do and I'm on it."

Because he'd promised Meri a lifetime of protection.

SHE'D CHOSEN The Lemonade Stand for three reasons. First, because she'd never been there before so she could be anonymous. Second, because they were privately funded and not as subject to unbending rules and regulations.

And third, because they were exactly what she was not—focused on comfort. Her focus was and always had been on practical matters. On survival—and serving others. She'd never choose anything fancy for herself. Not a car. A purse. Or a place to hide.

She wasn't fully in the mind-set of her abuser yet, but one thing she knew for sure was that Steve was confident to the point of being cocky about how well he knew Meredith.

The way to fool him, at least in the short run, was to act out of character.

It would keep her one step ahead of him. She hoped.

Everything she'd read that Sunday morning about the abusive personality reinforced this belief. And so, armed with a momentary sense of safety, and a burning need to be Meredith, Jenna escaped her prison Sunday afternoon.

Steve wouldn't expect to find her in public, at any of her usual haunts. And she had no doubt now that he knew all of them. That while she'd been daring to hope that she was free of him, he'd been quietly tracking her every move.

Today he'd be watching shelters, probably had others doing so, too, in big cities in surrounding states. Or maybe he had access to an inside database. Shelters worked closely with police departments and while Steve was no longer on the force, he could still have connections.

And running to shelters was what she always did. Ran to the closest state she could get to, contacted Victor, the broker she'd met in Vegas, for another new identity, and entered a new shelter. It might take Steve a bit to figure out her new name. He'd have to check all the new residents at all the shelters and figure out which one was her. But he seemed to enjoy the hunt—something else she had confirmed in her reading that morning.

But this time she'd run differently. She'd stayed close to home. And checked into what was essentially a resort—not a bare-bones place where an actual bed, in place of a mattress on the floor, was a luxury.

She'd stayed close because she wasn't running from him anymore. And still, as she rode the bus toward the ocean Sunday afternoon, she sat with her long dark hair pinned up and concealed under a big hat. Her cell phone was tucked safely in her bra beneath the too-big silk blouse she'd chosen out of the garment supply at The Lemonade Stand to go with the blue cotton capris—also a little big— to conceal a shape Steve knew only too well. Meredith didn't carry a bag. She had money tucked in her pocket and her passcode for reentry into the private section of The Lemonade Stand, firmly tucked away in her brain.

The passcode wasn't her birthday. Or Max's or Caleb's, either. It wasn't her wedding date or the date her final decree had been recorded. It wasn't either one of her folks' birthdays. Or even Chad's— her little brother who'd died way too young.

No, the code she'd chosen as her "key" to her temporary home was the numerical coordinates for the name of her imaginary friends when she'd been a kid. Only her mother had known that she'd called them "my fellas." Yet it was something Jenna would never forget. Not even under duress.

And who knew how long it was going to take Steve to figure out that she'd changed her M.O.? She could hope for months.

It had taken him that long to find her in the past.

As the bus pulled to a stop only a few miles from the Stand, Meredith focused, taking in the entire area, behind her, in front of her, next to her, inside and outside the bus. A group of people stood gathered in the parking lot a few steps away. They appeared to be waiting for more people to join them.

Standing at the exact time as others did, she exited the bus after a couple of people had gotten off but while there were still a few behind her. She walked as closely to the woman in front of her as she could without making her uncomfortable— with the plan that if the woman turned, she'd tell her she loved her shoes and was just trying to get a closer look at them.

They were interesting. Black wedge sandals with gold and silver embellishments. Not her style…too flashy…but she liked them.

She'd chosen tennis shoes off the shelf of new shoes in her size at the shelter. Running shoes.

As luck would have it, the woman in front of her headed straight for the group of people gathered in the parking lot. But instead of joining them as Meredith had hoped, she turned right before reaching them and headed toward the beach.

Meredith's goal was the beach. If she could get there without drawing attention to herself. At that moment, the woman who'd been her cover turned away, and Meredith slipped in between a couple of people on the periphery of the big group. It didn't take her long to figure out that she was in the midst of a gathering of distant family members, many of whom didn't know each other, brought together by a cousin who'd done their familial genealogy and had arranged a picnic on the beach.

She moved through the group. Smiling at anyone who noticed her. And as they started slowly walking toward the beach, she traveled with them.

"You must be Brian's wife," one woman said to her. Meredith smiled and excused herself, pretending to see someone she knew—her gaze taking in everything around her, and searching for one familiar sight—her husband and son, enjoying their regular family Sunday afternoon at the beach.

UNLESS THERE WAS an emergency at the hospital, Sunday afternoons were family time. Max reflected that he and Meri had made it a point ever since Caleb was born to take him to the ocean, even if only for a brief visit that one day a week. Meri had insisted.

I want him to grow up with an ingrained sense of freedom, she'd said. She'd told him that it hadn't been until she'd arrived in California, stood next to the ocean for the first time, that she'd really believed she could recover from her past.

Standing at the ocean, she'd said, put life in perspective. Possibilities were so much larger than the limitations others tried to place on people. She'd just needed to see to believe.

She wanted their son raised to believe that anything was possible.

Her insight had opened his eyes.

And that Sunday afternoon, Max was left caring for an out-of-sync two-year-old, and feeling blind as a bat.

As tempting as it was to just sit at home in front of the television and take the opportunity to introduce Caleb to football, he knew better.

He wasn't giving in. Or giving up. They'd find Meri. She'd be back home soon.

Until then, he had to carry on with his life. Which meant taking his son to the beach as was their Sunday afternoon tradition.

And maybe some of the inspiration his wife seemed to get from being there would rub off on him, too.

Caleb sat quietly in his car seat as Max drove. At first Max thought he'd fallen asleep. But when he glanced in the rearview mirror, he saw his son staring out the window, a wide-eyed, serious expression on his face.

Max wished he could see into his son's mind. To know what the boy was thinking. To know how best to help him.

"Sand!" Caleb squirmed in Max's arms, wanting to be let down, as soon as they reached the section of public beach that had become their regular spot not only because it was next to the playground, but also because it provided the most unfettered view of the beach strip.

No hiding places, Meri had said.

"You want to play in the sand?" he asked Caleb, as he adjusted his step to keep his son within arm's reach. Meri would be holding Caleb's hand, but it was time for the boy to spread his wings. To find his wings and learn how to use them might be a better metaphor.

Because Meri kept them clipped and tied? Had she been right, that wise woman who'd so completely stolen his heart? Had she been telling the truth in the letter she'd left him? Had she believed that she'd been holding their son back with her paranoia?

Had he been so blind that he hadn't recognized the extent of his wife's personal struggles?

Max didn't think so. Meri was careful. But she also gave in when Max put his foot down. They made a good team, she'd said. "Daddy, sand!" Caleb sat and pounded the ground beside him.

Though there were many people about, the beach wasn't overly crowded that Sunday in September. The weather had cooled over the past week and even in the jeans and long-sleeved T-shirts he'd dressed himself and his son in, he could feel the first hint of winter's chill.

With a glance around, checking out the few people scattered across the beach and seeing nothing out of the ordinary, he sat.

"Cassie, cassie," Caleb said, pounding the ground again. *Castle.* The toddler wasn't laughing. He wasn't running and throwing sand and showing other signs that a happy, extroverted two-year-old might show, but he wasn't whining, either, which was a blessing after four days of little else.

So Max dug his hands down to damp sand and did his best to form enough of a lump to satisfy his son that they had a castle in front of them.

"This is the moat," he said, finding the sand sifting through his fingers therapeutic, and enjoying his son's rapt attention. He dug a trench around the lump he'd built. "There's pretend water running all around it here, see?"

"Fish!" Caleb said loudly enough for people several yards away to hear, as he picked a small piece of debris out of the sand at his side and threw it into the trench.

"Good!" Max said, smiling. "Fish are good. I think we need more." He struggled to hold the smile. He wasn't feeling it. But if collecting beach debris in a small circle around a nondescript mound kept his son occupied, he'd gladly force a lot more than a smile.

And would gladly stay on the beach as long as Caleb was happy there, too. The sand and the breeze, getting lost amongst people who were milling around as though the world was perfectly normal, was far better than facing a closet full of clothes that weren't being worn and wondering if they ever would be again.

"Mama!" As though Caleb could read his father's mind, he cried out.

"Mama's not here," Max said. "Look! A big fish. Maybe we should name him."

But Caleb had no interest in the sea bark he'd just unearthed from the sand. The boy was staring across the beach. "Mama!" he said. Not as though he was lonely. Or asking for her.

But as though he saw her there.

Following his son's gaze, Max saw a big group of people walking together as they crossed from the parking lot to the beach. A family reunion of some kind? Maybe a church group?

But he didn't see any sign of Meri. Still....

"Mama!" Caleb called again, scrambling to his feet to charge off in the direction he'd been looking as fast as his chubby little legs could carry him in the sand.

On his feet in seconds, Max was already at a run as he settled Caleb on his hip, holding the boy with both arms. "Where, buddy? Where did you see Mama?"

"Mama!" Caleb's call turned into a cry. "Mama!" he screamed.

They'd reached the edge of the beach and were approaching the bushes that separated the sand from the sidewalk.

"Mama!" Caleb cried again, tears in his voice now. He hitched himself up and down on Max's hip as if he was riding on a horse, kicking Max in the groin as he did so. "Mama!"

They rounded the corner to the parking lot. A couple was exiting their car. A mom was strapping a baby into the infant seat in her van.

There was no sign of Meri. Or even anyone with her height and build.

"Mama gone," Caleb said and started to cry. "Mama gone."

Not even the allure of French fries could console the little boy as Max drove home, no closer to having any answers or insights into his wife's disappearance.

CHAPTER TEN

DAY FIVE.

I saw Caleb today. After standing around in the parking lot for an ungodly length of time, the reunion organizers finally decided everyone had arrived and moved the group toward the beach.

I took a couple of steps and there he was, playing in the sand with his father.

He saw me, too.

He stood up. Ran toward me. Oh, God, I almost lost it. Almost ran to him.

But his father picked him up and I slipped away before Max spotted me. I can't think about my husband, about how much I am hurting him. I won't have the strength to carry on if I let myself dwell on Max.

He's a man who shoulders the cares of all those around him. He's the calm in the storm. Reason in the face of drama and fear. He's loyal and kind and honest.

And he has a heart that is as vulnerable as mine. Sometimes I think more so because mine has been hardening since I was twelve. His hurts are far newer.

I know how sensitive he is about losing his wife. I know how close he came to not asking me to marry him for fear that he'd lose me, too, like he lost Jill. And, for now, I've made his worst nightmare come true. I've left him.

But it's the only way we'll ever have a chance of being happy together. If I ever get back to him. If he'll be willing to take me back if I make it out of this alive.

Getting Steve out of my life is the only way Max will ever be able to live without the constant threat of losing me. He doesn't understand Steve. He doesn't want to believe that we're in danger. I know differently.

If I don't stand up to Steve, he will return again and again. And someday he'll kill me. And maybe them first just to make me suffer for choosing them over him. Which is why I had to go. So he'd see that I didn't choose them, either.

Jenna stopped, staring at the wall in front of her. Her hands trembled and she drew in shaky breaths. She should never have left the Stand that day. It had been too soon.

She wasn't ready.

Thankfully her housemates had been out when she'd returned a little over an hour before. She'd avoided the sidewalks that meandered through the property and walked between buildings to get to their bungalow and then come straight to her room.

They'd be expecting her to have dinner with

them, though. They'd raided the shelter's pantry together the evening before, choosing what they needed to prepare a Sunday dinner together. Each of them had chosen a favorite recipe. Her potato casserole, Carly's parmesan chicken breasts, and Latoya's dirty pudding, minus the gummy candies because they couldn't find any.

And while the pantry was there for anyone to take what they needed, Jenna had left money in the donation box from her stash of cash after the other two had left the room. Too many women needed the free facilities offered at the shelter—those who had no money whatsoever because their abusers controlled all of their income. And while The Lemonade Stand had enough to go around, she wasn't going to take from someone who was more in need.

Now she wished she'd never agreed to the dinner. How on earth she was going to keep up appearances, or be of any benefit to the two women sharing her space who were hurting so badly, she had no idea.

Jenna was strong. Capable. Tonight she just felt broken.

She'd slipped through the buses as soon as Caleb started toward her that afternoon. She'd run as fast as she could without drawing undue attention to herself. And as she'd rounded a corner, heading toward a bus stop she knew of on the next block, she'd tripped and fallen. She was fine. Picked herself up. But not before a police officer had seen. Stopped her and asked if she was all right.

She'd tripped because she hadn't seen the uneven crack in the sidewalk. Because she hadn't been able to see much of anything through her tears....

She'd been a fool to go.

And couldn't afford to be a fool twice.

"YOU NEED TO EAT, son." Max sat at the kitchen table with Caleb on Sunday evening. He'd only been able to convince the toddler to sit at the table when he'd moved the booster seat to Meri's chair.

"Mama," Caleb said, his eyes big and moist as he glanced at Max. It was the only word the little boy had said since leaving the beach.

"You love hamburgers and French fries," Max said, pointing to the opened paper wrappings spread in front of Caleb. He had his own disposable container in front of him. And took a bite of a sandwich he didn't want, chewing on the cardboard-tasting substance, to convince his son that it was the thing to do.

And wondering when Chantel would call. Another day had passed. With Meri still out there.

"After you eat, we'll go get ice cream," he said, pulling the words from the pool of desperation settling in his midsection. He'd been an active dad from the moment of Caleb's conception—eagerly sharing in every part of raising him that he could, from bringing him into the world to midnight feedings, first bath, first everythings....

He'd thought himself fully capable of every aspect of parenting.

He'd never realized how much Meri had done without him even being aware. He'd never realized quite how much her nurturing had filled up their son—and him, too....

He jumped when his cell phone rang, eager for news about his wife.

And then he saw who the caller was.

"Hi, Mom," he said, answering because he knew she'd worry if he didn't. "How was your week?"

He patiently half listened as she told him about her doctor's visit, about his father's refusal to slow down, and about a country-and-western show they'd seen at the clubhouse of their San Diego resort community the night before.

"How are Meri and Caleb?" she finally got around to asking the question he'd been dreading. He'd been debating what to tell his elderly parents, who'd taken Jill's death hard. Because they took anything and everything hard if it had to do with their only son—a late-in-life baby that they'd never expected to have.

"They're fine," he said. "Busy as always." And what in the hell was he going to do if she asked to speak with Meri?

"Did you go to the beach today?"

"Yes."

Caleb was quietly eating his French fries now. Wonder of wonders. So Max continued, "We built a castle and then found things in the sand to serve as fish for the moat."

"Any new words this week?"

Not unless you considered hearing *Mama* screeched over and over again with heartache. "No."

"Dad and I would sure love to see you," she said next. "It's been a couple of weeks since you came down and kids grow up so fast...."

"We'll talk it over and set a date," he said, hating the lie, and the desperation pushing him into it. If he told his folks Meri was gone, it would be an official part of their family memories.

He wasn't ready for that.

Or for the myriad questions her disappearance would raise. He didn't have any answers to give them.

He couldn't afford to worry about them worrying....

"I know Meri has a client going in for surgery this week and she'll want to be around afterward, for as long as the recovery takes."

"Is that the throat therapy she was talking about?"

"Yes."

"Well, that little girl needs her," his mother said. "Just let us know and we'll put you on the calendar," she said, easily enough.

His mother, who would be eighty on her next birthday, generally went with the flow. Unless she was worried.

And after her bypass surgery the year before, he didn't want to worry her at all.

He asked about his father. Watched Caleb eat over half of his hamburger, squeezing the bun between his fingers, and getting mustard on everything he touched.

Meri knew how to get mustard stains out.

And the internet would know, too.

Telling his mother he loved her, sending love to his father, and promising to share their love in return with Caleb and Meri, he rang off, hoping against hope that he'd bought himself another week before he'd have to answer to his mom again.

And that by the time that week had passed, his wife would be home to do the answering for him.

RENEE WASN'T IN Jenna's group counseling session. Nor was she in the class Jenna had signed up to take on the basics of business management, in an attempt to appear to be a normal resident. Then again Renee didn't have a husband with his own medical practice who might benefit from the class.

The older woman didn't have a child who stuttered and so wasn't involved in Jenna's first professional sessions at The Lemonade Stand, either.

And yet, over the next couple of days, Jenna

saw as much of Renee as she did anyone else, her housemates included.

Renee sought her out. And maybe she sought the other woman out, too.

"I'm worried about the bruise," she told her new friend as they sat together at the kitchen table in Renee's bungalow. Renee had three other women living with her, but they had all gone to a fashion show at the main building on Tuesday evening, leaving Jenna and Renee to have a quiet dinner of salad and iced tea together.

Renee glanced at the expanding mark on her forearm, one that was turning a dark red instead of changing to purple and yellows as it healed, and shrugged. "It'll heal."

"I think it's more than a bruise," Jenna continued. It was the first time she'd seen Renee without sleeves, and only then because the bungalow was warm enough that Renee had taken off the cardigan sweater she'd had on that day. "Brian did that to you, didn't he?"

Renee's silence was answer enough.

"When?"

The other woman poked her fork around her salad. Jenna suspected then that the bruise wasn't healing because it was new.

"You saw him on Sunday, didn't you?" She'd looked for Renee after her stint at the library. And again later that evening when, after her dinner with Latoya and Carly, she'd felt like taking a walk on her own. The other woman hadn't been on the grounds as far as she was aware.

Dropping her fork in her bowl, Renee laid her arm on the table with obvious care and looked up. "I called him," she said. "I asked him if we could meet together with the head pastor of our church."

From what she'd read, when it came to abusers and victims, attending counseling sessions together wasn't recommended. At least not in the beginning.

"And?"

"He agreed to meet. I told the pastor what had been going on in our home and asked him to help us."

Jenna held her breath.

"Brian responded with contrition and shame and asked for a sabbatical from the church so that he could enter an abuse counseling program immediately."

Renee shifted in her chair and Jenna's eye fell on that bruise at the same time her heart sank.

Renee's eyes had filled with tears, though the older woman wasn't crying. Jenna recognized the look. The pain was there, but buried so deeply it couldn't be released.

"Thinking that all was well, the pastor left. We'd met in the public park by the amphitheater downtown and...."

She could have filled in blanks. "There were people around. I thought I was safe...."

"What did he do?"

"He grabbed my arm." Renee was looking at Jenna, but her arm jerked on the table, as though remembering....

"He told me that I was a traitor to him, to his father, and to God. He said that I was evil for trying to come in between him and God's work. And he said that if I didn't want to end up in a home for the elderly, I would never, ever embarrass him like that again.

"He also told me that I could expect to pay all of his bills until he could get back to work."

Glancing at Renee's arm, Jenna asked, "He did that just by grabbing your arm?"

Renee gently covered her bruise with her free hand. Did she think she could make the problem disappear if she could just stop feeling the pain?

Did Jenna?

"He gave my arm another hard squeeze for each accusation." Renee's throat caught on the words. "I felt something snap. I think he may have cracked the bone."

Jenna's chair scraped across the floor as she stood up. "We've got to get you to the clinic. You need to have that set or it won't heal properly. It'll hurt you for the rest of your life. It also might continue to bleed and cause more problems."

She wasn't a medical professional, but she was married to a doctor and knew enough to know that Renee's injury could have serious repercussions.

"I can't." The other woman shook her head. "If I

go to Lynn, she'll be under obligation to inform the police and I'm not going to have my son arrested."

Lynn Bishop—the newly married chief medical officer at the Stand—was a nurse practitioner. Jenna had met her briefly her first day at the Stand. And had seen Lynn and her little daughter Kara walking across campus a time or two. She'd yet to meet Lynn's new husband, the man apparently responsible for the beautiful grounds at The Lemonade Stand. He and his older brother also lived on the property.

And Renee's son deserved to be arrested…and worse.

"I know what you're thinking," Renee said, her expression ancient, yet calm, as she glanced up at Jenna. "I'm not excusing his behavior, but I know my son. If I have him arrested he'll only get angrier. And blame me rather than taking accountability for his own actions.

"He agreed, in front of Pastor Johnson, to go through the recovery program. Pastor Johnson will see that he does so. If he's in jail, that won't happen. If he's in jail, he'll have much less hope of ever getting back to preaching. And if he doesn't see that as his goal, he's not going to be influenced by Pastor Johnson…."

Renee had good points. And obviously had given the matter a lot of thought. Clear thought.

"I'm under no illusions where my son's treatment of me is concerned," she said as Jenna continued to stand over their half-eaten meal. "But neither can I walk away. He's my son."

Jenna had fought too hard and too long to accept that there were options other than leaving. Hope kept you captive.

"Do you have any children?"

The question shot at her out of the blue. Two days after she'd nearly fallen apart at the sight of her son.

And she realized too late that her silence was answer to Renee just as earlier Renee's silence had been answer to Jenna.

"One? Two?"

With her hands gripping the back of her chair she said, "One."

"Boy or girl?"

"Boy."

"Is he safe?"

"Yes." She answered with absolute conviction. And as long as she stayed away, Caleb would continue to be safe.

"And if he wasn't, you'd do whatever it took, sacrifice your life if that's what it took, to try to help him to safety, wouldn't you?"

Jenna knew by the knowing look in Renee's eyes that Renee knew she'd won this round. The older woman just had no idea how close to home her words had hit.

CHAPTER ELEVEN

"WE HAVE TO get that arm looked at," Jenna picked her half-eaten salad and bowl off the table and carried it to the undermount stainless-steel sink in the bungalow's decent-size kitchen. Granite countertops completed the elegant space.

Shaking her head, Renee stood, too, though a bit more stiffly than Jenna had, more stiffly than a woman in her mid-sixties should have needed to, and Jenna figured she was witnessing years' worth of beatings in the other woman's slow-to-move body.

Renee's abuse had to stop. The woman deserved so much better.

"You've been at the shelter for how long? Six weeks?"

"About that."

"And no one knows you saw Brian Sunday."

"That's right."

"So why would the shelter's nurse have to report an injury sustained while you were apart from your abuser?"

"She's going to ask what happened."

"From the way Carly talks about her, I don't think Lynn will press for any answers that aren't critical to your immediate safety and physical health."

After they rinsed their bowls and Jenna helped Renee straighten up the rest of the kitchen, Jenna hung up her towel and looped her arm through Renee's good one. "Come on," she said. "I'll be there with you and I'll answer anything you can't."

Lynn didn't press Renee for any answers she wasn't willing to give. She'd gone to the park in town Sunday afternoon and come back with an arm that needed attention, and no, she didn't need to have the police called. There had been no surprise visits from her abuser. And her injury had been caused by pressure to the arm. She'd gone on to say that perhaps she had osteoporosis, a hypothesis that Lynn didn't react to one way or another as she x-rayed and taped Renee's cracked, but not broken, bone.

Lynn's parting remark, "Make sure you bring up the incident in your session with Sara this week," was the only indication that she suspected the whole truth wasn't being told in that room that night.

Jenna walked Renee home and wondered if any of them would ever live a life free from the secrets they all kept safe.

MAX PRETENDED TO himself that he was surprised when Chantel showed up shortly after he'd put Caleb down for the night on Tuesday. He'd known his first wife's best friend was off duty at three that afternoon.

"If you'd said you were driving all this way, I'd have told you not to," he said in greeting as he opened the door to her.

She came into the house as though she'd been doing so for years, the bag over her shoulder telling him she was planning on staying the night.

"Why do you think I didn't let you know?" she asked, dropping her duffle bag on the floor of the living room.

"You've heard something, haven't you?"

She nodded. "This afternoon. My friend on the Santa Raquel force, he called and said he'd been talking to another guy in the locker room this morning. He'd just asked the guy to keep an unofficial lookout for Meredith. He showed him her picture, and the guy recognized her. He'd seen her at a bus stop on Sunday not far from the beach.... She had on a hat, but he was sure it was her...."

Chantel continued to talk as all of the blood drained from Max's face. He felt it go. And could count his pulse without feeling for it, as it roared through his ears.

She'd been there.

Caleb *had* seen his mother. "She'd been running, Max, and tripped."

Running because Caleb had seen her? Or running because someone was after her?

He was elated—surely it hadn't been a coincidence that she'd been at the beach during their regularly scheduled family time. And he was also more worried than ever—she'd been running from something.

"Did he see where she went? Who she was with? Did he talk to her?"

Chantel sat on the edge of the sofa that Meri had picked out and, with her fingers lightly threaded together said, "He asked her if she was okay, she said she was, and ran off to catch the bus."

So she'd been running for the bus? Not running from something?

"Which bus? Where was it headed?"

She named the street.

"That's downtown. Only six or seven miles from here...." Santa Raquel wasn't that big. "It means that she's close," he said, taking the seat next to Chantel, turning to look at her as his mind raced in various directions. "She's never stayed close before when she ran. Does that mean Steve's not after her? Or that he has her and is holding her someplace close by?"

"She was alone when the cop saw her. Got on the bus alone."

"Steve could have been watching."

"Not likely. Why would he let her get on a bus by herself? She could have alerted anyone. Gotten off at any stop."

"Maybe he was already on the bus."

"Then why would she get on it? Why not alert

the cop when she tripped and he stopped to help her?"

He couldn't answer that.

"You told me Sunday night that you were at the beach that afternoon," Chantel said slowly, watching him. "You said Caleb saw her."

"That's right. And obviously he did. She knows we go to that beach every Sunday. It was her idea to begin with. She was there to see us, Chantel, I'm sure of it."

"Then why not wait and say hello?"

"Because Steve had to have been with her. Someplace. He had to have been watching her. Or she was afraid he was."

"Or maybe she just wanted to make sure that you two were getting along fine without her as she moves on with her life. It's clear that she loved the two of you, Max. Even if leaving is the right thing to do for her, it still has to be hard. I understand how difficult this is for you, too, Max, but maybe you have to face that it's you she didn't want to see."

"You said she was running for the bus."

"Yeah."

"What woman does that unless she's either late for an appointment or afraid?"

"She was afraid you were going to see her, to force her into a conversation she isn't ready to have. Or maybe she'd seen what she'd come to see and didn't want to have to wait around for the next bus."

Her words made him angry, even while Max knew that she was just doing what he'd asked her to do. Find Meri. Find the truth.

"You don't know her."

"Has it occurred to you that you might not know her as well as you thought you did, either?"

Hell, yes, it had occurred to him. Every day since she'd disappeared on him without a word. After promising that she'd do everything she could not to break his heart....

And then he'd climb into their bed at night, smell her perfume on their sheets, her shampoo on her pillow, and careful not to touch either, so they didn't lose that scent, he'd lie there next to her space and know that whatever Meri was doing, it was because she loved him.

Steve had to have threatened her somehow. He didn't know how. When. Where. And sure as hell couldn't explain why she hadn't wanted him or Caleb to see her. Unless, as he'd thought before, she thought she was somehow protecting them. It didn't really make sense, not when he knew—and had told her often enough—that his police connections would keep them all safe.

"You have to find her, Chantel," he said now, more certain than he'd been since Meri had disappeared that she needed him. "She's in trouble. I know she is."

"That's what I'm here to tell you, my friend. We did find her."

JENNA WAS ON her way home from walking Renee back to her bungalow Tuesday night when her cell phone rang. She'd already spoken with Yvonne, Olivia's mother, and knew that the little girl had come through surgery just fine. She'd agreed to meet with the two of them on Thursday at the home of a woman Yvonne had met through work for Olivia's first therapy session.

And Yvonne didn't have her cell number.

No one did. Except for Lila.

The managing director wanted Jenna to come to her office.

The other woman's invitation didn't include tea. It sounded formal.

With her heart in her throat, Jenna hurried over.

And felt her stomach cramp as she entered the room to find a uniformed police officer standing there.

Something had happened to Max. Or Caleb. They were there to tell her that she'd lost everything in the world that was dear to her....

She felt as if she was going to faint. Sat down. Unable to breathe. And folded her hands together, reminding herself that she wasn't weak.

And no one knew where she was, or who she was.

The officer looked at a picture in his hand. "Are you Meredith Bennet?" the officer, about forty with graying hair at his temples and a kind expression on his face, asked.

"Has there been an accident?" The words came out on a squeak. She coughed and repeated them. More clearly.

"An accident?"

"Are you here to tell me that...." Her throat was so dry the words wouldn't come. "Has there been an accident?" she repeated, aware that Lila stood just off to her right, with one hundred percent focus.

"No, ma'am. Not that I'm aware of. Were you in an accident?" the officer asked gently, as though he was proceeding with utmost caution. Sizing up the situation.

And suddenly she was scared to death. Steve had sent this man. He'd found her and this was his way of saying so.

He wasn't going to wait for her to move out of the shelter this time.

"Jenna...are you Meredith Bennet?" Lila came forward, sat next to her, not touching her, but seeming to hold her up at the same time.

Not that Jenna needed holding. She didn't. "I'm Jenna McDonald."

"Yes, I know. But...."

"So you aren't Meredith Bennet?" the officer said, coming closer. Looming over her.

Lila had a gun. Jenna might be the only resident who knew that, but the woman had told her about it the night she'd been in her apartment. The night she'd told Jenna to get to her if she was ever in trouble—no matter what it took.

And when Jenna had tried to find out why the woman had a gun, to find out anything at all about Lila's private life, she'd found herself up against a wall of steel.

"Because if you're not Meredith Bennet, I'm very sorry, ma'am," the officer continued, backing up a step now. "I didn't mean to upset you...."

She wasn't upset.

"Jenna? You're white as a sheet, dear. Do you feel okay?"

"So you don't know Dr. Max Bennet," the officer said, almost at the door.

"What do you know about Max?" The words were out of her mouth before she could stop them. So there *had* been an accident. Or Max was ill. Or in trouble. It had been two long days since she'd seen her boys healthy and at play....

This wasn't about Steve.

"You do know Dr. Bennet?" The officer was back again.

"Sir, I think it might be best if you take a seat." Lila's voice came from her right. The officer was on her left. And Jenna was scared to death.

"Thanks, Wayne."

Max stood, hands in the pockets of his purple scrubs, picking at the threads there, while Chantel took the call that had just come in on her phone.

Presumably her cop friend on the Santa Raquel police force.

The officer who'd discovered earlier that day that a fellow officer had seen Meredith on Sunday. The one who owed Chantel a favor.

He'd spent a couple of hours going over business surveillance footage nearby the stop where Meredith had vacated the bus.

He'd been going to talk to Meredith.

And then call Chantel. Who wouldn't tell Max where she was.

If she was in a hospital, he'd find out soon enough. As soon as Chantel got off the phone and gave him whatever report she was going to give him.

He was a respected pediatrician who worked with all of the area hospitals, not only the two in Santa Raquel, but those in surrounding cities, as well. His consultation work took him as far as Los Angeles.

"I'll let you know tomorrow," Chantel was saying.

Max waited. Staring at the laces in his orange tennis shoes as he rocked back and forth on his toes. The high-tops matched the orange-and-purple dinosaur shirt he was wearing.

Color put kids at ease. Put him at ease, too, truth be told. Because some days weren't good. Some days he had to cause pain to make things better.

And some days even painful treatments couldn't save a life.

"I will. And yes, lunch sounds great."

He'd lost a patient that day. A youngster who'd been born premature, had experienced a brain bleed at birth and had suffered permanent neurological damage. The boy had had little chance to survive from the beginning, but he'd hung on for more than two years.

"No, burgers are fine. Really."

Tommy was at peace. His parents were at peace. Max still felt as if he'd let them down.

And Chantel was discussing burgers.

CHAPTER TWELVE

CHANTEL STOOD AS she hung up the phone. With her hands on her hips, hips that looked smaller in the jeans she was wearing than they did in the uniform she'd arrived in the week before, she faced Max toe-to-toe.

"Wayne spoke with Meredith."

His shoulders sank. Every bit of nervous energy drained out of him, and Max knew a second of sheer relief.

It was only then that he consciously acknowledged that deep down inside he'd been afraid that Steve had killed her—his sweet, beautiful, vulnerable wife.

"Where is she?" he asked as the tension seeped back.

"I can't tell you," she said, looking him straight in the eye.

"But, obviously, since Wayne had just gotten off duty when he went to see her, she's still close by."

Chantel stared at him.

"And she's okay?"

"She's fine."

"I check the hospitals in the area every morning...."

"She's in no need of a hospital. She's fine."

No, she wasn't. She couldn't possibly be fine. She wasn't home.

"Was she alone?"

"No."

"She's with Steve."

"No."

"She has to be. Maybe not that she's saying, but I know he's behind this."

She wasn't alone. Thoughts came and went in no apparent order. "Who was she with?"

"I can't tell you that." Chantel's expression, her voice, held more pity than anything else.

If she wanted him to believe that Meri was with another man...that she'd left him for someone else....

"There's no way you're going to convince me she's having an affair...." Not ever. Not Meri. It was just something he knew.

"I'm not trying to convince you of anything, and I have no evidence whatsoever that suggests there's another man involved here. More that Meredith just wants her freedom."

"Her freedom." The words didn't make sense to him. How did he apply them to the Meri he knew, to the son he and Meri shared, to their marriage? "I didn't realize she was feeling trapped." He shook his head. He was not a stupid man. Or an overly spiritual one, either. But he knew his wife.

"What did she say?" He needed Meri's words. Not an outsider's interpretation of them.

"She's using an assumed name," Chantel said.

Another wave of relief consumed him. With a fear chaser. "It's Steve," he said. "There's no other reason she'd use an assumed name."

"She has identification under the alternate name, Max. It takes time to get that. This wasn't a spur-of-the-moment plan."

That stopped him. For the moment it took him to remember that his job was to remain calm. "It's because of Steve. I'm telling you. She knew someone in Vegas, a broker, she called him, who supplied her with identities. He'd been Steve's snitch at one point, I think. I'm telling you Steve found her and she ran." Because she didn't trust him to be able to help her? "Tell me what she said."

"Wayne asked her if she was Meredith Bennet and she said no. Several times."

"Who did she say she was?"

"I can't tell you that."

"But you know."

"Yes. I asked only so that I could use it as I investigate Steve Smith. If he's using her assumed name in conjunction with anything he's doing— the purchase of plane tickets, for instance—I'll get a hit."

One thought rang clear in that second. Chantel

wasn't giving up. Because of something she'd heard that she wasn't telling him?

Or just because he'd asked?

"You're still looking for Steve."

"Yes."

"Because of something Wayne told you?"

"Let's just say that something that occurred today leads me to believe that while Meri isn't in danger, it might be good to be certain that Smith hasn't been in touch with her."

She knew something she couldn't tell him. Something pertinent. Her expertise was far beyond his. As was her reach. This was why he'd called her.

Max sat down. He wasn't going to do anything, ask her anything that would jeopardize her job. Or put pressure on her to tell him things that, ethically, she shouldn't.

He was scared to death.

"So she never admitted to being my wife?"

"Wayne asked if she knew a Dr. Bennet. He could tell by her reaction that she did. After that, she opened up. She told him that she was your wife. That she was Caleb's mother. He asked if she was okay. She assured him several times that she was.

"He asked if she needed any help. She insisted that she didn't."

It was hard to sit there and listen to that. "Steve had to be within earshot. Maybe he's got her bugged." Okay, his imagination might be running a bit wild. "Maybe he was in the other room."

"I can assure you he was not."

"But you don't know whether or not he has her wired. He's a former cop, Chantel. He'd play it out like a cop."

Her brown eyes softened and he felt like a stupid kid. It was a feeling he hadn't experienced in twenty years.

"I can't guarantee that she wasn't wired, no," Chantel said. "Because she wasn't searched. But I'd bet my life on the fact that she wasn't. We have ways of finding out if someone is being coerced," she said. "In this case, Wayne wrote on a piece of paper, asking her if she was on the run. She shook her head. She was calm, Max."

"This person she was with, was it a professional?"

"I can't tell you that."

"But you know."

"Yes."

"Is she staying with this person?"

"No."

"But Wayne knows where she's staying."

"Yes."

"How certain can he be that she's safe there?"

"As certain as it's possible to be."

And he knew.

"She's at The Lighthouse, isn't she?"

"No, Max. She's not. Now, please, stop this. I did

as you asked. I found her. I'm certain she's okay. Leave it at that, okay?"

He had more questions. Too many of them. And needed a few minutes to figure this out. To understand what Meri was doing, what she was trying to tell him.

"She knew that I was behind this evening's visit?"

"After a time, yes."

"Did she have a message for me?"

As Chantel's chin dropped, his gut got hard as rock. His friend looked over at him and he wanted to end the day. To wake up in the morning and start fresh, a married doctor with a two-year-old son and a wife who didn't want their toddler in day care.

He'd play it differently. He'd tell Meri that she could keep Caleb with her if that was what she wanted. He'd trust her to raise their son into an emotionally healthy young man.

Chantel's hand covered his, bringing his attention back to her. "She said to tell you that she didn't need your help, Max. Or ours. She asked that you let her go."

His chest burned.

And he sat down, a stabbed man with a big gaping wound.

"I HAVE SOME other news."

Chantel's voice broke into Max's private hell. He'd promised Meri he could handle being married to a woman with an abusive ex in her past. And he wouldn't put it past Meri to say whatever she thought she had to say for whatever reason she had to say it. She would not have left him, just to get away from him, without telling him. He would bet his life on it.

She would not have left Caleb just to go start a new life.

Something else was going on.

"Max, did you hear me? I have other news."

Chantel sat down next to him. She was there to help him. He needed her. "What other news?"

"Steve Smith. He quit the force with a perfect record, but I talked to someone today— a person someone else had told me I might want to talk to— and this person intimated that Smith might have quit before his record could be tarnished."

"He was in trouble?"

"From what I heard, an internal investigation was never opened, there's no record of anything, but there was talk that one might have been opened if he'd stayed."

"For what?"

"I don't know yet. I'm getting this all second- and thirdhand, and cops don't talk bad about their own to their own, let alone to someone they don't know."

"So how do you know there was talk?"

"A daughter of a woman who spoke at a Las

Sendas library fund-raiser is a dispatcher in Las Vegas. She asked around."

"What were you doing at a library fund-raiser?" For a second he was twenty-five again. Sitting in his living room with Jill and Chantel, having a glass of wine to take the edge off long hours at the hospital with no pay.

For just that second he wasn't a man trying to assimilate facts about his wife that just wouldn't come together. His head dropped to the back of the couch.

"I read books, Bennet," Chantel said, with a small smirk, before growing serious once again. "Sandra, the dispatcher, put me in touch with a detective who she thought might be able to help me. I'm waiting to hear from her."

He stared at the ceiling, looking for the energy he needed to get up in the morning, get his son out of bed, and tell Caleb, when he asked, as he inevitably would, that his mother wasn't home yet. How long would it be before Caleb quit asking?

Chantel settled back, as well. It was late. It had been a long six days.

"Does this detective know you're calling for personal reasons?"

"Yes." She turned her head just as he turned his and they were facing each other, lying back against the couch.

Max sat up. "I don't blame you if you don't believe me at this point, but I know without a doubt that Steve is behind all of this," he said, his thoughts finding clarity all on their own. "I can't explain it to you. I can't tell you why Meri is still in town, or why she didn't ask for help. I can't tell you why she didn't come to me before she bolted. But I am absolutely certain that her ex-husband is behind it all. Find him and we'll find our answers."

"And what if those answers turn out to include the fact that Meredith no longer wants to be married to you?"

The question was a hard one. Asked in the gentlest way.

"What if she really can't stand the stress of worrying about Caleb every day?"

He knew better, but he didn't expect Chantel to believe that.

"Women who are abused…they've experienced something that none of the rest of us will ever understand, Max. The aftermath, a lot of times it's worse than the actual beatings. Paranoia is a very real, very painful consequence. Its real power comes from the fact that, for abuse victims, it's based in truth. In having experienced the horror which everyone fears most—being betrayed in the most heinous ways by the one person in the world you thought you could trust."

Meri had said things like that before. But her words had been less concise, mixed with example and emotion and tears, all things he'd had to contend with at the same time she was delivering her message. He'd needed to comfort as well as understand.

Hearing those same words from Chantel—they took on new meaning. Frightening meaning. And then something else occurred to him.

"How do you know this?" Meri had told him that one in four women suffer from domestic violence. He'd found the statistic staggering. And kind of hard to believe.

He'd carefully watched the mothers coming into his exam rooms with their children. If he saw eight kids a day that meant eight mothers. Statistically, two of every eight had been or were currently being abused.

"The Las Sendas P.D. required every one of us to take a course on domestic violence."

"The women you mean?"

"No, I mean all of us. Every single officer on the force, no matter how junior, has had training to recognize and deal with potential DV-related situations. Every one of us has to respond to a DV call at some point."

It made a sickening kind of sense.

"I'm just saying, Max...." Chantel was closer to him, leaning toward him. "It's possible that Meri knew her paranoia was out of hand, getting the better of her. It's possible that she knew she couldn't control it anymore and saw that it was already starting to have an effect on Caleb. The way you describe her, as devoted as she was and as committed to serving others…I just think you need to consider that she's done exactly what she told you in the note. She's loving you and Caleb the best way she knows how. By removing herself from your home before Caleb is infected with her paranoia."

He didn't want to consider anything of the kind.

He was a doctor; he understood that mental issues were medical issues. He knew that they could be treated, and that sometimes treatments failed.

But he also knew Meri. She talked to him about her fears. About Steve's ability to hunt her down. His tenacity and patience with undercover work. But she'd been through counseling and knew how to control her fear.

"If she'd come to you, would you have let her go?" Chantel's voice was too close now. Softly working its way in when he just wanted to be alone with Meri.

"Or would you have promised to support her, tend to her, help her back into counseling, stand by her…."

"Of course I would have supported her, stood by her, tended to her, helped her in any way I could." It's what a spouse did. Which was why marriage vows said "for better or worse" and "in sickness and in health" and…

"Exactly. She'd have known that. So maybe she'd reached a place where she knew that none of the above was going to work anymore. She knew what you did not, that the treatments didn't work…."

No. He was not going to listen to this. Not now. Not ever.

He stood up. "Steve's behind this, Chantel," he said, while doubts pressed in on him from all sides. "I won't turn my back on her. I won't give up. I'm going to find this fiend. Somehow. Some way. Either with you or without you."

He hoped to God it would be with her. He didn't know if he could do it on his own.

"I understand." She stood, too, toe-to-toe with him, not backing down. "I just need you to know that when we find him, it might not be what you think."

The panic eating up his insides let go. "Fair enough."

"Okay." Turning, she reached down to the floor, slinging her bag up over shoulder.

"So—" just to be clear "—you're still in?"

"Of course. I was never out. I'll see you in the morning."

Without another word, she turned and made her way down the hall. Max was still standing in the living room, right as she'd left him, when the door to the guest bedroom closed quietly behind her.

CHAPTER THIRTEEN

JENNA TOSSED AND turned most of Tuesday night. She could handle whatever was handed to her. She knew how to put one foot in front of the other, how to get up in the morning and start off the day with the belief that she could make it a good one. She knew how to take things one moment at a time, to find even the smallest positive if that's what it took to get through.

She just couldn't figure out how to fall asleep.

Lila had asked her if she wanted to stay and talk. And Jenna knew the woman had been asking her to do so. She'd told her the same thing she'd told the policeman. She didn't need anything. She was fine.

One of her bungalow mates got up just after three. Latoya, she figured. The older woman couldn't make it through the night without a trip to the bathroom. She'd suffered bladder damage the last time her husband knocked her to the ground and kicked her.

Jenna heard movement. Waited for the swish of water going through the pipes as the toilet flushed. She counted sheep and thought about making oatmeal for Carly and Latoya in the morning. They both needed to eat more. And both had early-morning sessions at the main building. Latoya was starting a job as a sales clerk in the TLS gift shop, Pretty Dreams.

And Carly…she had her first physical therapy session tomorrow morning, to help her regain full use of her left shoulder, which her boyfriend had damaged by shattering her rotator cuff.

Yes, she'd make oatmeal. And at ten she was meeting her little client who was stuttering. It would be good to work.

She'd also met a woman the day before who wanted to lose her heavy South American accent with hopes of becoming as Americanized as she could. Romar had come to the States as a mail-order bride and loved the country, but had become a victim to the man who'd purchased her. Fighting for her freedom was made harder by her inability to make herself understood. Because helping people lose accents was part of the work of a speech pa-thologist, Jenna was going to work with her every day for as long as the two of them were residents of The Lemonade Stand. She'd made it clear there were no promises after that.

She lay in bed, making mental lists. And when each thought ended, she found herself right back where she'd started. Face-to-face with an image of the husband she'd left behind.

At four, when darkness and panic finally won

the battle she'd been having with them, when she started to shake and her stomach had knotted to the point of hurting, she gave up trying to sleep. Throwing the covers back, she rolled out of bed and took a seat at the antique desk she liked so much.

The little things. They would see her through. She just had to focus. The antique-white color of the desk was nice. It reminded her of a bedroom set she'd once seen in a magazine. She'd been about ten and sitting with her mother waiting in some office. She'd long since forgotten what they were waiting for. But she remembered the magazine, and showing her mother the picture.

She'd come home from school a month later to find a similar set furnishing her bedroom. Complete with a canopy bed.

Jenna pulled her knees up to her chest, hugging them. And when the tears threatened to come anyway, she knelt at the side of her bed, pulled out the diary she hid there every night, and, sitting on the floor with her back against the bed, she began to write.

DAY SEVEN.

Tonight I gave my husband away. I cannot pretend otherwise.

Officer Wayne Stanton. It's a name I will never forget. At first I feared him, as I fear most people in uniform. The uniform, after all, is a shield that protects those who wear it from being accountable.

But that's old news.

Officer Wayne Stanton. As soon as he told me that he was there on a mission for Las Sendas P.D. Officer Chantel Harris, I knew what I'd done. I sent Max straight back to Jill's best friend. The woman was in love with him, even if he wasn't aware of that.

I've never even met her, and I knew she loved him. He told me some of the things she'd said, but I also saw the cards she sent. Every Christmas. When Caleb was born. Anytime anything special happened in our lives.

They were addressed to both of us but the messages had been highly personal. And clearly only for Max.

He'd said it was because she didn't know me yet.

But he never offered to introduce us.

And now I've given him reason to call her. To seek out her help.

Hands trembling, Jenna glanced over what she'd written, hardly able to read the scribbled words. And still she felt the pain of them.

She'd had to let go before. So many times. Why did it have to hurt so badly this time?

The dark of the night belongs here, in the only place left where I can truly be myself. These pages.

Max hasn't accepted that I left him. I really thought that the keys in the cup holder would do it.

She had to pause again as tears blurred her vision. She'd cried when she'd left those keys there, knowing that by doing so she was stabbing Max in the heart.

But a little stab now was so much better than the grief he'd feel if Caleb was hurt. Better than loving Meri for another few years, making more memories and maybe even another baby, and then losing her. She knew that. Knew that she was being kindest in the long run. Knew that she had no other choice. And still…

Sometimes I wonder when I will reach the point that it's all more than I can bear. When is enough, enough?

No. She couldn't go down the road to nowhere. She'd traveled it for too long. And wasn't going back.

She wouldn't give Steve that satisfaction. And she wouldn't do it to herself, either. *I have to let Max know that I'm okay. And that I honestly and truly want to leave him so he'll tell Chantel to stop looking for me. I can't have them finding Steve. They'll never get him. They'll only piss him off. Make him more inclined to hurt them. Or Caleb. They're taking away the time I need to plan. Forcing me to hurry.*

I have to convince him to back off.

I convinced Officer Wayne Stanton tonight. I convinced Renee and Yvonne, too. And now I have to find a way to convince the dear sweet man that I love more than life that I don't want a life with him.

Please God, if I'm going to die seeing this mission through, take me soon.

ON WEDNESDAY MORNING, Chantel called Max at work. He'd just come in from a patient and was voicing his chart notes into his computer when the phone rang.

"Do you have anyone who covers for you there?"

"I do," he said. And as soon as he got off the phone, he was going to ask the other pediatrician who worked at the clinic to take his appointments for the rest of the day. It would be the second day in a week that he'd asked for the favor.

"What's up?" He'd dropped Caleb off at day care on his way in to work that morning so Chantel had the house to herself. And the freedom to come and go as necessary.

"I have a dinner appointment with that detective I told you about."

"She's in Santa Raquel?"

"No, it's in Laughlin. She doesn't want to meet in Vegas. She says there are too many people who know people there and she's not sure who's still friendly with Steve and who isn't. I guess he was in good with the police commissioner and I'm guessing that's why he still has a perfect record."

"Laughlin's nine hours from here."

"I can get us booked on a flight to Bullhead City just across the river if you can leave by two. We'll be home by eleven o'clock tonight. Wayne and his wife said they'd keep Caleb for us. They'll come to your house. I think he's curious to meet you and Caleb after seeing Meredith last night."

"He believes her."

"Yeah, but he also understands your position. It's a tough one. Like I said, we all deal with DV issues, Max. And I knew you wouldn't leave Caleb unless you were absolutely certain he'd be safe."

"Thank you. I'm in."

Max finished charting, rescheduled his well-checks, and moved the rest of his appointments to the office next door. He did the same for Thursday's appointments, as well.

He had no idea what he was going to find out in Laughlin.

But he walked with new energy in his step.

He was going to get some answers.

Finally.

JENNA MANAGED TO avoid Lila on Wednesday. She avoided the cafeteria and, except for her speech therapy appointments, she avoided the main building.

For that one day, she avoided the library as well, opting instead to take a break at the resort's kidney-shaped outdoor pool.

Steve was not her first priority that day.

Convincing Max that she'd left of her own accord was her number one priority. If he didn't stop looking for her, Steve would get mad. He might do something to Caleb, just to show Max who was more powerful. Lying facedown on a lounge chair in the one piece suit she'd picked up from the TLS thrift store, Jenna closed her eyes.

After her restless night, she was exhausted.

And still couldn't sleep.

She never should have married Max. Tears sprang to her eyes at the thought, but it was true. She knew Steve better than anyone. She'd known he'd never leave her alone. She'd wanted so badly to have a normal life. To have a family of her own. To love and be loved.

She'd wanted to believe that all she had to do was have the courage to start over. To open her heart and let trust be reborn. To hope and dream.

But she'd known, with some part of her, that she couldn't have a normal life. Steve wasn't just an abuser. He was her owner. *In his mind.*

And still she'd married Max. She'd given birth to a child.

Knowing that they could be in danger someday.

Now it was up to her to fix that mistake.

"I've been looking for you."

She didn't need to open her eyes to know that Lila had taken the seat next to her. But she opened them anyway.

Sitting sideways, facing Jenna, Lila was fully dressed in beige pants, a cream-colored blouse and a beige sweater. Her graying hair was pulled back into a bun. Jenna concentrated on the toes of the plain beige flats on the woman's feet.

She didn't say anything.

"Thank you for being out here," Lila said softly. From her supine position, Jenna couldn't see her face. She saw the older woman's hands folded together, resting on her knees.

"The pool's been open for almost a month and only a handful of people have used it. Mostly moms who come out to let their kids swim."

There were certain hours when the pool was open to children. And there were adult-only swim times, too.

"I was hesitant at first about having a pool installed," Lila continued. "Most of our women… they've got scars to hide outside as well as in… and then it occurred to me that that was exactly the reason to have a place where they can remember the joy of sluicing through the water or lying out in the sun without having to be self-conscious. And maybe…if they get used to it here, they'll continue to go to the pool or the ocean when they leave here, too."

Jenna had scars. On her back. Both upper arms. On the back of her neck and the front of one thigh. When had she stopped thinking about them? Remembering to hide them?

Turning over, she sat up.

"Max made me feel beautiful," she said. Lila knew about Meredith. Officer Wayne Stanton had agreed to keep her whereabouts and her name change secret. Last night, in her office, Lila had, too.

Neither of them knew why she'd insisted they not tell anyone. And that if they did, she'd leave the shelter.

Lila would never condone Jenna's plan to confront her abuser alone. But that was the only way Steve wanted her. The only hope she had that he wouldn't immediately go on the defensive....

Glancing at Lila, Jenna was surprised at the warmth in the other woman's eyes. Lila was a professional. A woman in her position couldn't afford to get emotionally involved with the hundreds of women who made their way through the shelter.

"I didn't realize it until right now, you know," Jenna said. "I didn't realize that I'd lost that feeling of being...physically ugly. I cover the scars out of habit, not because I'm consciously aware of them, or aware of the questions they'd raise in other people." She shook her head. "I can't believe I forgot that."

Max hadn't just told her she was beautiful. He'd shown her. The man had been so hot for her she'd barely been able to get him to put clothes on when she was around. He was a little better since Caleb had been born. A little more circumspect. But his sexual appetite hadn't waned one bit.

Neither, for that matter, had hers.

An astounding feat for a woman who'd grown to hate sex and everything about it.

"Your Max sounds like a pretty incredible man."

Jenna's eyes narrowed. "What do you know about Max? Have you been talking to someone?"

She didn't mean to sound accusatory, but this was her problem. She'd created it. She'd fix it.

And if she succeeded with Steve?

Then, if she was meant to be with Max, he'd be available.

"Jenna?"

She looked up at Lila.

"Yes?"

"I didn't talk to anyone. About you or Max. And I won't. But I want you to talk to me. Please."

She understood the position Lila was in. She had regulations she had to follow.

But Jenna didn't have anything to say.

"Did Max hit you?"

"No!"

"So you really aren't running from him."

"No."

"Then why not speak to him? It's obvious the man's worried sick about you. He's got two different police forces working on a missing person who isn't missing."

"Max won't listen." That much was true.

"But you are on the run."

No. Not anymore. But… "Yes."

"From an abuser."

"Yes."

"Were you married to him?"

"Yes."

"He gave you those scars?"

Jenna pulled her wrap around her shoulders and tucked her towel around her legs.

"Yes."

Lila nodded. "You're safe here."

"I know."

"Does Max know about him?"

"Yes."

"And he thinks he can take him on," Lila guessed. "You know better."

Okay. It was sort of true. Max thought that the law could take on Steve. He believed that she could live free and happy. She shrugged. And knew that Lila took the action as an affirmative response to her question.

"And you're sure you don't need legal assistance?"

The thought was almost laughable to her. Except that she would never be at a point where she could laugh about anything to do with Steve Smith. "I don't."

Lila hesitated. And then asked, "Do you have a plan, then?"

"No. I just…."

"You need time to figure out how to deal with an abusive ex-husband while married to a good man."

She didn't answer.

"You know there's family counseling for survivors of abuse and their family members."

"I know."

She'd insisted that Max attend a program with her before she'd agreed to marry him.

But they all assumed the threat of abuse was in the past.

"I'm glad you're helping Romar. Sara said she thinks it'll go a long way toward her healing. Romar has somehow associated her inability to communicate with her abuse and also with her low self-concept."

Lila was now speaking to her as a professional to another professional. Jenna noticed the shift.

And she was grateful for it. They spoke about a couple of other residents who could benefit from Jenna's services.

And then Lila said, "Because you wish it, you will remain Jenna McDonald here," she said. "I ask only one thing."

"What's that?"

"That if you're in trouble, you come to me right away."

"I will." She would if she could.

She liked the woman. Felt a peculiar kinship with her. And didn't miss Lila's skeptical look at her last comment.

She knew Jenna was up to something.

CHAPTER FOURTEEN

"YOU DIDN'T TELL me the dinner date was in a casino." He'd changed from scrubs into jeans and a pull-over, but was still wearing the lime green high-tops he'd had on that morning. He'd been in a hurry.

Caleb had clung to him when Wayne Stanton and his wife, Maria, had first arrived. But Maria soon had the toddler engaged and Max might have been hurt by how easily he'd been able to slip away if he hadn't been so relieved.

"Detective Kolhase chose the spot." Chantel, also in jeans, had been pretty closed-mouth about the upcoming meeting, though she'd been talkative on the flight over. Reliving the past. Things he'd forgotten. Like the time Jill had come up behind him while he'd been making a peanut butter sandwich, grabbing his arm from behind in a playful attempt to bind him, and sending a glob of peanut butter from the knife to Chantel's face. The glob had landed on her upper lip like a mustache and the three of them had laughed until it hurt.

"How do we know what this detective looks like?

How do we find her?" And what was she going to tell them?

"She's in a navy suit, slacks and jacket, and will be carrying a red purse. She's got short dark hair."

Lights flashed, music played and the sound of slot machines rang all around them. Max had been to casinos. He'd played blackjack a few times. He'd just never been able to relax and enjoy giving his earnings to chance.

"That must be her." Chantel's tone changed from casual to all-business as she headed toward an alcove with a couple of couches and a table along a corridor lined with various eateries.

Diane Kolhase approached them, a confident smile on her face, and a sense about her that she could take the world by the hand and make it safe. She had a table in an Italian restaurant and led them there, letting their waitress know that they'd arrived.

So far he was impressed.

"I'm sorry for all the drama, bringing you here, rather than just meeting in Vegas," she said as soon as they'd ordered and finished with introductory pleasantries. "But when you mentioned Steve Smith…"

Any sense of relaxation Max might have felt fled. As did his appetite.

"Did you know him personally?" he asked, not waiting for Chantel to conduct the interview.

"Yes. For a brief time I was his partner."

"Why a brief time?" Chantel asked. "Was his behavior inappropriate?"

Diane, who was probably in her late thirties and looked as lithe and hard as a football running back, shook her head. "He was promoted," she said, arms folded on the table as she leaned toward them. "Back then I was as impressed by him as everyone else was. The man has a mind like a steel trap. Nothing gets away from him. He walks into a room and could walk back in five minutes later and know if anything had moved even an inch. He could pull facts from a year before into a current case and come up with missing pieces before some of us even knew pieces were missing."

Max leaned back in his chair, listening. And growing more desperate by the minute.

DAY EIGHT.

It's just after nine and I've retired for the night. Not because I'm tired but because I just couldn't keep up appearances any longer.

I invited Renee to have dinner with us tonight. She's down to only one roommate and the woman works in the cafeteria, so she's never home for meals and I didn't want her to have to cook for herself.

Latoya and Carly liked Renee, too, as I suspected they would. Carly, bless her heart, likes anyone who is kind to her, which could be part of what got her into the situation she was in. Latoya's a harder nut to crack, but she was the one who took Renee's plate from her when she was going to carry it to the sink. And filled her tea, too.

I talked to them all about having a pool party next weekend. They liked the idea and we started planning the food and talked about some games we could play. It's more than a week away and I wonder, will I still be here then? And what of Max and Caleb? Will they be well into learning to live without me?

I have to hope so. As much as the selfish part of me wants to matter more than that to them, I need to know that I'm not hurting them as badly as my own heart is hurting.

The pool party. I was talking about the pool party. It would be an opportunity for all of the women to be in swimsuits in a safe environment. Hopefully, Lila will be pleased. I don't ever want her to think that I'm just using The Lemonade Stand for my own ends.

Jenna wrote a bit more about the day, cataloguing her activities as though she was talking to a much older Caleb—a young man who would hopefully be reading with an open heart, seeking to understand why his mother had done what she'd done. Seeking the love for him that she was pouring into these pages.

And Max? Would he read them? With another woman by his side, perhaps?

Why do I torture myself with images of Max with

another woman? Sometimes I'm afraid that maybe, secretly, I want that for him. I love him so much and it kills me to think of another woman touching him—and worse—him touching her. But wouldn't that be better for him? I want my love for him to be clean and pure and that means I have to always have his best interests at heart and what if that's not me?

Here, at The Lemonade Stand, I'm coming face-to-face with myself. Not part of my plan, but I can't seem to help it. The truth is I'm not pure and clean. I'm dirtied by a choice I made so long ago. The choice to marry Steve Smith. Max and Caleb, they're too...precious to me...too...clean... to be sprayed with Steve's mud.

Her arm cramped, but she wasn't at all tired. Her time alone that day, her talk with Lila at the pool, had filled her with wild energy as she contemplated what lay ahead. She was going to do this. She was really going to take Steve on. By herself. She was either going to find a way to convince him he no longer wanted her, or that it was in his best interests to let her go, or she was going to die trying. Because she wouldn't live with him again. And he'd never let her leave again, unless he himself decided to let her go.

Tomorrow I see Yvonne, and sweet little Olivia. I called again today to check on the little one and to confirm tomorrow's appointment. Olivia is home and was up playing this afternoon. The surgery only took half an hour and she didn't seem to be in any pain.

Finally something went right for those two. Lord knows they deserve it.

And while I'm out, I know what I can do to convince Max that I left him....

She wasn't going to think about that now. She knew what to do and she'd do it. She didn't have to dwell on it.

Her task was to dwell on Steve. To prepare herself.

I know now what it means to be alone when you are with other people. I am on this journey completely alone. I have no other voices giving me opinions or helping me plan the task ahead of me.

As I read more, as I go back in my mind to when I was with Steve, immerse myself in everything I know about him—good and bad—I feel as though I am becoming Steve.

I can see him so much more clearly, now. And as I read, I can feel him, too. I never could before. I couldn't understand how he could be so incredibly good at his job, so committed to catching the bad guys, so protective of the innocent, and then....

Well there are some things it won't pay to relive. I know that pain well enough.

And I know, just somehow know, *that right now Steve is cursing me for having escaped him. He waited a long time for this reunion. So much longer than the other times he returned to claim me.*

And this time his victory was going to be the sweetest of all because he was taking me away from a life I truly loved. A full, beautiful, healthy life.

I don't believe Steve is angry that I married Max. Or had Caleb. Though he's incensed that I slept with another man. He's glad about my Bennet boys because it gives him more power over me. There wasn't a lot he could do anymore that would faze me. I just didn't care enough about anything.

Until Max. By marrying Max I gave Steve more than he'd probably hoped for. He's got me now. Well and completely.

Because just as I am getting inside of him, he's been inside of me for almost half my life.

He knows that I'll do anything he says as long as he leaves Max and Caleb alone.

My fate was sealed the day I said "I do."

I am so, so sorry, Caleb. I didn't know then. I hadn't figured it out yet.

I will make this right.

Goodnight, Little Man.

The last words smeared as her tears fell to the page.

MAX COULDN'T REMEMBER much about the food he ate. And he would forever remember that Laughlin casino as one of the darkest places he'd ever been in. Flashing lights could do nothing to dispel the feeling of dread that came over him as he paid the dinner bill and followed the two policewomen out of the restaurant and down to the river walk.

Diane Kolhase had suggested that he should at least see it before she drove them back across the Colorado River to the Arizona airport where they'd catch their flight back to California.

In truth, she'd probably realized that he couldn't just sit in one place and listen to the things she was telling him.

Or maybe she hadn't wanted to continue the conversation in one place—where someone might inadvertently overhear them.

"You've been hinting all evening that you know something in particular," Max said, walking in between the two women on the wooden sidewalk that ran behind the strip of casino hotels along the Colorado River. There were a few couples out strolling, but that Wednesday was a quiet night in the casino town.

"I do." Diane had done a fine job painting a picture of a larger-than-life cop that everyone would want to know. She'd spoken of awards and commendations. About Steve Smith risking his life to rescue a little girl from the hands of a pedophile before any irreparable damage had been done. About the man saving the commissioner's recalcitrant daughter from a drug dealer she'd fancied herself in love with. About his fearlessness where the underground powers in Vegas were concerned.

If he hadn't been concerned with saving his wife's life, Max would have been intimidated.

"Tell me what you know," he insisted.

The Vegas detective, a few inches shorter than he was, glanced up at him. "Chantel told me your first wife was killed saving a fellow officer." The words that came out of her mouth were unexpected.

"That's right." Jill had come around the corner to see a man pointing a gun at a junior officer and had taken the perp by surprise from behind, knocking his gun from his hand. He'd knocked her to the ground and managed to get his gun and get one shot off before the other officer killed the man.

The one shot had been all it took to end Jill's life. She'd bled out on the street.

"Chantel said the other officer was on a routine domestic violence call and the perp ran. Your wife was backup."

"We all heard the call come through on the radio," Chantel said, from Max's other side. The sound of her voice in the cool darkness was calming. Familiar. The voice he'd first heard as he'd stood over that puddle of blood in the street, telling him to walk away.

To come with her.

Chantel had seen him through those first horrible hours. She'd been at the funeral home with him, helped him make decisions he'd never expected he'd have to make. Jill's family hadn't arrived yet.

"Jill was the first on the scene."

And in the space of a second, her life was over. And his had been irrevocably changed.

It wasn't going to happen again. "Tell me what you know," he said to the detective.

"Steve Smith was having an affair with a woman he'd saved during a robbery attempt. She was young. A dancer. Making it on her own. These two hoodlums looking for drug money grabbed her from behind...."

Max heard only one thing. "Did Meredith find out about the affair?"

"I have no idea."

"Did you know Meredith?" It was a question he'd wanted to ask, but hadn't yet.

"I met her a couple of times, but no, I wouldn't say I knew her. I don't think anyone on the force really did. Steve liked to keep his private life private."

Not a bad practice. Unless you were hiding something.

"She left him while the affair was going on. After Meredith was gone, Steve wanted the woman to quit her job. She was in one of the classy shows in one of the elegant hotels on the strip, but apparently he didn't like her on stage at all. His partner at the time was a guy I used to date and he told me about a phone call he overheard between Smith and the girl. He was saying that even the greatest couples have their low moments.

"The girl wouldn't quit. Six months later she ends up dead."

Max kept walking and listening. Chantel's grasp on his wrist kept him focused.

"What was the C.O.D.?" Chantel asked.

Cause of death. Max recognized the term.

"Car accident."

He started to breathe a little easier.

"She'd been drinking and hit a tree."

"But you think Steve had something to do with it?" Chantel asked.

"He was with her that night. And when the autopsy came back, the coroner said that she'd been beaten—before the accident. I figured there'd at least be an internal investigation, but next thing I knew the report was sealed. The beating didn't cause the death and that was that. But talk was that there'd been a witness, a neighbor, who'd heard Steve and the woman fighting. She'd fled the apartment and a couple of minutes later and three blocks away, she wrapped her car around a tree."

"She'd been running from him," Max said.

"I'm sure of it."

"Why didn't anyone pursue this? They had the neighbor's testimony."

"The guy was high at the time. And drinking. He couldn't remember some pertinent details and his testimony would never stand up in court. There's no way the LVMPD would bring up one of their own on such flimsy evidence. Most particularly when you were talking about a decorated officer with a clean record who was in with the commissioner."

Chantel's fingers squeezed harder around his wrist.

And Max asked, "Do you know if Meredith ever filed charges against him?"

"Not in Las Vegas she didn't. I'm not saying she didn't talk to someone about Steve, but if she did, no one came to her rescue. You have to understand, Doctor, the job we do, it requires a certain bit of steel around the edges. Sometimes that steel can be misinterpreted, or come up against something soft and...."

"Surely you aren't condoning a man getting rough with his wife."

"Of course not! And neither would the LVMPD or any other police force I know of. But at the same time, the force might be more apt to suggest anger counseling, or some other assistance, before they'd ruin a man's exemplary record with formal charges."

"Cops are generally controlling by nature, Max," Chantel reminded him, in a tone that probably told Diane Kolhase that Chantel and Max had had the conversation before. "That doesn't make them abusive."

Jill had been a control freak. He'd teased her about it. And she'd not only admitted to it, but been extra careful to control her need to control.

"Is there any way for you to find out if Steve Smith ever had anger management counseling, or any other assistance? To find witnesses from the night his girlfriend was killed? Or to see if anyone knows where he is now?" he asked, staying focused because if he didn't he wouldn't be able to remain calm.

"I can do some checking. It might take a few days."

Max nodded. They walked. The night air chilled his ears. And kept him from burning up inside. He wasn't a violent man.

He was a man who'd dedicated himself to saving lives.

And right then, he wanted to end one.

CHAPTER FIFTEEN

LITTLE OLIVIA HAD a G-tube, which they'd planned for. She needed it only until she could swallow on her own.

That was where Jenna came in. Helping the little girl learn to swallow again.

She worked with Olivia for an hour, in five minute spurts, in between which she kept up a steady flow of light conversation to avoid any chance of Yvonne asking personal questions.

The woman whose house they were using wasn't at home, but had already arranged different homes for them to meet at every day for the next week. Jenna agreed without hesitation to the plan. One thing she and her sister victims had learned was how to be savvy.

It was good, felt healthy, to be living part of the life she'd loved. To stay in touch with that self, even if only for an hour a day.

Or so she told herself.

In the end, this time wouldn't change things for her. But it could matter a whole lot to Olivia. And Yvonne.

Still on a high from seeing Yvonne's relieved smile as Olivia moved her tongue slightly, in the manner they'd practiced before surgery, she left the house, slipping through trees in the neighborhood, silently apologizing to homeowners as she cut across lawns, and made it to the closest bus stop just as the bus was pulling up.

She'd planned the trek well, and had waited out of sight until she saw the bus one street over, on its way to the stop.

She had to know the routes. And she prayed that if Steve was in the area, if he'd already figured out that she hadn't run, that she was off her normal course, that he wouldn't try anything out in the open.

That had never been his way. Steve had a reputation to protect. His public image mattered to him.

It was a fact that had nearly gotten her killed the time she'd dared to tell someone at the LVMPD about his problem. The LVMPD family counselor she'd sought out had gone straight to Steve, supposedly out of respect. Steve had been humbly embarrassed, begging for the whole thing to be forgotten for her sake, because she was a jealous fool who'd lied to try to make him pay for a supposed liaison that had never happened. She'd had no bruises at the time, no proof. She'd expected her cry for help to be protected by confidentiality laws. Apparently those didn't apply when the psychiatrist worked for the police force.

She'd never spoken to an LVMPD official again. Partially because he'd made certain she never dared get close to one. The scar on her thigh was her reminder.

Two stops, a transfer and a shortcut through a neighbor's yard and she was at her next carefully planned destination.

A place for necessary business. Nothing more.

Keeping her eyes trained only on what she had to see to complete her task, she pulled the spare shed key out of her pocket, a key she'd stored with a spare house key in the magnetic holder on the underside of the glove box in her car. Coming from the back side of the shed, keeping trees between herself and the house, she hurried to the door, had it unlocked and was inside in fewer than thirty seconds.

The box was right where she knew it would be. Right where she'd left it. She only had the one pair of black dress pants and a white blouse to go with them and she tried to keep them clean as she climbed over the lawn mower, up onto the trunk behind it, and reached behind a can of nails for the box that held all of the drill bits.

Opening the box, she lifted out the top tray and reached inside for the mint tin. That was all she needed. The mint tin.

Shoving it into the waistband of her pants, she reversed the order of her activity, until she was once again standing on the floor in front of the lawn mower.

She didn't glance out the shed's small window. If the roses were wilting there wasn't a thing she could do about it.

And if… No, Caleb wasn't there. He'd be at the day care, going every day now, she was sure, which was just what his father had thought in his best interests from the beginning.

Children needed to be socialized. They needed to learn how to take turns and stand up for themselves at the same time. They had to learn pecking orders and how to get along in groups. They had to find their own inner strength, without relying twenty-four-seven on the parents who were there to protect them.

She didn't disagree with any of that. They were all necessary lessons. She just didn't think Caleb needed to learn them before he was able to speak up for himself. Until he could tell someone if he was mistreated.

She didn't think he needed to join the track team before he could run.

Still, Max had never taken an unscheduled day off from work since she'd known him. He had patients and he'd be at the office. Which meant Caleb wouldn't be home.

Which was why she'd chosen that particular time to visit.

With fumbling fingers, she pulled open the little

metal tin in her hand. The five one-hundred dollar bills were there, just as they'd left them. Max had teased her the day she'd insisted on stashing the money. He'd had both hands on her waist as she climbed up to reach the shelf, and had lifted her down, sliding his hands up her body as he'd done so.

They'd made love in the seat of the riding lawn mower.

That had been before Caleb. Or maybe the day their son had been conceived.

Those five one-hundred dollar bills had been the first she'd earned as a fully licensed speech pathologist. They'd symbolized freedom and a new life to her. All the things Max had been telling her she had. She'd wanted to give them back—to them. She'd told him they'd put those exact bills away, hide them ceremoniously, and get them out on their thirtieth anniversary to spend on whatever they wanted.

The vow they'd made that day, even more than their wedding vows, had bound them to a lifetime together.

They'd vowed to be together thirty years from then. To spend the money together.

Trembling, she took the dollars and shoved them into her bra, the side opposite her untraceable cell phone. She wasn't going to cry.

It would serve no purpose, and might call attention to her as she made her way back to the bus stop.

Back to The Lemonade Stand where, for now, her secrets were safe.

Closing her mind to voices from the past that would weaken her ability to take care of the task at hand, she closed the box and strode for the door. All that was left was leaving the tin box where Max would be sure to find it empty.

A movement out of the corner of her eye caught her attention. Something had moved in the yard.

Flattening herself against the wall of the shed, she moved toward the window, looking sideways and tilting forward only enough to see out.

Steve was back. She just knew it had to be him out there someplace.

She'd underestimated him. Again.

Without conscious effort her mind began cataloguing everything in the shed. Things she could throw. Things she could use as tools. Tools that could be used against her if Steve got his hands on them.

She was on her own property. He was there uninvited. It would be self-defense.

She had to know how much time she had…could she get out the door and to the other side of the tree trunk before he knew she was there? She had to get him away from this house. Away from Max and Caleb.

She wasn't ready for the showdown. Was only

just beginning to figure him out and didn't yet know how best to use the information to get the better of him, other than some half-formulated idea of getting him to confess while she had her phone on so that someone else could hear the whole thing.

The plan, in its current state was too simplistic. Implementation didn't stand a chance against Steve's powerful mind. At the moment, a plan didn't matter. All that mattered was getting him away from Max's home.

She stole another glance out the window, formulating her next move.

It wasn't Steve standing out there.

Shaking from the inside out, Jenna pulled back, pressing against the wall of the shed she'd helped Max build. He was in their driveway with another woman. The image of him and Chantel Harris played over and over in her mind.

She'd never met Chantel Harris, but she knew that the woman standing there with Max had to be her.

She'd seen pictures. Knew from Wayne Stanton that she'd been helping Max. And the cop uniform was a dead giveaway.

She just hadn't realized the woman had been staying with her husband and son in their home.

But if that duffel bag slung over her shoulder was anything to go by, she had been. Jenna should have looked at the house before she'd come into the shed. She'd have seen the unfamiliar car parked in the driveway.

She wondered what had happened to her van. Did Max have it back? Parked next to his in its usual place in their garage?

She couldn't leave. Her legs were too unsteady to carry her as quietly and quickly as she'd need to go.

And her heart wouldn't bear the stress of a run. Not in that moment.

Her Max. With another woman.

Someone who'd had the hots for him. He'd told her how she'd come on to him the night he'd finished his residency. How she'd been there during the funeral. And how he'd left town, partially to get away from memories of Jill, and partially to avoid breaking Chantel's heart.

Like some kind of masochist, she took one more peek and pulled back instantly.

Max was hugging her.

Where was Caleb? Already at day care?

Why wasn't Max at work?

And how was she going to gather the strength to get herself out of there?

She didn't blame Max. She'd left him.

But maybe she hadn't known him as well as she'd thought she did. Maybe he hadn't loved her as much as she thought.

Yes, he'd known Chantel a long time, before Meri even, so something could form between them quickly.

But this quickly?

And what about Caleb? Was Chantel even interested in a package deal?

Jenna slid down to the floor of the shed, falling apart in the most inappropriate space. She couldn't afford to do this. Had to get out of there and back to the safety and privacy of her room at the Stand.

She couldn't let Max see her. One look at him, one touch, and she'd be done. She needed him more than she needed air.

She needed to rest her head against his chest, feel his comforting heartbeat and believe, once more, that life really could be good. But this wasn't about what she wanted or needed. Not anymore. It was about the love she felt for Max and Caleb.

She'd thought that if she took the cash they'd put away for their thirtieth wedding anniversary, he would finally get the message that he had to move on with his life. Turned out he already had.

She should be happy. She was doing this for him. Honestly and truly wanted him happy.

But her heart was going to need a few minutes to catch up with the plan.

She heard the slam of a car door. The car started, and pulled down the drive.

She held her breath. Would Max come out to the shed? She'd closed the door behind her. There'd be no way for him to know that it was unlocked.

But maybe he'd need something. Ant killer. Or…

The French doors off the kitchen opened. She

heard the squeak as the latch stuck, just as it did every time the door was opened or closed. Max had offered to fix it more than once.

She'd asked him not to. She liked knowing any time a door opened or shut. The alarm in the house told her when a door opened to the outside, but it didn't distinguish between doors.

The garage door had its own slightly echoing sound. The front door was solid. And the French door to the backyard squeaked.

It squeaked a second time as Max shut it. And she knew it was time for her to go.

No need to leave the tin for him to see. He no longer needed her message.

Sliding it into the front pocket of her pants, she took one more glance outside, and as stealthily as she'd arrived, she slipped out of the shed. Out of Max's life, taking a small piece of him, of their dream.

She'd cherish that five hundred dollars. It had his kiss on it, and hers. A promise to each other to stay together, no matter what.

She'd made the promise even knowing, deep inside, that Steve was out there, able to prevent her from keeping any promise she made.

And now she had to pay the price.

CHAPTER SIXTEEN

As soon as Chantel left on Thursday, Max turned off the TV, packed his son into the van, and drove.

He wasn't going anywhere in particular. He had juice boxes. Extra diapers. Vanilla wafers and a couple of Disney movies downloaded on the tablet. And he was driving. On every single street in Santa Raquel.

"Sha sha!" Caleb called out, kicking the back of the seat in front of him. Max had already seen his son's favorite restaurant. He was the one who disapproved of feeding Caleb fast food.

But he knew that Meri did. Once a week.

She'd been gone more than a week now.

And before he really thought about what he was doing, Dr. Maxwell Bennet found himself in the drive-thru for the second time in fewer than seven days.

He strained to see inside the joint. Maybe Meri was there. In honor of Caleb. Clinging to pieces of the life she'd left behind.

One thing was for certain.

Meri was here someplace. At least she had been as recently as two days ago.

And he had the rest of the day off.

He couldn't sit at home knowing that she might be out there somewhere in the same city. Even if he just had a glimpse of her—one second to see the bounce in her step, or a smile on her face—he would feel better.

Hell, just being out driving, knowing she was there somewhere, made him feel better.

And if Steve Smith thought that Max's being hopelessly in love meant he was weak, he had another think coming. He was going to find the bastard.

And have him put away permanently.

The guy was never going to have a chance to bother Meri again. Ever.

JENNA COULDN'T SLEEP Thursday night. And couldn't stay cooped up in her room, either.

Caleb was young enough that he wouldn't even remember her, wouldn't need to be hurt by her past life, or her abandonment. If his father was providing him with a new mother, she wasn't going to get in the way of that.

She wanted to, though. So badly that it was eating her alive. She wanted to order Chantel Harris to get away from her men. To stay away.

She wanted to go home.

Instead she quietly made her way out to the

living room she'd yet to use except as a corridor from the front door to the kitchen or her bedroom.

She wasn't going to turn on the television. Didn't want to disturb her housemates.

But there was a library out there—a collection of fiction—as there was in every bungalow on the premises. She used to love to read.

She couldn't remember the last time she'd picked up a book. Sometime after her marriage to Steve, but when?

He hadn't liked her reading, she remembered. He'd said that her reading made him feel lonely, had tried to distract her with butterfly kisses any time he'd seen her with a book in the early days.

Later there had been fights. He'd resented her time with her romance novels. He'd said the books were filling her head with dangerous notions about women's roles, giving her false expectations of relationships. They were coming between them, ruining their marriage. The books were changing her.

Standing in the living room, perusing shelves of novels that were unfamiliar to her, a tiny bit of anticipation started to grow within her.

She couldn't remember making a conscious decision to give up reading. But she remembered feeling guilty for wanting the escape.

Remembered sitting in the bathroom, pretending to do her business so she could finish a book after Steve got home.

She remembered the broken wrist she'd ended up with the time she'd pulled one of her novels out of the drawer in her desk, looking for an excerpt to use as proof of an example of something she was trying to explain to him. She'd long since forgotten the conversation. It had had something to do with differences between men and women, a statement a character had made that resonated with her. But she remembered that he'd grabbed for the book, he'd said, in attempt to understand, to share it with her, and had grabbed her wrist instead.

Who grabbed a book with a grasp hard enough to break a wrist?

But she'd wanted to believe him, she guessed. Because she'd stayed. She'd been a stay-at-home wife back then and had let him take her to the emergency room, telling the doctors that he'd accidentally broken her wrist as he saved her from tumbling down the stairs.

Once again he'd come out the hero.

And now, here she was, in the middle of the night, pondering a book choice and still looking over her shoulder for Steve. She'd come full circle.

But this time she was going to make a different choice. She was going to choose a book, instead of giving them up.

Studying the spines, she pulled one out, returned it and then pulled out another. There were so many choices.

She heard something. Heart pounding, she froze, trying to ascertain just where the sound had come from.

Outside? Or did the noise come from within the house?

It had sounded like a scrape. Like metal against wood. A window jamb being jarred?

Slowly, Jenna let go of the book she'd been about to pull out and turned, looking for signs of anything amiss.

Both of her housemates' doors were closed. She prayed the women were safe behind them.

Had Steve found her? Had he grown bold enough to breach a shelter in his quest to have her?

And then she heard it again. Definitely a scraping sound. Coming from outside. As if someone was trying to get in.

The inside grounds of The Lemonade Stand were completely secure, accessible only by personnel with individual key cards for tracking purposes. There were also security locks and alarms on all of the windows and doors.

None of which would stop a man like Steve Smith, who knew all of the devices on the market and how to manipulate them. How else did you rescue a young victim from a pedophile kidnapper?

Steve would know how to disarm the devices.

But how had he gotten inside the grounds? Even he wasn't able to scale ten-foot high walls and become invisible to the security cameras set up all over the grounds. Those cameras were manned twenty-four hours by the police.

And there were four security guards on duty at all times, too.

As she moved toward the kitchen, the sound came again. Not from that direction, but as if it was coming from Carly's suite. Heading quickly toward that part of the bungalow, she stopped only long enough to pull her cell phone out of her bra and send a 911 call to the Stand's emergency broadcast line. She gave only their bungalow number before hanging up to lessen her chance of being overheard.

Then, without waiting for help, fearing that Steve would get inside and hurt Carly, she quietly opened the younger woman's door, entering slowly.

Carly was wide-awake, frozen in her bed, staring at Jenna as she came in.

The scraping sound came again, loud, now, and was clearly coming from the window.

Dropping down to her hands and knees, Jenna made her way to the side of the bed opposite the window.

"Slide out of bed," she whispered to Carly. "I'll get in."

"What?" Carly mouthed the word. "No."

"He's not coming for you," she whispered as fiercely as she could without making noise. "It's me he wants. Get out of here, now. I've already called for help. They'll probably be here before he gets inside, but just in case, go to Latoya's room and stay there with her. Quickly." She pulled at Carly's wrist just enough to get the girl moving.

Within seconds, Carly was out of the room, closing the door behind her, and Jenna, in the nightgown she'd borrowed from the clothing room, was lying beneath the sheet and comforter on Carly's bed.

Waiting.

I should be afraid, she thought.

But she wasn't.

CHANTEL WAS WORKING second shift on Thursday, Friday and Saturday and then would have three days off before going back on days for two weeks. Las Sendas police schedules changed on a regular basis to keep officers from seeing the same people on the same streets at the same time every day— an attempt to prevent complacency.

The changing schedule had once ruled Max's life, as he never knew when to expect his wife to be home. When to plan dinners with his folks. Or a night out with fellow residents from the hospital.

Jill had never seemed to mind the unknown when it came to her working hours. She lived to work. Any time she was on was fine with her. It was the off time that she seemed to find more challenging.

But then, her family was all in upstate New

York. Max had only met her immediate family once before the funeral—when they'd flown out for their wedding. He'd never met the myriad aunts and uncles and cousins she'd left behind at eighteen when she moved to California. And her only friends, other than Max, whom she'd met while on a call in a hospital emergency room, had been work associates.

Waiting up for Chantel's call Thursday night brought back memories of other nights he'd waited up for Jill to be off duty and safe.

His full day of appointments on Friday loomed just as they'd done back then.

He was lying in bed when his cell phone, set on vibrate so as not to disturb the sleeping toddler in the next room, started to buzz.

He greeted Chantel, hand over his eyes, as though he could somehow hide his desperate wish that it was Meri's call he'd been awaiting. "How was your day?" he asked. Because it was the decent thing to do.

And for the same reason, he listened as she gave him a briefing on the meth lab she and her partner had stumbled upon that afternoon. She'd taken an attempted rape call, too, near the college campus.

"Did you hear from Diane?" he asked as soon as Chantel fell silent.

"No, but don't get discouraged, Max. You heard her say it could take a few days."

How could he not be discouraged, every single

night that he slept alone, wondering where Meri was sleeping—and with whom?

Wondering if, while he lay in the big soft bed he and Meri had purchased together, on sheets she'd washed and put there, she lay somewhere frightened for her life.

And wished for the thousandth time in a week that he'd made her talk more about her years with Steve Smith. Wished he'd been able to listen to the horrors without getting upset for her, and thus shutting her down.

"How are you holding up?" Chantel's tone had softened. Become more intimate than friendly.

"Fine."

"What did you do with the rest of your day?"

It was a Meri question. A wife question. "Drove every street in this city looking for my wife," he answered honestly. Because he needed both of them to remember that Meri was the light of his life.

And if she was gone, his heart would be in permanent darkness.

He wasn't going to be in the market for another woman. Though he was starting to strongly suspect that Chantel was in the market for him.

"She's safe, Max." The tone of voice didn't change. And he didn't want to like it.

"She was two nights ago."

"She's safe tonight. Wayne's...in touch. He called earlier this evening to let me know that she's in for the night."

"He's got a watch on her?"

"Not exactly."

"But she's keeping in touch with him?"

"No."

"Then…"

"Don't, Max. Don't ask. Please. Just trust me and know that you can get some rest. Meredith is where she chose to be and she's sleeping in a nice bed in a nice place."

Nice place. Okay. That ruled out some of the horrors he'd been imagining.

And where she chose to be. Which was not with him.

"You're a good friend," he told the woman who was giving him so much of her time when he hadn't tried once to see her in more than four years.

"You're a good man, Maxwell Bennet," she said in return.

And he worried that they'd just turned onto a road he didn't want to travel.

CHAPTER SEVENTEEN

IT WASN'T STEVE at the window. Jenna was still reeling from the news.

"You're going to be fine, now," she said softly, sitting on the sofa in the bungalow with a still-shaking Carly.

They were close, curled up with cups of green tea laced with just a hint of brandy, given to them by Lynn Bishop. Their feet were touching.

Latoya was there, too, in a chair next to them, sipping on the same brew.

"They got him, girl. I saw them haul him away."

Carly nodded. "I know. Lila told me."

Lila, Lynn, TLS security, the Santa Raquel police had all been there. Sara, too. And they were all gone now. Because the three women had assured them they'd be fine.

As fine as any of the three of them were ever going to be.

They talked for another hour. Reliving the horrifying experience of having one of their abusers invade their safe place. Carly's ex-boyfriend. He was being held not only for trespassing, breaking and entering with intent to harm, and attempted kidnapping but for stabbing a security guard and knocking out another, as well as tampering with security devices. Jenna wasn't the only one with an ex who'd had special training. Carly's had been a marine.

Latoya, who had an early session in the morning that she still intended to attend, finally excused herself and went off to bed, leaving her door open as they'd all decided they would do for the next couple of nights, at least.

"You can go, too," Carly told Jenna. "I'll be fine. You have that little girl to help in the morning, and then a couple of appointments here."

She'd told her housemates a bit about her work when she'd returned that day. Latoya had seen her come in, before she could clean herself up and put on fresh makeup, and she and Carly had both wanted to know where she'd been. In another situation their curiosity might have been considered nosiness.

But at the Stand, it was an inherent part of their sisterhood that they watch out for each other. Victims of domestic violence couldn't always trust themselves, and, like any kind of an addict, needed a support group. Except that it wasn't alcohol or drugs that held them captive. It was the need to love and be loved that did it to them.

So when Latoya had asked where she'd been,

she'd told them about Yvonne and Olivia. Fellow sisters.

"I wouldn't sleep if I went to bed," Jenna said, more for Carly than for herself, but knowing the words were true just the same. She wasn't going to sleep, but she'd be okay in her room alone.

Carly wouldn't.

"I just can't believe you did that for me. That you risked your life like that."

"I thought it was…someone else."

"At my window?"

"He could have been at the wrong window." But she had wondered, as had Lila and the others, how Trent Compton, Carly's dishonorably discharged marine ex-boyfriend, had known which bungalow was hers.

As it turned out, he'd been watching them from a rooftop for the past week. And had seen Carly come and go. He must have seen her at her window at some point, too, to know which room was hers.

Carly was shaking her head. "He used to watch my window in L.A." Her voice was soft as she shook her head. "My folks were…I don't know… they, neither one of them had careers, you know, but just worked as store clerks and my dad worked in a factory for a while. They were into motorcycles, smoked and drank a lot and hung out with a pretty tough crowd. My brother got into riding, too. We lived in a rough neighborhood and when they'd take off on weekend rides, I'd be home alone.

"And there was Trent. He lived in the apartment across from ours and he promised me he'd keep a watch on me, to make sure I was safe. He had all these sight things, like for guns, but they were more like binoculars. He'd ordered them off the internet. He said he was into stars and wanted to study space travel.

"I thought it was cool then...."

Because girls were vulnerable sometimes when it came to their own protection. Until they learned that they were the only ones who *could* keep themselves safe.

"It probably was cool, then," Jenna said. "It was probably just over time that it got creepy." Which was part of the problem. How could anyone predict how another person might change?

"I just don't get it. It's not that Trent was a bad guy. He was into animal rescue and fighting for the underdog...."

Steve had rescued human beings, and had put his life on the line every day to see that they were protected.

"What happened to him?" Carly's blue eyes filled with tears and she started to shake again.

Jenna had an answer. An odd burst of clarity in a mind that had been foggy....

The research she'd done over the past week, her trying to get into character...she was more prepared than she'd thought.

"Somehow he wrapped up his own sense of

value, his sense of self-worth, in his possession of you," she said slowly. Softly. "As long as he has you he is rich. Anytime he feels like he might not have complete control of you, his prize possession, his sense of self is threatened. He goes into survival mode. Those types of people will stop at nothing to survive. He starts to feel powerless so he has to exert his power. Only when he is certain that you will do only and exactly as he directs, is he at peace.

"You're a living being he has to own, in order to feel safe, but you have a mind of your own and are escaping him, which makes you an enemy to his basic sense of survival."

Jenna's heart started to pound as she spoke. And she knew she was on to something important. Knew that she was stumbling across the key to beating Steve.

"He becomes filled with the anticipation of the hunt."

"Kind of like those guys who spend a hundred thousand dollars for a chance to go out with some big game experience guy and shoot a bear or some other poor animal that's being held captive," Carly said. "All so he can take the pelt home and hang it on his wall and make everyone think he shot it in the wild. Like he's some big strong man who can take on bears and win. I saw a show on TV about it not long ago. It was disgusting. These guys killed animals who were doing nothing more than living the lives they were born to live, animals who weren't hurting or threatening anyone. Just so these losers could feel more manly among their peers."

"Exactly," Jenna agreed. "Or like the guys who spend two hundred thousand to do the same thing over in Africa. It's like an instinctive need with some guys."

"It comes, I think, from the the natural instinct to kill in the wild to provide food for his family…."

"Only completely twisted," Jenna added.

She was in Steve's mind-set now. Getting him. He didn't just want to keep her on the run so that he could keep her vulnerable to him. He wanted her on the run because he got off on the challenge of the hunt.

Because I dared to get down off of his wall and tell the world that he wasn't a great hunter at all.

"A man who can't hunt well can't feed his family," Jenna said, going with the metaphor.

"So a possessive guy who feels like he's losing control of his possessions, acts instinctively, as though, if he can't get the hunt right, he'll never have a family to feed. It's not that he needs me so much at this point as that he needs me not to be able to get away from him."

"Yes. Though this could be complicated by the fact that on some level he really does love you.

"And I think it gets even more convoluted when you add in the social factor of how everyone else views him. Like the man with the bear pelt on his wall that he has to show everyone who comes to his house—Trent thinks that when people see you with him, they think he's some great guy. If you leave him, he feels like less in the eyes of the world, like your rejection says there's something wrong with him. Or makes him somehow less."

Yes! She was getting it now. Pieces floated into place as though animated and on-screen.

Steve wasn't just an amazing brain plotting actions that no one could hope to outsmart. He was a fallible man with an emotional need that was being threatened.

He wasn't acting out of logic. He was acting out of emotion.

Which not only made him less likely to succeed and more likely to make a mistake, but made him more vulnerable, too.

There was something he cared about more than life. More than Jenna.

Something that controlled him.

His own threatened sense of self-worth.

That was her secret weapon.

Her mind raced as she tried to figure out how to use it against him.

MAX ARRANGED FOR the older neighbor lady who'd babysat Caleb a couple of times in the past, to come to the house and stay with him on Saturday while he made hospital rounds just around the corner from the clinic.

He saw patients all morning. Life had to go on. People needed him.

Caleb needed some semblance of normal.

But how in the hell did a guy do normal when his world was exploding around him and there was seemingly nothing he could do about it?

He talked to Chantel each day, too. Lived for her calls, and at the same time was glad the other woman was on shift three hours away. The comfort she offered was too tempting to a man ruled by grief and fear.

Until Sunday's call.

Saturday she'd told him that Diane had talked to someone who knew that Steve had undergone voluntary anger management counseling not once, but twice. She'd also added that he'd attended one of those times with his entire squad who'd been ordered to go as part of a continuing education LVMPD initiative that the human resources department had implemented.

On Sunday, she didn't even bother with hello. Or to get home from work, for that matter.

He'd just hung up from lying to his parents— telling them that Meri was in the shower and would call later in the week—and was still treading around his bedroom barefoot, getting ready for bed, when she called.

"Max. I just listened to a voice mail from Diane. She tracked down one of the anonymous witnesses from that dancer girl's death. As it turns out the guy across the hall still lives in the building—on the top floor. He owns the place now. And still remembers that night. He says there's no doubt in his mind that the girl was running from Steve when she left the apartment. She wasn't the partying type. And took cabs if she'd ever had more than one drink. He says there's no way she would have gotten in that car if she hadn't thought her life was in immediate danger if she didn't do so."

Suddenly wide-awake, with nerves on the edge of needing a run, Max said, "Because why would you trust a call for help, a call to the cops, when you had a cop in your apartment."

"Exactly."

"So what happens next?"

"She's going to try to build a case. I can't promise that anything will come of it. Chances aren't good that a grand jury would indict an ex-cop with an exemplary record on circumstantial evidence, but if she can build enough of a case, she might be able to get an order to have the woman's body brought up."

This was not normal bedtime conversation.

"You really think they might do that?"

"Do you remember that case in Chicago a few years ago? The cop who was charged with killing his second or third wife, but they couldn't find her body, so they brought up the body of his first wife who'd either committed suicide, or been ruled accidental, I can't remember which right now, but they brought her body up. Did an autopsy. Her death was ruled murder and he was later convicted."

He didn't think he'd ever heard of the case. But was glad that Chantel had.

"Okay," he said now, pacing his room, frustrated as hell that he didn't have Meri with him to discuss this newest development. "Keep me posted and let me know if there's anything I can do to help."

If only he'd known these things years ago—if only Meri had...

"She just needs us both to keep quiet about this for now," Chantel told him. "That means you can't tell anyone, Max. Not anyone. If Smith gets wind of what she's doing before she has a chance to build a big enough case, he could make it go away just like he did before. And if not, then he'd definitely be out to get her. He's already got the death of one woman on his slate, what's one more if it'll keep him looking clean?"

He hadn't thought of that.

"Of course I'll keep quiet. Who would I tell, anyway?"

"Well, it's just...she's put things in motion and if, by chance, you were to talk to Meredith, or she came home, she can't know about this, Max. We don't know what hold Smith has on her, or what she might tell him if, for instance, he threatened you or Caleb...."

Beads of sweat popped out on his lip. "You really think Caleb could be in danger?"

"Not now, I don't, or you can bet I'd be doing something about it. But if Meredith were there with you, the stakes could escalate a bit."

The words quelled his fear, slightly. But they also hit home. "What you're inadvertently saying is that she might have left to protect us from him," he said. He'd had the thought earlier, but had never quite been able to follow the reasoning through, knowing as he did that they'd have full police protection and knowing that Meri had been fully aware of that fact, too.

But it didn't sound as if she'd have trusted police protection....

Problem was, he didn't know at this point what she thought or whom she trusted.

And then something else occurred to him. By calling in Chantel, who was working on this privately as a personal favor, he'd put her in danger, too.

"I want you off this case," he said, louder than he'd intended, the words filled with absolute intent. "I will not have you hurt because of me."

"I'm not on the case, Max," Chantel said with a soft chuckle that sounded as satisfied as it did amused. "Wayne is handling things in Santa Raquel. And Diane has it in Vegas. I'm just the conduit that sends news your way."

She was more than that. But she was right, too.

"I have no jurisdiction in either place and no

personal knowledge of him. Hurting me would do him no good at all."

She made sense.

"Okay, you've convinced me."

"Good, because I'm not going anywhere, whether you're convinced or not."

He told her he was glad.

And then figured he probably shouldn't have done so.

But dammit, he'd been a good friend to her for years, including her in his and Jill's life, lending her money to buy the condo she'd wanted, helping her get a car when she'd totaled hers....

And now he needed a friend.

More than that, Meri needed her. Max was a pediatrician, not a cop. When it came to finding Meri, without Chantel, Max was powerless.

CHAPTER EIGHTEEN

JENNA WAS THE talk of the Stand over the weekend, and hated every second of the notoriety. By Monday, she was actually eager to leave the place to meet with Yvonne and Olivia, and when she returned, kept her speech therapy appointments and then sought solace in the Garden of Renewal.

Plans were underway for the pool party. It was going to be for adults only. Shelter employee Maddie Bishop, who was six months pregnant, was going to be the unknowing guest of honor. Her husband, Darin, along with his brother, Lynn's husband, Grant, had volunteered to watch the seventeen underage residents. A group of women were planning snacks and games for the kids to keep them busy and happy.

Jenna meandered through the Garden and smiled at the few women there, but didn't stop to speak. The Garden was meant to be a peaceful retreat, not an area for socializing.

She'd never spent any time there and on that afternoon she tried to open up and allow the privacy, the towering trees and the beds of glorious, sweet-smelling flowers, to heal even a tiny part of her. But it appeared she was immune to the salve.

And so she started to pull weeds. Because there were a few, scattered about, and she'd met Grant Bishop and his mentally handicapped brother, Darin, over the weekend and knew that the men had their hands full keeping up with Grant's landscape design business and yard maintenance at the Stand, as well. She knew only because Darin had told her.

He'd also told her it wasn't anything his brother, Grant would ever tell anyone.

You had to look hard to find anything on the grounds of The Lemonade Stand that wasn't immaculate. But when she saw some weeds growing at the base of some of the trees in the thick woods that set the Garden off from the rest of the grounds, she dropped down to pick them.

She left them in piles as she worked, with the plan to come back and gather them in her blouse to carry them up to the trash. She worked quickly. Quietly. Undaunted by the fact that there were easily three or four acres of woods surrounding the Garden.

The earth felt good beneath her hands. Dirt under her trimmed nails. Kept short in deference to the baby she'd tended, the diapers she'd changed.

And for every weed that wanted to play tough, that gave her a hard time, she held a mental victory celebration as she hung tougher and succeeded in pulling it out by its roots.

This was what she was going to do with the memories of Steve. Pull them up by their roots and throw them in the trash.

When she'd rid her life of him.

Didn't matter if there were acres of memories. Or tough ones to excavate. Didn't matter if she got it all done in one day, or had to repeat the effort over and over again for the rest of her life.

She could pull them out and throw them away.

And if they regenerated, she could pull them up again. Throw them away again.

Her life could be as beautiful as this Garden. She just had to....

A sound behind her had her freezing on the spot.

Carly's ex-boyfriend had managed to break through the security at the Stand. And while security was tighter than ever before, with added guards on duty, more cameras, and more outside patrol as well, Steve was far more skilled at knowing how to break and enter than Trent would ever be.

Another twig snapped. Several feet behind her and off to her left. She didn't turn around. Didn't want him to know she was on to him.

She had to get to her phone. Push the TLS emergency speed dial.

Another movement. A little farther to her left.

No one knew where she was.

She didn't even know how far she was from the

actual Garden. She'd been pulling weeds. Mentally expostulating about life. Not paying attention to her surroundings.

Reaching into her bra, she opened her phone and felt for the number three on her dial pad. Pushed.

Security would be there soon.

Jenna pulled a weed. Carefully added it to the small pile she'd begun to form between two closely planted trees.

She'd broken her number one rule. Be aware of your surroundings. At all times.

How could she have been so foolish?

Or felt so safe?

This place had gotten to her. Given her a false sense of security. It was a lesson to her that even she could be wooed into letting her guard down.

A lesson that could cost her.

When she heard another twig snap, Jenna slowly stood. It would be far better that Steve get her now rather than giving him a chance to hurt anyone else. She'd leave quietly with him.

And figure out the rest from there. Security should be there in seconds to protect everyone else.

She just didn't want anyone to get hurt. With very little fear, she turned.

And saw a body bending over by the base of a tree. And farther off in the distance, another body. And on the other side of her, even farther away, a third.

Residents. Her sisters. Helping her pull weeds.

And she'd thought no one knew where she was.

"WE ALL HEARD Darin the other day," Renee, the weed picker who'd been closest to her, walked with Jenna as she left the Garden almost an hour later. Security had been and gone. "Julie saw what you were doing and called up to the main building to let anyone who was free know that you could use some help."

She didn't know Julie well. But had recognized her as the woman sitting alone on the bench in the Garden when she'd taken her walk earlier.

"I didn't even know you guys were there."

Renee shrugged. "Everyone knows the Garden's a place for quiet contemplation. Some people contemplate while pulling weeds. As busy as you are, I figured you had something pretty important to work on to be out there pulling at dirt."

It was as direct a question as Renee would probably ask.

Feeling the weight of responsibility for the example she set, just by existing among needy women who looked to each other for help and support, Jenna shrugged.

"I'm not used to the attention I've been getting here lately. I needed a…break." She picked the words that she could speak.

And left the rest.

"You do a lot of weeding in your past life?"

"Nope." Not until she'd moved in with Max. And even then, she did more spraying and hiring of landscapers than actual weeding.

"I grew up pulling weeds in my mama's garden," Renee continued, walking easily beside her.

And strangely, as they talked, Jenna didn't mind the other woman's presence. In spite of the fact that she'd gone to the Garden looking for escape.

"When my Brian was little he lisped...." Renee was holding one end of a sheet and Jenna the other. They were alone in the laundry room Monday night. Renee had signed up to do TLS laundry once a week, which included anything used in any common areas, including physical therapy and the cafeteria. Towels mostly.

Jenna had offered to help. It gave her a chance to get her own few things washed. And to keep busy.

She'd been so tempted to go back by Max's house that morning after she'd seen Olivia. The bus stop was only one past hers. She'd thought about it the whole way. And then watched out the window as the familiar area sped past.

Movement cured all ails. Or it had to this point in her life.

Was there a cure for seeing the man you loved with another woman?

"The kids at school teased him and my instinct was to coddle him, to fight his battles for him. Gary insisted that we make him tough it out and go to school and stand up to the bullies...."

They came together and Jenna took the sheet, finishing up the last fold and placing it on the large table that currently held over a hundred towels all washed and neatly folded, while Renee picked up another sheet, found the ends and handed two to her.

"I wish I'd stood up to Gary then," Renee continued. "Brian was such a sensitive creature. We should never have forced him to go against his nature…."

Renee needed to understand her abuser. And she was the mother bear, protecting her young at the same time.

An untenable position.

Far worse than having an abusive husband.

Far, far worse than knowing that your husband would have someone to help him bear the pain you'd caused.

"My little brother lisped," Jenna said, jumping at the first thought that came to her brain that wasn't about Steve, or Max and Chantel. The sound of the machines running, tubs filling, the cottony spring scent of softening sheets, even the warmth generated from the dryers were nice. Steady.

Familiar.

Renee glanced at her as though she was waiting for more. There wasn't any more. Chad had had a lisp.

"That's partially why I became a speech pathologist," she said. Everyone at the Stand knew she was one. Nothing to hide there.

"Did he have troubles at school?" Renee asked.

"Yeah. I remember him coming home from kindergarten with a fat lip. He wasn't crying at all. But when Mom made him tell her why he'd gotten into a fight, and he'd had to admit the kids said he talked like a baby, he started to bawl. And I remember the woman who came to our house a lot after that, doing mouth and tongue exercises with him. By second grade the lisp was gone. I kind of missed it. It was cute."

"The last thing boys in school want to be is cute."

Caleb was cute. And in one of his last pictures, looked just like a picture she had of Chad, too.

Would he also have his uncle's lisp when he fully started talking?

"I didn't know you have a brother. You've never mentioned family."

"Yeah."

"What's his name?"

"Chad." And now it was time to get the next batch of towels from the dryer. These were smaller, from the kitchen, rather than the larger ones used in physical therapy and the gym.

"Is he local?" Renee's tone had changed, becoming more like Lila's every second. Jenna tensed.

"No."

"You don't want to talk about him."

"No." She gave her refusal gently.

"Of course you know that they say when you don't want to talk is when you should."

She couldn't tell Renee about her plans, couldn't

tell any of the women that the programs that worked for them, that they were supposed to believe worked for them, didn't work for her.

"I don't talk about them because my family was killed," she said, taking the folded sheet from Renee and putting it with the last one they'd done.

And while Renee stood there, hands empty, she rolled the cart over to the dryer and pulled out the next load of towels.

Her few things were done. Underthings neatly folded. Clothes hung and ready for her to take back to the bungalow where she could have done her laundry. If she hadn't been helping Renee.

"Killed how?" Renee didn't fold. She just watched her.

Picking up a towel, Jenna made short work of the task at hand. "In a car accident. It was a long time ago."

So long ago she hardly thought about it anymore.

"How long ago?"

"Twenty years."

"You were just a kid."

"I was twelve."

"Oh, my God, Jenna, I'm so sorry. What a horrible thing to have had happen. I don't know what to say…."

"No one ever does. Which is why I don't talk about it. It was horrible. But like I said, it was a long time ago."

"Was it just the four of you, then?"

"In the car? Yes."

A towel hung in Renee's hands. "I meant in your family."

"Yes. They were my whole family."

"You were in the car with them?" Renee asked next.

"Yeah." Jenna looked at the towel. Heard a clank as something went around and around in one of the dryers. Probably a fastener in some of the donated clothes Renee was sending through the wash before putting on the shelves in the store room.

"And you were the only survivor."

"Yeah."

"I can't imagine…."

She folded. "I know."

"Were you conscious? Do you remember anything?" Renee's tone held more compassion than Jenna could take at the moment.

"Unfortunately, I remember it like it was yesterday," she said. Because they weren't talking about Steve. And she wasn't having to think about Chantel and Max and Caleb. About how she'd feel if she lost her men in a car accident when she hadn't even told them goodbye….

"I used to have nightmares," she said. "But I don't much anymore." Not one since she'd climbed into bed with Max Bennet. Until last week, when she'd climbed out again.

"We were hit by a garbage truck. On the driver's side. The guy had fallen asleep at the wheel." She was the only one who'd been thrown free. She'd been hurt, but hadn't felt any pain. She'd jumped up, run back to the car, pulling at the mangled steel. She could see her little brother's hand. Her mother's hair. Part of her father's shirt. And couldn't get to any of them.

And if she'd let Chad sit where he wanted to....

"I was told they were killed on impact."

That had been the only blessing she'd carried away from that day. The fact that her family hadn't suffered. Or even known that something horrible had happened.

But they must have known that she didn't go with them.

"Did you have relatives?"

"A grandfather who wasn't in good health. An aunt with six kids who fought with my dad more than she was nice to him."

"Who did you go to?"

"I went into foster care. Neither of them had the financial means to care for me."

She'd known, even back then, that neither of them had wanted to take her in. Her grandfather, she understood. He'd died within a year of the accident. But had come to see her every single week until he got too sick. And then he'd arranged for her to travel to see him.

"Oh, my...I'm so sorry, Jenna. Such a little girl, too young...."

Renee had tears in her eyes.

Jenna shook her head. "No, really, it was a long time ago," she said, wishing she hadn't said so much.

She never said that much.

Not even to Max. It served no purpose. Except to make people feel sorry for her.

She folded. And stacked. And moved another load from the washer to the dryer.

"I imagine, being the only one left behind, would be a hell all in itself. Even apart from losing your loved ones."

She'd had counseling. "I had things left to do here."

Renee's arm slid around her waist and, surprised at the contact, Jenna jumped back and dropped her towel.

"I didn't mean to startle you," the other woman said. "But this isn't just another room and another conversation, Jenna. I've trusted you with my deepest pain. And you understood, without judging. It was the greatest gift anyone has given me.

"And I'm thinking maybe you need a gift, too. Maybe you need someone to understand that someplace inside you you're still that little girl who's had to carry the weight of the world on her shoulders all alone."

"No." She shook her head. Picked up a towel. "I'm fine, really."

"There was a young woman at church once who was having a hard time staying out of trouble. Brian counseled her in our home and I couldn't help overhearing a few things through the door. She and her twin sister had been out in a storm and a tree had been struck by lightning and fallen. The twin sister was struck in the back and was paralyzed. The girl blamed herself. And spent the next several years involving herself in every destructive behavior she could think of, punishing herself...."

"Luckily, I got counseling."

"You don't think denying yourself the right to ask for what you want, to demand what you need, is destructive?"

Renee didn't know that that was exactly what Jenna was doing. She was demanding her right to be done with Steve, once and for all.

"You blame yourself, don't you? For not dying with them?"

She'd wondered many times why not her. "I just know that I was left on this earth for a purpose and so I try, every single day, to give as much of myself as I can give to those around me, hoping that I'm fulfilling that purpose."

"To justify living when the others didn't?"

Counselors didn't get as in your face as Renee was doing. But anyone who'd been through counseling would be able to ask these same questions. She'd been through them all. More than once.

"To make lemonades out of lemons," she said, quoting the slogan of The Lemonade Stand. She glanced at the wall opposite them with the full mural of a lemon grove and the words painted in colorful script winding through the trees.

She knew she was on the right course. She'd applied herself to the programs and counseling.

If she'd blamed herself for anything, it was that she'd lived and Chad hadn't.

But she knew that it had been fate that had taken her little brother, not she.

CHAPTER NINETEEN

MAX KNEW THAT Chantel was off on Monday. He just didn't expect her to be in Santa Raquel. He'd suggested, the night before that, until there was something more to go on, she stay home and get caught up on her life there.

He'd been trying to tell her nicely that he didn't think it was a good idea for them to be spending so much time together.

For her to be staying over so much that Caleb was getting used to having another woman there.

It had been two days since the toddler had asked for his mother. He hadn't asked for Chantel, either, but when she showed up at their door just before nine, catching him watching the end of yet another Disney movie with his son—keeping the boy up an hour past his bedtime to boot—Caleb said "Chan," from his place on Max's hip.

"Hey, Caleb," Chantel said, pulling a teddy bear from behind her back. "This is Henry. He's a friend of mine and he wanted to meet you."

"Hen'y." Caleb took the bear, but didn't smile. He was sizing up Chantel. And when she leaned in a little farther toward him, he leaned back.

"He's a tough egg to crack, isn't he?" she said, depositing her duffel bag on the floor as she walked into their home.

"He's a lot like his mom," Max said. He needed Meri there.

"I know I'm taking a huge liberty packing a bag and showing up without calling first," Chantel told him, following him into the living room where the movie was on pause.

"Ca...." Caleb made the demand without an ounce of little boy excitement. "Ca," he said again, as though to be sure that Max had clearly understood what had to happen next.

Max picked up the remote control and restarted the *Cars* video for him.

"I've got news, Max," Chantel said, sitting on the edge of the armchair perpendicular to the couch.

His gaze flew to her.

"That's why I'm here. Wayne's off in the morning and I'm meeting him to check out a few places."

"Is it—" He glanced toward Caleb.

"She's fine. Still at the same place," Chantel said. "Planning a pool party from what I understand."

"She told Wayne to tell me that?"

"No. Just something he overheard and told me."

"Because he doesn't think she's on the run. He thinks her reasons are the ones she gave." He chose his words carefully, in the remote chance that his son was following any part of the conversation.

"Correct."

"But she knows that Wayne is reporting to me?" Chantel shook her head.

"So whoever she's staying with is keeping me informed?"

"That's correct."

Good. They were getting someplace. "So whoever this is must think that there's a chance for our marriage."

"No." Chantel's eyes filled with that damned sympathy again and he was starting to feel pathetic.

Is that how he looked? Like some kind of sap who couldn't accept that his beautiful wife had left him?

Is that what he was?

Wallowing in disbelief rather than accepting facts and getting on with his life?

"Wayne understands your concern and doesn't want you to worry that she's in danger. That's all. On another note, we might have something on Steve."

She had news. That was what mattered. And he had to get his son to bed so that he could find out exactly what Chantel had driven all this way to tell him.

JENNA FINISHED WITH the laundry, walked partway to Renee's bungalow and continued on to her own, her arms laden with clothes. She put her things away. Stopped at the kitchen table to ask her roomies how the brownies were. Latoya had done the baking.

And Latoya and Carly were sitting over a plate of them with glasses of milk.

"Good. You want one?" Carly asked, jumping up. "I'll get you some milk."

"No." Jenna chuckled. "But thank you. I'm still full from dinner." Or from the knot in her stomach. She wasn't sure which.

"I cleaned your bathroom and vacuumed your room for you," Carly piped up. "I hope you don't mind. It was my week to do the living area and your door was open."

Making a mental note to herself to keep her door shut—not because she didn't trust Carly in her room, but because she wasn't going to have the younger woman think that she had to do special favors for her now—Jenna said, "Oh, Carly, what a sweet gesture. Thank you. You didn't have to do that."

"I know." The girl's mouth said one thing, but the almost adoring look in her eyes said another. And Jenna figured a talk between them was in order.

She wasn't a hero. She just wasn't going to have anyone else dying because of her.

"What is it?" Latoya asked as she bit into a brownie. "You just went white."

"I... Nothing," Jenna told her, feeling like a deer caught in headlights. *Anyone else dying because of her?*

Where had that thought come from?

Had the conversation she'd had with Renee planted it there?

"I…uh…I forgot I have a meeting up at the main building," she said.

"At nine-thirty?"

"It was the only time that worked. I just wanted to bring my laundry back." She was backing away from the table. Toward the door. "I'll see you guys when I get back. If you're still up."

"It's dark out," Carly said. "I can walk with you if you'd like."

"No, I'm fine. The walk is well lit and I have my phone."

"Well, at least make sure you call security for a ride back," Latoya reminded her. It was a newly instated rule that anyone out and about on the premises after ten o'clock had to be accompanied by security.

"I will." Jenna was at the door. She reached behind her for the knob and hurried out.

She wasn't sure where she was going. But she needed to think. To figure out what was going on with her. To be certain that she could trust her own mind.

It had been a long time—since leaving the first shelter several years before—since she'd doubted her own instincts.

And that fact, far more than a man at the window in the night, scared her to death.

WHEN MAX CAME out from putting Caleb to bed, Chantel was in the kitchen, doing his dinner dishes.

"I was going to get to those," he said. There were two days' worth in the sink.

"I'm not good at just standing around," Chantel reminded him. She'd been known to dust their living room, or mow the lawn when she visited. Anything to keep busy.

He'd asked Jill once why Chantel couldn't ever just chill out. She'd shrugged and said that she was borderline ADD or something. He couldn't remember exactly.

And wished he'd paid more attention.

Coming up behind her, he put his hands on her shoulders and squeezed. "Really," he said. "You don't need to do my dishes for me. Sit. Have you had dinner?"

"I grabbed something in the car on the way up."

"Then how about a beer?"

"You didn't have any last time I was here."

Neither he nor Meri were big drinkers.

"I picked up a six pack."

He pulled out a bottle. Opened it and handed it to her before pulling out a second. While she sat sideways on a chair at the kitchen table, hands on the back as she watched him, he finished loading the dishwasher in exactly the way Meri liked. Moving some of the dishes that Chantel had already placed to make that happen.

He washed the pans and plastic container by hand.

And then, also to please his wife, he wiped down every single counter, although he hadn't used them all during his food prep. They'd eaten soup and sandwiches that night.

When he was done, he took his first sip of beer, then joined Chantel at the table.

"What did you find out?" He'd put off knowing for half an hour. Avoiding what he knew he wasn't going to like.

"Steve Smith told someone in the LVMPD, a guy he ran into in a casino about six months ago, that he'd purchased a little place on the beach."

"Here? In California?" This was bad.

Really bad.

"We don't know. But it bothered Diane enough that she thought I should check it out. I talked to Wayne about it and he agreed that it's suspicious enough that it's worth checking into, so tomorrow he and I are going to canvas areas around here. Tonight, our job—yours and mine—is to search public records of home and condo sales in the area since Meredith has lived here, and see if we get lucky and Steve's name pops up. Though I suspect that he'd have paid cash using an assumed name. Or put the property in somebody else's name."

Max's blood ran cold. His skin felt clammy.

Had Meri's ex been watching her, watching them, all this time? "I'm not at all sure this'll turn into anything, Max," Chantel said, arms on the table as she leaned closer to him. And for once he wished she'd reach out and touch him. Because it would be inappropriate for him to touch her, and he could sure use a bit of human contact at the moment.

"According to Diane's source, Smith had been drinking at the casino and the guy wasn't sure whether Steve had been talking big, or if he was being serious. And there are a million beaches in the world...."

But not a million in a town where an ex-wife—whom he'd already stalked through three states—lived.

"Wayne's using official means and time to do this?"

"And working on his own."

"Why? Surely he's paid off his debt to you by now."

"You're a citizen of Santa Raquel—one he's sworn to protect. As is Meri. You've expressed suspicions. With your wife's sudden choice to leave you, and your inability to accept that she really just wants out of the marriage, he feels it's his duty to check things out."

She was playing this down. But he didn't need or want to be coddled.

"Diane's convinced Meri could be in trouble, isn't she?"

"Diane has a dead woman on her mind."

"And witnesses that make that woman's death look like a murder that was covered up."

God, Meri, what are we into here? Why didn't you tell me everything?

Did I ever give you cause not to trust me?

They were questions he couldn't answer.

So he thanked Chantel, once again, for having his back. And sipped his beer.

And just before he drifted off into a restless sleep later that night, he sent a message into the air, hoping that by some miracle it would find its way to his wife.

Please stay safe, my love.

JENNA DIDN'T HAVE a conscious plan to end up at the door to Lila's private suite after leaving her bungalow Monday night. The managing director might not be there, since she had her own place a few miles from the Stand. But Jenna had seen her heading to her on-campus apartment late in the evening, off in the distance, when she'd been coming back from the laundry room.

She knocked softly on Lila's door, intending to leave as soon as her knock went unanswered. But the door opened before she could think about turning around.

"Jenna!" Lila, dressed in black fleece pajama pants and a T-shirt that said, "Best Mom Ever", pulled the door opened wide. "Come on in."

"I'm sorry," Jenna said, backing away instead. "You're ready for bed. I should have called."

She was still in the jeans she'd worn to pick weeds that afternoon.

Seemed like a lifetime ago.

"It'll be hours before I attempt sleep," Lila said. "I was just curled up with a book," she said, smiling and looking gracious and capable and welcoming. "It's a guilty pleasure when I'm here overnight. At home there's so much to do, so many responsibilities. Laundry, cleaning, bills to pay…but here—" she shrugged, smiling again "—I don't have to do any of those things. Please, come in."

She'd disturbed the woman. She couldn't also disappoint her.

"I'm not in trouble or anything," she said, almost stammering. Wasn't that rich, for a speech pathologist to stumble over her own tongue?

Lila had told her to find her if she was in trouble. Not to bother her because she didn't want to go back to her own room and face the voices in her own mind.

"I'm fairly certain you wouldn't tell me if you were," the older woman said, leading Jenna into her small sitting area.

"Can I get you some tea?"

"Can I have some without milk?"

She moved slowly around the room as Lila disappeared into the kitchen. There were pictures on the walls, but none had people in them.

"Are these places you've visited?" she called

out, recognizing Monte Carlo and the Mediterranean Sea.

"No. Just places I've always thought I'd like to go," Lila said, coming back into the room.

"You hang pictures on your walls, but don't take a vacation and go?"

"I know." The woman smiled again, looking around the room. "I've got too much else to do right now. But maybe someday." She left the room again and Jenna heard china rattling. A refrigerator opening and closing.

She wondered about Lila's private life. Her family.

Wondered why she was so dedicated to this place.

And when Lila came back with her tea, curling up in one of the armchairs, Jenna took her same place at the end of the couch.

"How are you doing?" Lila asked, folding her legs beneath her as she sipped her tea, looking as if she'd be happy to sit and chat all night long.

"I'm fine."

"Good. I'm glad to hear it."

Jenna nodded. And stood up. Carrying her tea with her, she wandered the small room. Studying pictures, landscapes, she'd already studied.

"I…have a question," she said to a photograph of the Leaning Tower of Pisa, when it seemed as though Lila would let her wander the room for the next week.

"I'll answer it if I can."

Jenna turned and looked Lila in the eye. "How do you know when to trust your instincts and when your mind is just playing with you?"

She'd had this down once. And she'd obviously lost some key piece of the puzzle.

"I'm not sure you ever do know for sure," Lila said. "At least not that I've found."

"But…they teach…we're supposed to listen to our hearts, to trust ourselves, not our abusers."

"That's true," Lila said, her expression dead serious as her gaze followed Jenna around the room. "Trusting yourself is a vital component to recovery and survival on the other side of abuse."

Jenna frowned. "But…."

Lila shrugged. "The mind plays tricks on us," Lila said. "All of us. At one time or another."

It wasn't the answer she'd been seeking. Nothing she'd ever heard in DV counseling in the past.

"So how do we know that we aren't the ones to blame?" The question tore out of Jenna with such force her throat burned.

"Because no matter what you do, you are not responsible for the actions of others," Lila returned with cold conviction. "It is illegal for someone to enact violence on another. No matter the provocation."

Jenna agreed. But….

"There are means for handling situations where others are acting out or acting inappropriately.

Even being unfaithful. There is never an excuse for violence."

"I know."

"But we aren't talking about an abuser, are we?"

"I don't know what we're talking about," Jenna admitted, completely deflated as she sank into the couch. She put her tea on the table and sat back, staring at the ceiling.

This self-doubt wasn't something she was used to. Not anymore. She'd come through all of that. Was in touch with her inner self. Knew her flaws, her issues, and took responsibility for them.

"I'm sure of something, you know?" she said to the room at large. "I know it." Steve was after her.

"But something happened today, and I reacted, certain that I knew what was going on, but I was wrong."

She'd heard a noise in the garden and she'd been certain it was Steve.

"And what it was had never even occurred to me."

She never would have imagined that someone might notice her picking weeds and come to help.

And then there'd been the incident outside Carly's bedroom window. She'd been so certain it was Steve outside that window that she'd risked her life to prevent him from hurting anyone else.

And at the house…Steve hadn't been outside the shed, hunting her down. Max and Chantel had been there. Hugging….

"You can't expect to be aware of every possibility in the world," Lila said in that reassuring tone of hers. "Anyone, all of us, can only make determinations based on our own perceptions and perspectives. Just because you were wrong about something doesn't mean you can't trust your instincts."

Yes. Right.

"What if your instincts are wrong?"

There was no movement from Lila's chair and Jenna lifted her head and glanced over. The woman was staring right at her.

"You don't always know," Lila said. "That's part of the challenge of being human," she said. "You have to remain fully alive, every minute of every day, always aware that what you see in front of you might not be there at all."

"And what you don't see could be sitting right in front of you."

"Exactly."

"So the key is to not get set in your ways."

"Maybe. And maybe there is no key. Maybe each day is meant to be lived for what it is."

"So how do you stay safe?"

"Ah, so that's the real question, is it?"

She wasn't sure. "What's the answer?"

"I don't have it."

It wasn't the response she'd been expecting.

"I was so sure that if I kept my mind on what

I knew to be true, stayed in control, mentally, I'd be fine.

"But when you try to stay in control mentally, when you stay focused only on what you know, you close the door to knowing differently."

"Yes, you do."

It all felt so hopeless. She felt so helpless.

"I think I blame myself for the fact that my family was killed in a car accident and I wasn't. I was thrown from the car and I lived."

Hearing her own words, Jenna cringed. Obviously she'd lived. She was sitting right there.

"I really believe that I was saved because I have more to do here on earth. I certainly didn't save myself. And I know there was no way I could have saved any of them. I was a kid. I wasn't to blame for the accident. I was too young to drive and had nothing to do with any of it. But…I don't know, could I still, deep inside, be blaming myself?"

"I think the fact that you're asking the question says that you are, on some level, taking some sort of responsibility for what happened. Tell me about the accident."

She was so messed up, so desperate for clarity, that for the second time that night she spoke of something that she normally kept buried in the deepest recesses of her psyche.

And as she talked, she remembered little things that she hadn't known were buried there. Like the chocolate bars.

"Anytime we took a trip, my mother would buy us each our favorite candy bar," she said, remembering her favorite. And those of her mom and dad and brother, too.

And there was the cheeseburger Chad had ordered when they stopped for lunch. He'd taken so long to finish it their folks had let him bring it in the car. She'd sat there watching him eat it, one little bite at a time, and wished that she had one, too.

"I remember my father looking in the rearview mirror, watching to make certain that we both buckled our seat belts when we got back in the car," she said slowly, back in that car, seeing her father's raised brow. "I pretended to put mine on. I made it click, but didn't fasten it. I hated the way it dug into my hip bone."

Feeling sick to her stomach, Jenna fell silent. She'd been the only one without a seat belt on.

That was why she'd been thrown from the car.

That was why she'd been separated from her family. And had to grow up alone.

"I'd say that a young girl who thought she'd lost her family because she'd disobeyed might be subconsciously driven to do whatever she was told from that point on," Lila's soft words, several silent minutes later, held possibility and no conviction, but hit her powerfully.

Was that why she'd stayed with Steve for so long?

And was still doing what he wanted? Leaving

Max and Caleb because she knew Steve would never allow her to live her happily-ever-after with them?

Could it be that she'd thought she didn't deserve a family because she'd disobeyed her father and lost the one she'd had?

Was she dreaming up this whole Steve thing then? Had the note on her car really been a mistake? Meant for another van, another person? Had there been no one following her after all? And no reason to leave her beloved husband and son?

CHAPTER TWENTY

"DR. BENNET? THERE'S a woman here to see you."

The words came over Max's intercom as he was finishing up some charting Tuesday afternoon.

"Did she say who she is or what she wants?" he asked the office assistant, Jennifer.

"She said it's personal."

It had to be about Meri.

Tripping over his bright red high-tops, he smoothed back blond hair that had grown a little shaggy and burst through the door into the waiting room.

Chantel stood there, her eyes filled with a nervous energy that reminded him of Jill.

Nodding to Jennifer, he ushered his friend back into his private office.

"I'm sorry to bother you here, Max, but you pick up Caleb on the way home and then we can't talk until after his bedtime, and I couldn't wait that long."

She glanced around, seemingly taking in the full wall of books, the leather chairs with gold braid and cherry frames and the cherry wood desk with one quick look. And then she made a slow perusal of him, up, down and back up again.

"Did you find Steve's place?" he asked. He'd been watching the clock all day, wondering if they'd get lucky.

And wasn't sure what lucky would have meant: Finding that his wife's stalker had purchased a home nearby? Or that he hadn't?

Lifting one hip onto the corner of his desk, Chantel shook her head, giving her messy blond hair a sexy windswept look. "Not for sure. But maybe.

"There's an older one-bedroom home across the street from the beach. It was purchased four years ago and is titled in the name of what appears to be a bogus company. Neither Wayne nor I could find record of it doing business anywhere. The problem is the buyer paid cash so there's not much of a paperwork trail.

"I called Diane and she's never heard of the business, either, but get this, it's the name of a dog she's certain that Steve Smith used to own. Pepper, Inc. is the name of the company. Did Meri ever mention having a dog named Pepper?"

He stood with his hands in the pockets of his cartoon scrubs, rocking back and forth in his high-top tennis shoes, and listened to his heart pound. "No."

She'd never mentioned having a pet at all.

Or wanting one, either.

"The place sits off by itself," Chantel continued,

her gaze locked on his. "No one was home, and there wasn't anything to tell us if it had been occupied recently. The outdoor trash can was empty, but he could take the trash with him when he goes. There's no city service to the place. It's on septic and a well. The yard is hard dirt, so wouldn't show footsteps. It's in decent repair. Blinds were closed. Not a lot of cobwebs or debris on the front step."

Max just didn't know what to do with any of this. He didn't need more possibilities. He needed answers. Needed to know that the man who'd spent years stalking his wife wasn't after her now.

Or needed to know that he was and stop the guy before it was too late.

"The drive was paved so we couldn't see evidence of fresh tire marks if there were any," Chantel was saying. "But we talked to a guy who lives about two blocks away. He said he wasn't sure who owned the place, but he'd seen someone there a time or two. Said he drove a white pick-up truck. Wasn't sure if it was rented or not. We showed him Smith's picture. He said it could be him but he wasn't sure. Said he was friendly, though. Waved anytime he went by."

Was he disappointed? Or relieved? At the moment Max wasn't feeling much of anything, except lonely. And frustrated.

Steve Smith had apparently been highly liked in Vegas. By a lot of people. It wasn't a stretch to think that neighbors could find him friendly.

"He did say that he'd seen a local work truck there a month or two ago. He couldn't remember which company, but he remembered thinking that maybe the owner was going to fix the place up and put it on the market. Or rent it. Says it's a shame to have it sitting there empty so much of the time. He'd been planning to stop and ask the guy if he was interested in selling it to him, but hadn't gotten around to it."

"Now what?" And why couldn't Chantel have just called him with this news? Shamed at the thought, he reminded himself that Meri's leaving him wasn't her fault.

"Now we keep checking. Wayne's going to watch the place, ask around some more. And we see what Diane comes up with in Las Vegas. We'll find this guy, Max. We just might have to be patient."

The problem was he'd run out of patience.

JENNA HAD HER speech therapy session with the little boy who stuttered on Wednesday morning. And afterward, she worked with Romar on mouth exercises, retraining the woman's muscle memory so that when she spoke she didn't automatically revert to the motions she made without conscious thought.

Then it was time to see Olivia. At yet another new house. She took the bus, as usual, and watched her back.

She just wasn't as sure anymore that she needed to be doing so.

Thirty-six hours had passed since she'd visited Lila in her suite. A day and a half to assimilate, do some soul searching, and listen to her heart. And she couldn't be certain what her instincts were telling her.

If Steve wasn't after her, if she'd left her life and the home and the man and the boy she loved because her paranoia and fear had snuck in the back door and ambushed her, then she had some very serious repairs to make.

With her husband. Her son.

And in counseling, too.

But as she rode the bus home, and thought about counseling, that didn't sound right, either. She could recite, by rote, the things she'd be told. The things she needed to do.

The things she was already doing.

No counselor could give her the clarity she needed. It had to come from within.

It just had to.

If she couldn't trust herself, she couldn't trust anyone.

And so, when the bus made a stop a block from Max's house, Jenna stood up. The few steps down the narrow rubber aisle of the bus seemed to take forever. She could hear each step she made. Counted them.

One, two, three, four and she was there. Down one step and then the next. One more and she was on the blacktop. Stepping up the curb to take two steps in the grass and then she was on the sidewalk.

She didn't trck through yards. She wasn't hiding. If there was no one chasing her, she could walk as normally as anyone else would. One foot in front of the other, enjoying the hint of coolness in the autumn air and the sun on her face. The smell of freshly cut grass.

Looking for the roses that had been planted at the house on the corner of her street, she noticed a new bloom since she'd left. A pink one. Perfect enough to be photographed. Like a work of art come to life.

And there was the fountain in the Thomases' yard. It wasn't on, but then it wouldn't be. They had it on a timer, set for four o'clock, so the fountain would be running when they got home from work.

She wondered how the Bradys' baby, Melissa, was faring. They'd been married fifteen years and she was their first child, born prematurely, but had been doing well.

And then she was…home. The house was dearly familiar to her. Standing there on the same street with all the homes it had stood amongst since the day it was built.

Her key worked the front door. And she used it there, not bothering to hide her actions.

No neighbors were about, not that she was surprised. There were many times that she and Caleb were the only ones home during the day.

The house smelled the same. Maybe a bit stale. Max wasn't big on dusting. Nor, she discovered, on cleaning the bathrooms. So she decided to do it herself. It felt odd, being there, a stranger in her own home. Like she was trespassing. She retrieved her cleaning things that were exactly where she'd left them, and scrubbed the toilet and the bathtub.

And while she was at it, she pulled out the dusting spray and disposable cloths. Might as well take care of that business, as well.

Max would have his hands full taking care of Caleb on his own. The refrigerator was stocked, but not the freezer. Almost all the meals she'd prepared ahead of time and frozen were gone.

The dishes were done, dishwasher emptied.

And the kitchen floor had been swept.

She was home. But it didn't feel like home.

She was moving about freely and didn't feel free.

Leaving the bedrooms for last, Meredith entered Caleb's first. The crib sheet had been changed. His blanket was folded and put on the end of the mattress just as she'd always done.

She picked it up and the softness clung to her hands, or maybe she clung to it. As if to a lifeline.

But in whose life?

When tears started to choke her, she kissed the blanket, and turned her back.

"I love you, my baby." Her voice broke as she left the room. And on the way to her own room across the hall—the one she'd shared with the husband she adored and missed so desperately—she caught a glimpse inside the spare bedroom.

That was when she admitted to herself that she was looking for a duffel bag. Black. With a shoulder strap.

It wasn't there.

But the bed had been slept in. The pillows weren't arranged as she arranged them.

The spread wasn't on as straight as she kept it, either.

She fixed both.

And skipped the master bedroom.

She couldn't go in there.

Because she knew, standing there in that home, that she'd left for a valid reason. She wasn't losing her mind.

Maybe things weren't exactly as she'd thought them to be. Maybe she had issues she hadn't dealt with.

But the Steve issue…the threat he posed…was real. Being in the home she'd put together, with the things she'd purchased and arranged, had quieted the confusion in her mind. Because the home she was standing in was a fantasy she'd created.

Her reality existed only inside of her.

She didn't belong where she was. She was a danger to Max and Caleb. Just as she'd known she was.

And being there was completely selfish. She had to get out, get away, and pray that Steve wouldn't punish her by taking her visit out on the two innocent Bennets.

The possibility that had occurred to her days ago, the idea that she'd always known she wasn't free to share her life with Max, that she'd made promises to him knowing that she wouldn't be able to keep them, was true.

It was the cold hard truth.

She'd wanted to believe Max when he'd told her she was suffering from paranoia. He was a doctor. Not a psychologist, mind you, but he'd had enough medical training to recognize fear-based delusion. She'd really wanted to believe that the threats were behind her. She'd wanted to do what Max had told her to do, which was to move on and be happy. To give them a chance to be a family.

But she knew Steve. He'd refused to acknowledge their divorce even after the judge had signed it into fact without him. He'd followed her to four states.

How many times had he told her she was his and he'd never let her go?

She couldn't go in the bedroom she'd shared with Max because her time there had been a farce. Based on lies.

Her lies.

To herself.

And to him.

And the only way she could right this most atrocious wrong, was to go back to Steve. She had to find a way to get him to let go of her, to somehow convince him that he wanted to let her go, or she would die trying.

She wasn't sure what her chances of success were. She might live. And she might not. But she didn't have anything to give to anyone until she rid her life of the demon.

Maybe she'd hoped, by going home that day, that she'd find out she'd been sabotaging her own life. That she'd prevented herself from being happy out of a sense of misplaced guilt.

Maybe, in the back of her heart, she'd planned a welcome home dinner for her husband that night—preceded by a phone call of course so he could prepare their son. And so she could be certain she was still welcome home.

Maybe she'd hoped that she could go back two weeks and pretend that Steve Smith didn't exist.

What she'd hoped was that the past two weeks had been a product of her mind playing games with her. She'd hoped that she could end the madness and crawl back into bed with the man she loved.

She'd let emotion take over, had tried to justify giving up on her plan by telling herself that there was no need to confront Steve. She'd given in to the weakness that would probably always plague her, the need to be cared for, to not be alone. To the temptation to lose herself in the love she shared with Max, at the possible cost of his life.

No. She could not risk being responsible for the death of another human being.

And she knew a way to prevent herself from waltzing back into her home and taking up residence again.

Quickly, so she wouldn't have time to change her mind, she reached into the bag she'd taken with her, pulled out the little metal tin, and placed it where she knew for certain that Max would find it.

And then she sneaked out the back door, and went around the shed, through the shrubbery....

And heard the bushes move behind her.

Turning, she thought she saw a branch move, but couldn't be sure. She picked up her pace, taking a different route than usual, cutting through yards she didn't know, and as she changed course, rounding a three-car garage, she saw a flash of color. Someone had just ducked behind the other side of the building.

Someone she recognized.

That was when Jenna stopped thinking and acted. Purely on instinct. Sliding in and out of places that should be too small for her to fit. Sucking in her breath, running without making a sound, climbing a half brick wall and hiding behind it until she heard footsteps go past.

She waited some more. To make certain they didn't come back. That he didn't come back.

Running, keeping an eye on her surroundings, staying one step ahead, was familiar.

She'd eluded him.

For now.

But she knew who he was. She'd seen his face. And she was done being hunted like an animal.

Soon, she was going to be stalking him.

CHAPTER TWENTY-ONE

"MAX? IT'S CHANTEL."

He knew that. He might be driving, but his phone was hooked up through a device in the car that let him speak through the stereo. And the stereo displayed the caller's ID.

"I'm in the car with Caleb," he said quickly, glancing in the rearview mirror at his son. He'd just picked up Caleb from day care and the boy had been listless. Was he coming down with something?

At the moment, he was sucking on his thumb and staring out the window. The whole thumb-sucking thing. They'd broken him of it. But sometime over the past week or so he had started doing it again.

The first time Max had noticed, Caleb had been sucking his thumb in his sleep as he lay in his crib at night.

Max had pulled his son's thumb out of his mouth that night. But he hadn't bothered to fight the habit since.

"Okay, got it. Wayne and I split up this morning, to cover more ground," she said, injecting a note of cheer in her voice, for Caleb's sake, obviously. "We didn't turn up anything and I was just getting on the highway to head back to Las Sendas…." She'd taken her bag with her that morning, planning to head home after a bit more canvasing. She was on shift at noon the next day, working three twelve-hour days in a row.

"But then Wayne called. He'd driven by the house we'd seen yesterday and…Caleb's there, right?"

"Yes." Another glance at his son and he saw the boy looking at him, not quite a frown on his face, but maybe a toddler version of one.

"Wayne was certain there was a light on inside the house," she said. "So I turned around and came back. If…well, I didn't know and…"

With an eye on the road, Max turned onto his street, and checked on his son once more. Still sucking his thumb, Caleb was back to staring out the window, his head against the side of his car seat.

He didn't look sick. Or even unhappy.

Just far too mellow for his father's comfort.

"So…is someone there? At the house?"

"It doesn't look like it. I've driven past several times. I'm just sitting down the street from the house right now. There's no sign of life."

"But Wayne thinks he saw a light?"

"He's not positive, Max."

"But he was sure enough that he called you."
Which was sure enough for Max.

"Yes. He also just checked to make certain that…
everyone he's been checking on…is okay." Meaning Meri. "Anyway, I thought I'd hang around here
a bit longer and then head your way, if you don't
mind. I'd rather make the drive back to Las Sendas in the morning."

"Of course I don't mind." He pulled into his
driveway, hitting the button to raise the automatic
garage door and pulled inside. "Have you eaten?"

"I can grab a burger."

"Nonsense. We're doing fish sticks and fruit, but
you're welcome to join us."

"What time's dinner?" She sounded as if she
was grinning.

It was four-thirty. "How about six?"

"I'll be there."

Max was certain she would be. And liked being
able to be certain. He just wished that his wife
would be there, too, to welcome his friend into
their home.

SHE'D BEEN THERE.

"Da, ca. Ca." Caleb squirmed down from Max's
grasp, and ran straight for the living room, grabbing the remote. He brought it to Max. "Ca," he
said again.

Max hardly heard him. Meri had been there.
The house smelled like it used to smell after

she'd cleaned. Like pine and flowers. Because she always sprayed floral air freshener after using the strong-smelling chemical cleansers.

The small bathroom off the living area had definitely been cleaned. He'd noticed the pink ring around the toilet that morning, but hadn't done anything about it.

It was gone.

The faucets were polished, no drops of water or any residue on them.

"Ca. Da-Da. Ca!"

Caleb had followed him into the bathroom and pulled on the edge of his Bugs Bunny scrub shirt. Standing on the toe of Max's gray high-tops, Caleb reached the remote up as high as he could get it, aiming for Max's hand.

"Ca, Da-Da."

And because he was sweating and as close to panic as he'd ever been, he walked almost zombie-like to the living room and set Caleb up with his favorite movie in the DVD player.

From there he raced through the rest of the house.

She'd been in Caleb's room. The blanket…he'd left it folded neatly in the crib. It was still there, but bunched. He picked it up, holding it to his chest with one hand while he went into the bedroom next door.

He could smell her there, too. And told himself

that she'd reclaimed the room that Chantel's presence seemed to have taken over.

The hall bathroom had been cleaned. Everything shone.

Max practically ran into their room. She'd have been in his shower, and probably scoured her garden tub, too. Cleaned their sinks and…

Throwing open the door he was only vaguely aware of the television blaring in the other room, of the music and voices associated with the movie he'd seen bits and pieces of many times over the weekend.

He didn't realize, until he felt the utter emptiness of his bedroom, that he'd been picturing Meri there on the bed, waiting for him.

She hadn't been in the room. Everything was just as he'd left it that morning. His closet door was still open. Meri hated open closet doors. The faucets in the master bath didn't shine. His towel was still wadded on the counter where he'd left it that morning. His dirty underwear hadn't made it to the hamper yet, either.

But more than the lack of Meri's touch was the stale smell. The absence of her energy.

She'd been home. But she hadn't come to their room.

Because she couldn't? Because it had been too hard for her? Because she missed him as much as he missed her and the pain was too devastating to bear?

Or maybe Smith had been with her. Wayne had seen a light on in the house by the beach.

But if her ex-husband had been with Meri, why come here?

And who would kidnap someone and then wait around while she cleaned house?

For that matter, why *had* Meri come home? And why had she stayed long enough to clean but then left again?

Leaving his room, he strode back to Caleb's. Maybe she'd left a note. Some sign for him.

And then he was back in his room. Maybe she'd been in there but only to get something. Maybe that was why she'd come home. To collect something she needed.

Which still didn't explain the cleaning.

He tore from room to room, managing to keep enough of his wits about him to check on their son on a regular basis.

Every time he looked, Caleb was sitting on the floor, the teddy bear Chantel had brought him clutched on his lap, staring at the television set.

He'd have to break that habit. Soon.

But not tonight.

Max checked the kitchen. He checked every room in the house and couldn't find anything missing.

So he checked the garage. Had she been in her car? Needed something from the glove box?

Left keys for him under the front seat—a sign that she was in trouble and needed help?

That was it! She'd come to ask for his help.

Running around the vehicle like a madman in Converse high-tops and cartoon scrubs, he banged his knee on the way to the driver's side, but didn't slow down. Grabbing the handle, he practically yanked the door off its hinges and dived for the floor. He felt everywhere. Under the driver's seat. The passenger seat. The backseats. He even checked the back hatch.

Everything was just as he'd left it when he'd pulled the van into the garage two weeks before.

Back in the house, he thought about dinner. Briefly. Checked that Caleb was still content on the floor and not asking to eat, and went back to check every room one more time.

Meri had been there. He wanted to breathe the same air. To take her breath inside him and keep her there. He needed her energy.

Hell, he needed her love.

He ran his fingers gently over the clean faucets and felt tears pushing at the backs of his eyes.

She must still love him. She wouldn't have cleaned for him if she didn't still love him.

Would she?

The knocking at the front door startled him. Feeling like an idiot, practically getting ready to cry over a bathroom faucet, he turned off the light and went to the front door.

"Am I on time?" Chantel came in, her ubiquitous duffel bag slung over her shoulder.

"Meri was here." He spoke softly so Caleb wouldn't hear him.

Chantel dropped her bag. "What? When?" Her happy expression was gone, but her frown wasn't so much displeased as focused.

"Today," he said, walking with her to the kitchen where he'd failed to get dinner started. "Sometime after I left and before I got home. She cleaned the bathrooms."

"She dusted, too," Chantel said, running her finger over the sideboard in the dining room just through the kitchen archway. "You could write your name in this thing last night."

He hadn't noticed.

"I think she wants to come home, Chantel. That's why she was here. She needed to be here. Needs us. Maybe this is all coming to an end."

She wasn't smiling. "Then why didn't she stay?"

"Because he's still out there. And she's not going to put us in danger."

"Then why not leave you a note?"

"Maybe he was with her. Or watching her. You said Wayne saw a light on at his house."

"We don't know for sure it's his house. And you really think he's going to wait patiently while she cleans your house?"

He'd had the same thought, but... "You got a better explanation?" he asked, angry, and knowing that it wasn't Chantel's fault. She'd been a godsend to him. And to Meri, too.

When this was over, they were inviting Chantel for Christmas. And Thanksgiving. And…they'd go to Las Sendas and take her out to dinner. Or introduce her to a handsome resident at the hospital or…

"I think she probably came because she needed something." Chantel's voice was soft. Caring. "She didn't have a chance to pack anything, Max. I'm guessing there was something here she wanted or needed. Maybe an important paper or something. Her passport…."

He shook his head. "She carries her passport in her purse."

"So it wasn't her passport." Chantel opened a cupboard, pulled out the spaghetti sauce. Took spaghetti off the shelf in the pantry. Got a pot out of the bottom drawer of the stove, filled it with water, and put it on to boil. "Clearly she needed something. It's also clear that she purposely came for it when she knew you and Caleb weren't going to be here."

He'd thought of that. But Meri wasn't the type of woman who would come waltzing back into their lives until she was ready to stay. Obviously she still had some things to work out. But she was coming home.

She wouldn't have let him know she was there, wouldn't have cleaned, if she wasn't coming home.

She loved him.

"Maybe she cleaned because she felt guilty for leaving you in the lurch like she did. Or maybe she didn't want her son living in filth. Maybe this was her way of letting you know you need to hire a cleaning lady."

Chantel didn't know Meri.

"Nothing is missing from this house," he said, completely calm now. He knew his wife. She was all about leaving messages in code that only the two of them would understand. He couldn't expect Chantel to get it. "I've opened every one of her drawers. Been through every room."

He'd had an hour and a half between the time he'd pulled into the driveway and Chantel had shown up.

"What about the garage? Maybe she had something hidden out there."

"I checked."

"Check again. She wouldn't have risked coming here without reason. She wouldn't have cleaned if she didn't want you to know she'd been here. And it seems to me that if she was thinking about coming home she'd have at least left a note. This almost borders on cruel, Max. Which you tell me she isn't. So she's telling you something. Go find it."

So while Caleb watched his movie about talking cars and Chantel made dinner, Max went through the house again, opening not just Meri's drawers, but all of them.

It was waiting for him in his top desk drawer.

Where he couldn't miss it the very next time he sat down at his desk.

That was something he hadn't done in a few days, but used to do daily. Back when reading the news on the internet while his wife made breakfast had seemed important.

With a feeling of dread weighing him down, he picked up the little tin in the drawer. But he didn't need to open it to know.

He checked anyway. He wasn't sure why.

And for the first time since Meri had disappeared, he started to believe that it was just as Chantel had been saying all along.

She'd left him because she wanted to.

Meri didn't want to be married to him anymore.

The missing money told him so.

She and her private, covert messages. Like keys under a car seat. She'd insisted on having predetermined ways they could communicate with each other without words, because she'd known what he hadn't. That her past wasn't just going to disappear.

She'd tried to tell him about the world in which she lived. A world where you might have to rely on coded messages, clues that no one else would understand, to communicate. A world where things were nothing like what they seemed on the surface.

He'd called her words paranoia.

She'd described a world where your husband, your protector, a decorated detective, could beat you and hound you and stalk you and you were afraid to say or do anything in case you were seen or overheard.

He'd figured her for a victim of post-traumatic stress disorder.

All along she'd known that she wasn't the least bit delusional.

He got it now.

Just as he got that he was too late.

Meri had left him because she chose to do so. Because she was afraid of what impact her past would have on Caleb. Exactly as she'd said in the note she'd left in her van.

And she wanted him to move on.

Taking their anniversary money was a message he couldn't misinterpret. Nor could he convince himself that that missing money was anything other than what it was. There couldn't possibly be a way anyone else would have known that money was there or forced her to take it.

If she'd needed money she could have accessed her bank account. Or their joint one. Or taken the emergency cash from the house. They'd had a thousand bucks stashed for "just in case." It was still there. He'd already checked.

No, she'd taken their anniversary money.

Because she didn't plan to have a distant anniversary with him.

She'd let him know she'd been there, not by anything as personal as a note, but by cleaning—a chore he could have hired someone to do.

And then she'd taken their special money and left him the empty tin. The message couldn't be any clearer.

Funny how, in that worst moment of his life, he didn't feel like crying at all.

He just felt dead.

CHAPTER TWENTY-TWO

THE LEMONADE STAND was abuzz with anticipation for Saturday's pool party. Some of the craftier residents were making decorations, some for the kids' gathering and others for the pool's christening, which was what they'd decided should be the theme for the party. A pool christening.

Jenna had suggested the theme and also put forth the idea that they use the party as a surprise baby shower for Maddie Bishop. They really wanted to surprise the developmentally delayed woman who cared so much about everyone and spread her perennial joy so freely amongst them.

Maddie's joy was as valuable to the residents as Sara's counseling and Lynn's medical skills.

Jenna attended Wednesday night's crafting and planning meeting, taking place at a building on the outskirts of the property, and threw herself into the preparations as much as the next woman.

Because she didn't want to think about anything else.

She'd said goodbye that afternoon.

To the only man she was ever going to love. The only child she was ever going to have.

To the only life she'd ever wanted.

And she *knew,* instinctively, emotionally and logically that she'd done the right thing.

MAX ATE DINNER. Then he bathed his son, playing boat and fish with him—a game Meri had conjured up with a plastic bathtub toy, soap and Caleb's fingers and toes. The boat carries the soap that then jumps out of the boat to fish for things to wash. He put Caleb to bed and rubbed his back until Caleb's breathing grew heavy, indicating that he was asleep.

He took a shower. Changed from his scrubs into sweats and a T-shirt and went back out to do dishes that had already been done.

Chantel had her laptop open on the table.

"What are you working on?" he asked, a glass of freshly poured tea in his hand. He should have offered her some.

"More record searches," she told him. "There's got to be some way to figure out who's living in that house. Electric was turned on in the name of the company, with the residence as the billing address. But that doesn't mean he has to be there to get the bill. He probably has it sent electronically."

"Or he could have it turned off for the time he isn't there."

"True. For that matter, maybe he has a generator."

"Maybe it's not his house."

"Wayne has a buddy who is helping him check out other possibilities, one by one," she said. "Since you, as a private citizen, made a complaint he thinks has merit, against someone who's being investigated for murder in another state, he's made the investigation into Steve at least pseudo-official. He's keeping it quiet."

Max nodded. Whether his marriage was over or not, he wanted the man who'd made his wife's life hell taken off the streets.

Meri wanted to be free and he wanted that for her.

"Diane called while you were in the shower," she said, looking over at him. He hadn't told her what he'd found in his desk drawer.

"She found a bartender who knew Smith and the dead woman. Said that the woman had told him she wanted to break things off with Smith because he was scaring her, but that she was afraid to tell him, afraid of what he'd do, so she was making plans to move out of state."

"And the bartender didn't come forward when she was killed?"

"He didn't know she'd been killed. It was a car accident. Not big news in Las Vegas. He just assumed he never saw her again because she'd moved as she'd said she was going to do."

"Is it enough to get her body up?" If they could prove definitively that the woman's body had been beaten to the point of trauma before she'd gotten in her car...

"Diane thinks so. She's putting in a request for a warrant first thing in the morning."

Good. Sitting at the table, Max noticed the open bottle of beer on Chantel's other side. Reaching for it, he took a sip.

"Diane said something else, Max." Her expression, while serious, held none of the pity he'd grown used to seeing there. Her blond hair framed pretty features—and a frown. "She paid a visit to one of Smith's old sources, some old guy, Victor something or other, who'd been a big-time drug dealer in his day and now lives comfortably in an active retirement community, playing golf and getting tanned. She knew that Smith and the guy had had a falling-out and wanted to know why. The guy had heard some rumors about Smith and one of Victor's girlfriends. Turned out they were false, but while he'd been watching Smith he overheard a pretty brutal fight between Smith and Meredith. He was outside their apartment and waited for Smith to leave before knocking on the door. He wouldn't tell her who he was, but he got her medical help after promising her that where he was taking her, they wouldn't call the cops. And he told her that if she ever needed anything to give him a call. He gave her a private number."

Max borrowed a second sip of beer and welcomed the burn as the liquid went down. He noticed his fingers tapping on the table and stopped them. Then started up again.

Meredith's life had been a living nightmare. And he'd blithely made assurances to her that she was fine and safe and just paranoid, promising her a happily-ever-after that he'd had no way of providing.

He'd been so self-righteous. So sure he knew better than she.

He hadn't had a clue.

And maybe she hadn't tried hard enough to explain her past to him. Except what more could she have said? She'd told him Smith was a decorated cop. That he'd stalked her from state to state....

"She used the number, Max. About a year later. She had bruises all over her arms, and that's just what he could see, but he said she moved like an eighty-year-old woman so he was pretty sure there were cracked or broken bones involved. He offered to get her medical help. She refused, said she didn't have time. She wanted a new identity. He gave her one. Said he heard from her a few more times after that. He couldn't remember if it was three or four, but that each time he'd send her new papers, no questions asked."

A burst of blood filled his mouth. He was gritting his teeth so hard he could barely part them to get words out when he asked, "Will he testify?"

"I don't think so. Even if he did, his testimony would never hold up in court. He's living on drug money. And clearly still has illegal connections. He also loses credibility because he'd accused Smith of philandering with his girl. Too much possibility of tit for tat, and not enough trustworthiness."

"So we still have nothing."

"We may not have enough yet for a conviction, but we have plenty enough to know that Steve Smith is a very bad man and that's enough to get badges working for you in two states, Max. We're going to find this guy. I promise you. And then your Meri will be free to come back to you."

He shook his head.

"What?"

"Funny, I've managed to finally convince you that Steve was behind her going, that she'd never just have left of her own accord, that she didn't want out of our marriage, that her paranoia was mostly a product of her imagination and that, first and foremost, she trusted me and would come to me before she'd ever do anything, most particularly before she'd leave me...."

She'd promised. She knew his aversion to opening up to the once-in-a-lifetime kind of love a second time. Even after he'd been lucky enough to find such a love twice in one lifetime. She'd known he'd rather die than go through losing a second wife.

"You live your love, Max. I don't think I've ever met a man as true to your marriage and commitments, as true to your heart, as you are. You give yourself to a woman and you are all hers."

Again he shook his head. "I'd convinced myself we'd had some divine connection," he said slowly, helping himself to the rest of her bottle of beer and barely noticing when she got up to get two more. The last two.

"But I'm beginning to think that it was only that—me convincing myself—and not some larger-than-life love holding us together. I needed to believe it was there so that I could believe it would hold us together no matter what, even after death. That way I'd never lose her. After Jill...I couldn't love another woman if I was going to lose her.

"My conviction was fear-based," he said now, his bare foot accidentally brushing up against Chantel's laced hiking boot under the table. Even in the summer Chantel wore jeans and hiking boots.

He'd never asked why.

"You're saying you didn't love Meredith?" she asked.

"Hell, no! Of course I loved her. Love her," he corrected himself.

"So you're doubting that she loved you."

"No, I'm realizing that love isn't always strong enough to overcome all the challenges life hands us. Meredith left me of her own accord, Chantel. You were right. She came here today for a reason. She left me...something. And now I know."

"What do you know?"

"That our love wasn't strong enough to overcome her fears. Or, I guess, mine either. I let mine bury my head in the sand rather than helping her deal with hers."

"So you don't think Steve is behind her leaving? Because I have to tell you, that's one bad dude, and I don't think any of us are going to stop hunting him at this point, whether Meredith wants to be with him, or is running from him or even has anything to do with him at all. The man is a danger and has to be taken off the streets."

"Of course Steve is behind it," Max said, needing to be completely clear on that one. He didn't want one ounce of energy taken from the hunt and was very clear on that point. He added, "Steve Smith was very clearly the impetus for Meri's deciding that it would be best for Caleb that she leave us. I'm just not certain that he's a current physical threat to her. Our marriage failed—I wasn't up to the task of being married to a woman who'd spent years being hunted like an animal."

The soft feminine fingers that covered his weren't a comfort. "Hey," Chantel said. "Don't be so hard on yourself."

"I didn't push her enough about all of the details of her past," he said. "I told myself it was because it upset her to talk about it and she'd been through counseling and knew what was best for her. I told myself I was respecting her. But the truth is I didn't push because I didn't want to know. I didn't want to have to worry. Or be afraid of losing her."

"You had every reason to believe that her past

was in the past," Chantel said, sounding like a cop now. A professional. Not someone saying what she had to say to comfort a friend. "Victims of abuse leave their situations every single day, Max, and many, many of them move on to new relationships. Healthy and happy relationships. With and without formal counseling. And, as you said, it had been quite some time since Smith had shown up. It was entirely possible that he'd moved on. Or that the restraining order had finally convinced him, a lawman, that he'd best leave her alone. They're all valid thoughts, Max. And we still have no proof that Smith is back in the picture. We only know he's a man who has committed atrocious crimes and needs to be off the streets."

All true. But....

"It takes two to allow a marriage to crumble," she added. And he nodded.

Meri had made mistakes, too. He got that. Maybe she hadn't tried hard enough to help him understand the magnitude of the horrors she had gone through. Certainly she hadn't trusted him. Or given them the chance to work through this latest crisis together before she'd just taken off.

But ultimately, the failure of his marriage rested with him. He'd refused to see the ugliness that his wife had lived with every single day. He'd wanted to pretend and he'd encouraged her to pretend, too.

"Let me ask you something." Chantel's soft voice

could have been a caress. He hadn't moved his hand from beneath hers and she didn't move it either.

He raised a brow to encourage her to continue if she really wanted to. He wasn't going to ask what she wanted. Wasn't going to encourage her that completely.

"Did you marry Meredith first and foremost because you were in love with her and didn't want to live without her, or because she was safe?"

"Safe how? I don't understand what you're getting at."

"Safe in that she didn't take risks. Her main priority was to keep your family and your home safe. Because safety, according to you, and from what I've seen here, is everything to Meredith."

He was head over heels in love with Meri. More even than he'd been with Jill, not that he'd tell that to Jill's best friend.

But was that why he'd asked her to marry him?

He wanted it to be. Wanted to be sure that he'd asked her to be his wife only because he'd loved her and not because he'd also loved her determination to always put safety first.

He just wasn't sure.

And did it matter at this point? He'd lost her.

He just couldn't believe it. Couldn't believe his marriage was over.

But then it had taken him a couple of years to believe that Jill was gone, too, and he'd seen her pool of blood in the street.

"I don't know," he finally told Chantel, pulling his hand from beneath hers to pick up his beer bottle and take a long swig.

She drank, too, watching him, and as she put her bottle down, her expression changed. Like something had come over her.

"I'm going to say something," she told him, looking him straight in the eye with a voice that was strong and sure.

He waited.

"After Jill died, I thought about calling you, about coming around, but I thought I needed to give you a chance to grieve for her. To heal and be ready to move on. I waited too long and you found Meredith and I thought I'd lost my chance. So I just want it known, right now, that when the dust settles and you get this figured out…if you end up single again, I want to be the first in line."

He didn't want to hear it. Not even a little bit.

"I don't expect you to say anything now," she continued, not faltering at his silence. "I know that this is really tacky and you couldn't possibly know, at this point, how you'll feel after you get through this, no matter who was offering. But a woman doesn't often get two chances at a dream come true and I'm not going to blow it this time."

"I have no idea what to say." She'd taken away the "absolutely no chance" option with her belief that he couldn't possibly know at this point how he would feel later on down the road.

"I'm not expecting you to say anything." With her arms folded on the table, she leaned in closer. "Except, maybe, yeah, I guess I am. I'd like you to promise me that if things don't work out for you and Meri, you'll at least give me a chance."

How did he make such a promise? He didn't think of Chantel in those terms.

Because she'd been his wife's best friend? And he was a married man?

"Would you have gone out with me if I'd been around after Jill died?"

She was giving him complete honesty. Laying her heart out on the table. So different from Meri's secret inner life. Her inner hell.

"I don't know," he said. And then, "Probably." Because it was also the truth.

"So, just this promise, Max. If you do become single again, we'll go out. At least once."

One date. It wasn't much to ask.

"How can I make that promise?" he asked. "You're helping me keep my wife safe and I'm praying with every ounce of my being that when Smith is out of the picture she'll come back to me."

"But you said tonight that you think the marriage is over."

"It might be." He didn't know. What if they did get Smith? Then Meri wouldn't have to fear for Caleb's well-being anymore.

He just knew he couldn't promise himself to another woman when he was still so in love with Meri.

"And until you know for sure, you can't think about making a promise to another woman," she said, with a small smile. A kind smile. And a knowing one. A familiar one.

"That's right."

"And that's exactly what makes you so special, Maxwell Bennet. So I just want you to know, my offer, it stays open. Indefinitely."

She said that now. But who knew what the future would bring.

Chantel was a bright, beautiful, giving woman. When the right guy came along and swept her off her feet, she'd forget she ever had a thing for a pediatrician who was besotted with the wife who'd left him.

CHAPTER TWENTY-THREE

JENNA CALLED YVONNE Thursday morning, just as she always did, to confirm the address for the day's session with Olivia. The little girl was making great progress and would probably be swallowing completely on her own very soon.

Yvonne's phone rang. And rang again.

Jenna had just finished a session with the little boy who stuttered. He knew his exercises well and, unlike a vast majority of the children she worked with, did the exercises on his own. Often. As self-directed and determined as he was, he was at a point where he could work fully on his own, or transfer to another speech pathologist without losing any ground.

Her work was coming to an end.

Yvonne's phone rang until it switched to voice mail. Jenna didn't leave a message.

She waited five minutes and called back. Waited twenty-five, in case Yvonne was on the road and not picking up, and then called a third time.

At which point she paced the secure parking lot at the Stand and called Yvonne's case worker at The Lighthouse—the shelter where she'd first met Yvonne.

Her bus stop was just through the door at one edge of the parking lot that led into the thrift shop and out onto the street. She'd heard the bus come and go twice. "I can't get Yvonne on the phone," she said as soon as the woman picked up.

"Meredith? I didn't recognize your number."

"I'm on a secure line," she said quickly. Explanations about her didn't matter at the moment. "I've been working with Olivia every day and she's making great progress and there's no way Yvonne would just not show up. I've called three times in half an hour."

"She's in the hospital." June's tone was personal, compassionate, as she delivered the news. "She took Olivia to see her paternal grandparents yesterday and Olivia's father was there. His parents said that he'd been through a program, that they'd had a long talk with him and they all wanted to turn over a new leaf. They asked her to give their son a second chance. They promised they'd do their part, check in all the time, and he said he'd do his. You know the drill. He cried...."

Jenna didn't want to hear anymore. Sick to her stomach, she asked, "What hospital did he put her in?"

June named the one across town from Max's clinic—the one he seldom visited.

"What room number?"

"391." The case worker gave a number that would not be given out at the hospital.

"Where's Olivia?"

"With her paternal grandparents." There were no maternal grandparents.

"And her father?"

"In jail. The parents pressed charges on Olivia's behalf. They weren't going to give their son the chance that Yvonne might change her mind again."

"I'll go see her."

"I'm sure she'll like that. She was worried about you but didn't have a way to contact you."

"She's conscious, then?"

"In and out. He got her pretty bad this time. Broke her shoulder. Busted her lip and one of her eyes is swollen shut."

She nodded, finished up the call, walked through the door of the shop and took the next bus out.

"Max, it's Chantel...."

Standing outside the door of exam room three on Thursday, Max listened to the voice mail that had come in while he'd been checking on a young patient with swollen tonsils.

"We've had two positive IDs for Steve Smith at establishments not far from the beach house. And a hit on a green car. It's from a few months ago. The attendant at a cash-for-your-car lot recognized a photo. He found a Notice of Transfer and Release of Liability form that's required by law for every sale, but it only required the purchaser to list a name and address. They were both bogus. He remembers a green car, but couldn't remember which one, so there's no way to trace it. Still, Wayne thinks he might still be in the area. I just wanted you to know."

Stepping into an empty exam room, he dialed her back with one push of a button.

"What about Meri?" he asked as soon as she picked up. "Has he alerted her?"

"He made a phone call. She'll be told."

"So she's safe?"

"Last reported sighting of Smith was a couple of days ago," she said. "Meredith was where she's staying this morning."

"So we can assume that, for now, she's safe."

"Correct."

He stared at his bright green tennis shoes. He was in Gumby print today. "She knew he was in town," he surmised aloud. "That's why she left."

"You thought that all along."

Yeah, but he'd also thought she'd been forced to leave. That Steve had taken her against her will. Or threatened her into going.

But she'd been back to the house. Taken their anniversary money. Very clearly of her own accord. No one else could have known about it.

"Either way, she'll know now," he said, feeling completely powerless. Meri was in danger. Probably had been through their whole marriage.

He couldn't pretend otherwise anymore.

And didn't know what to do to help her.

"Wayne alerted his captain to the situation, Max, and they're putting an extra watch out. She'll be protected as long as she stays where she is."

Okay. His muscles relaxed enough for him to draw a deep breath. "If she knows he's out there, she'll stay put," he said. That was one thing he could be sure of: Meredith always put safety first.

"I talked to my captain and got personal leave for the weekend," she said. "I told her about the case and asked for permission to come down to Santa Raquel and help Wayne for the weekend, since he's on shift and has regular duties requiring his attention. She called and made the arrangements."

A whole lot of people were taking Meri's plight seriously. The knowledge scared the hell out him.

And he was thankful, too.

"You're staying at my place," he said. It was the least he could do.

"I planned on it."

So. Good. For the next few days everyone had a job to do. Meri was keeping herself safe. Wayne, Diane and Chantel were going to get Steve. And Max....

His job was to remain calm.

"You din ha uh ca." *You didn't have to come.*

Tears filled Jenna's eyes as she sat at Yvonne's

bedside and watched her friend's distorted lips try to form words.

"Of course I had to come," she said. Lifting a hand to cover Yvonne's. Careful not to touch any other part of the woman's bruised and battered body, she said, "Now, don't talk anymore. There'll be time for that later. I just want you to know I'm here."

Because she'd been where Yvonne was, too. Not in a hospital, but in an all-too-familiar physical state. More than once.

When a tear dripped from the side of Yvonne's one open eye, she brushed it away.

"Stop that," she said, with a tender smile softening the command. "You'll get your sheet wet."

There were no words to take away the pain. Sometimes all battered women had was each other. Being with others who understood all of it as much as anyone understood any of it.

Yvonne's good eye closed and Jenna sat quietly, still touching her hand, not caring as the minutes passed, that her hand ached, or that her arm had fallen asleep. She'd cut off her arm if it would help ease the suffering of her battered sisters.

"He uhs ee." *He loves me.* Yvonne's eye didn't open, but if the injured woman had been asleep over the past half an hour, she'd reawoken.

"That doesn't give him the right to do this to you."

"I o." *I know.*

But knowing didn't always change things.

"You love him, too." Jenna tried to speak for Yvonne so she didn't have to. She'd been there. She'd loved Steve, too, in the beginning. Or thought she had. What she remembered feeling for him, even early on, didn't begin to compare with how bowled over she'd been by Max, on their very first date. Nothing would ever compare to the way she felt about him. Her connection with Max was soul deep.

And she was going to honor, with her life, her promise to love and care for and protect him.

Yvonne was crying again. Harder this time. Grabbing a tissue, Jenna dabbed at her eyes and nose when necessary. She tried to make out what words she could and just be there for the other woman.

"He egged e ot to ell." He'd begged her not to tell?

"Tell what?"

"at he it e."

"That he hit you?"

Yvonne's head moved in the affirmative. Once.

"And when you stood up to him and told him it was wrong and you weren't going to keep it quiet, he did this to you," she said, understanding.

Another affirmative half nod.

"I coun ell hi I o hi." The last word ended on a nasal sound.

"You couldn't tell him you love him?"

Yvonne blinked her good eye.

Doing what she had to do to help her friend, Jenna remembered back, put herself right in that bed with Yvonne, and said, "Because your heart is too bruised. You couldn't just open up and take him back wholeheartedly after what he'd done. Because you couldn't give him that power over you," she guessed.

Yvonne's nod was bigger this time.

"And that's why he hit you?"

A smaller nod. Accompanied by a wince. The asshole had obviously hurt his wife's neck, among other things.

"I o he ees I o." *I know he needs—love?* The nasally grunts preceded more tears. And Jenna knew how badly it was hurting Yvonne to speak. Recognized, also, that she needed to talk or she wouldn't be putting herself through the agony. Other than the top of the one hand Jenna was touching, most of Yvonne's visible skin was bandaged. It looked as if fingers on both her hands were broken. There was no other way for the woman to express thoughts that she clearly needed to get out.

So she guessed what Yvonne was trying to say. Made a wrong guess and tried again. Yvonne turned her head just an inch to the side, indicating another wrong guess. And waited.

"You know he needs your love?"

Yvonne nodded.

"Yvonne, you *are not* in any way to blame for

this." Jenna was standing now, not to tower over her friend, but to lean in closer than the chair beside the bed would allow. "Look at me," she said and waited for Yvonne to do so.

"This is me talking. I've been right where you are. Inside and out," she reminded her. And knew that Yvonne knew that she had. Which was why Yvonne was talking to her.

Counseling was good. Great. Necessary. And sometimes, it just wasn't enough.

Sometimes going where it hurt most was the only way to heal the hurt.

"Steve was the younger brother of my last foster mother." She told the woman something she'd never told anyone. Not any of the counselors. Not Max.

Because telling hadn't seemed necessary then.

Yvonne's good eye opened wider and her look focused.

Jenna swallowed. Longed for a glass of water. And said, "I was sixteen when I was placed with her. I'd been through a couple of different homes, I was withdrawn and they kept changing my home thinking that would somehow help."

At the time she'd thought they were all forgetting that she'd lost her entire family and would never be happy again.

With the clarity of passed time and some more years of life experience, she understood that no one knew what to do with her. There was absolutely no way anyone was going to be able to fix what ailed her. Or to somehow change her back into a normal girl.

And doing something was better than doing nothing.

"I met Steve at the party his sister threw for my high school graduation party. He was a beat cop then, but he'd already won a commendation for preventing a robbery and saving the old couple inside the store from being hurt. His sister had practically threatened him that if he didn't come to my party she was going to disown him," Jenna remembered aloud.

"I think she was afraid there wasn't going to be anyone there. I didn't have any friends. And obviously, no family. She'd been widowed young and had a son in college. He and his girlfriend were coming and she'd sent out invitations to other people in town, but…"

She stopped, realizing that she'd been going on about something that had nothing to do with what Yvonne needed to hear.

"Go o," Yvonne said. Her eyes told Jenna how intently she was listening.

"Steve was one of the first ones there. His place was about an hour away and he practically lived for his job, volunteering to work holidays because he didn't have a spouse or kids like most of the officers in his squad, which is why I hadn't met him before."

She wasn't getting the timing right on this, but

was telling it as it came to her. It had been so long ago. So long since she'd remembered....

"He took one look at me and I was a goner. The weird thing was, he was, too. Even weirder, he needn't have come at all. Turns out while I didn't have any friends, there was a community full of people who knew of me and came to that party to show me that I wasn't alone. To cheer me on in my success since my parents weren't able to be there to congratulate me themselves."

She paused, waiting for the choked-up feeling to pass. And then said, "I didn't know a lot of them, but the gesture meant the world to me."

A light came to Yvonne's eye. Jenna smiled at her friend and in the midst of the pain, they shared a few seconds of joy.

CHAPTER TWENTY-FOUR

"IT TURNS OUT that my foster mother and Steve were half brother and sister." Jenna was sitting now, with a cold glass of water, provided by the nurse who'd come to check on Yvonne and administer another round of meds in her IV drip. "They shared a mother, who died when Steve was little. My foster mother was already in college by then. He was brought up by his father who, as it turns out, wasn't a kind man. He didn't ever hit Steve, nothing overtly abusive, but he belittled him every chance he got. Steve wet the bed until he was ten and any time he had an accident, his dad would rub his nose in the sheet and make him wear a diaper to school. He'd take it off the second he got the chance, of course, but sometimes that wasn't until he got to school. He used to die thinking about someone finding out."

The question in Yvonne's eye had Jenna shaking her head. "No one did. But I guess as he got older, and bigger, his father would threaten to tell someone about the diapers if Steve acted out. That was his worst nightmare, the thought of other people finding out. He was so humiliated, and afraid of what people would think. Steve didn't play sports. He didn't even like to watch football. He wasn't into fast cars. His father was hugely disappointed in him and never failed to point that out to him...."

"...lane i..." *Blame him.* The nasal attached to the words gave Jenna their meaning.

"He blamed Steve for his mother's death," Jenna said and watched for Yvonne's affirmative, which came now in a blink of the eye. Her friend was growing sleepy. Probably due to the meds, but she also looked much more relaxed.

"Which wasn't fair because she died of breast cancer and that didn't have anything to do with him, but she'd breast fed Steve and his father had somehow attached everything bad to that act. Steve's lack of being man enough, and his wife's death, too."

"elau...."

"Jealous?" She waited for confirmation. "Yeah, that's what I told Steve," she said.

She tensed. She'd forgotten how much she'd cared about Steve in the beginning. Because her heart had ached for him.

"I not only found him attractive, but I admired him so much," she said out loud. "He'd come through all of that, gone to college, gotten a degree in criminal justice and was far more of a man than his father would ever be.

"We had a lot in common, too," she continued,

almost to herself as Yvonne closed her eye. "We'd both lost our mothers young and grown up feeling isolated. We had a lot of talks about how alike we were before he told me his secret. I was the only person he'd ever told. As far as I know, I still am. I think that's part of the reason he can't let me go."

Yvonne opened her eye at that.

"It wasn't until after we were married that I found out that in some ways he wasn't man enough at all. Even to himself. He was constantly having to prove his manhood. On the job. And with women...."

"I tried to understand. He was my life. And I loved his sister," she added. She'd had a family again. A mother figure. A husband.... "I finally tried to tell her what Steve was doing to me, one time after he'd beaten me unconscious. But he'd gotten to her first. Told her about one of his affairs." She wasn't even sure Yvonne could still hear her, but the words kept tumbling out. "He made it sound like the girl was the only one and that it had only been once. He'd been so upset with himself. So contrite. He told her he'd come to me immediately and begged for my forgiveness, but that he was afraid I was going to do something horrible to get back at him. I didn't know this, of course, so you can imagine how I felt when I finally worked up the courage to tell her everything and she not only didn't believe me, she accused me of trying to ruin his career and said she'd do whatever it took to protect him, which included testifying against me, including my inability to fit in socially during high school, if I ever told anyone else what I'd told her."

Yvonne opened her eye and was clearly drowsy. "Ga i ana...." *Gave him another*... She broke off, then winced as she forced out, "Ance...chan...."

"I gave him another chance," Jenna said, and when Yvonne closed her eye again she added softly, "Too many of them." She'd actually lost count of the number of times she'd given Steve another chance. Because she'd loved him. And he'd been a good man in so many ways, had helped so many people.

Yvonne's breathing deepened and Jenna watched her body struggling to gain air, to heal.

And she saw herself. Had she really stayed because she'd loved a man who'd done *that* to *her?*

Or had she stayed because she'd been afraid to face life without him? Because it meant she'd be alone in the world?

And then another thought occurred to her. Steve had known her deepest fear. He'd known how desperately afraid she'd been back then to be alone.

And he'd used the fear to keep her with him. Every time. He'd reminded her that if she left him, if she even tried to turn him in, he'd have everyone in the Las Vegas Metropolitan Police Department defending him, from the commissioner on down, and she'd have no one.

He used her fear because he'd known it would work. He'd known it was the one way to control her.

But she wasn't afraid to be alone anymore. She'd married Max because she was in love with him. And loved him enough to leave him, too.

Yvonne breathed. Her machines beeped. And Jenna knew how she was going to beat Steve at his own game.

Hearing her story out loud for the first time, the beginning part of it, she'd remembered so much. Remembered the man he was, someplace inside of the twisted, evil human being he'd become.

Steve's biggest fear was losing Meri. He, like her, feared being alone and unloved. And he needed her, in particular, because she was the only one who knew the whole truth about him. Not even his sister knew about the bedwetting. If anyone had known, Steve would have been rescued from the cruel man who'd fathered him. If anyone had known, Steve's father would have lost his power over him. So Steve's father had made sure his son was too humiliated to tell anyone.

Sitting in the safety of a hospital room filled with monitors, with medical professionals available at the push of a button, Jenna could let the thoughts just flow. The thoughts weren't a threat to her there.

Steve had told her after one of his affairs that she'd never have to worry about other women. That they meant nothing to him. That she was the only one who'd ever loved him for who he really was.

He'd seemed to think that the words would some-how heal the chasm he'd slashed in her heart. Or at least appease her.

She'd hated him that night.

He'd told her another time that he would go to any lengths to keep her with him.

When she'd lived with him he'd had his profes-sional reputation to worry about, too. That had car-ried almost as much weight as her acceptance had.

But he was no longer on the force. Which left only her....

He was a hunter. His need to look good to the outside world mattered to him. All the things she'd learned, everything she'd figured out—it was all coming together.

And she knew what she was going to do.

MAX TOOK CALEB to day care on Friday. Then he went to work. Chantel and another off-duty offi-cer were going to hang out in neighborhood estab-lishments around the beach house, and spend some time on the beach, as well. Chantel had brought her swimsuit with her and left with one of his and Meri's beach towels under her arm.

Armed with a photo of Steve Smith courtesy of the LVMPD, they were hoping for any glimpse of a man who resembled him. Diane, in the mean-time, had been granted the warrant to exhume the body of the woman Steve had been seeing who'd wrapped her car around a tree.

Unmarked cars were keeping an eye on wherever Meredith was living. Funny, he'd had no idea that she'd known anyone well enough to have another place to stay in town.

None of their friends or associates knew she was even missing. Not knowing where Meri was sleeping at night was slowly killing him.

So he worked. Picked up his son from day care. And went home.

He made dinner.

He bathed his son. Put him to bed. Was cordial to Chantel, listened as she told him that they'd had another sighting in a restaurant a short distance from the little house.

A more recent sighting.

And he tried to stay calm.

"YOU SEEM...DIFFERENT." Lila spoke softly, as she stood off to the side of the food table at the pool-party-slash-baby-shower on Saturday, replenishing snacks and drinks as necessary.

Everything was pink, in honor of the fact that Maddie had just found out she was having a girl. Lynn, a certified midwife, was going to be delivering the baby right there at The Lemonade Stand.

So they now had pink popcorn. Watermelon. Ham. Pink bread to make sandwiches. Strawberry Jell-O. And someone had even managed to sneak some food coloring into the au-gratin potatoes.

They might look kind of gross, but everyone said they tasted good.

And they were drinking pink lemonade, of course. It was The Lemonade Stand; there had to be lemonade.

"You look different, too. Must be the swim attire." Jenna came up with a response to Lila's statement. The two of them were the only two women not in the pool where all the games were going on. Right now everyone else was involved in pinning the disposable diaper on the noodle. There were eight floating six-foot-long swimming noodles in the water. The participants were blindfolded after they got in the pool, all the noodles had been dropped in the water and the women had to try to pin their diaper on the pink ribbon drawn on the pink noodle. "I don't think it's the attire," Lila said, like Jenna, watching the residents enjoying themselves. More than half the women living at The Lemonade Stand were there.

"You look good in a swimsuit," Jenna told the managing director who was technically off duty that afternoon.

"Thank you."

"You ought to take off that cover-up and get some sun on your arms and back," Jenna added.

Lila glanced at her, and the look she gave her wasn't directorish. For a second, Jenna was reminded of Renee—who was currently busy running the games portion of the afternoon's event.

"You didn't seem the least bit surprised when I told you that your ex-husband had been spotted in Santa Raquel on more than one occasion."

The managing director had told her that she'd had a visit from the police. They were doing a follow-up on their earlier visit regarding Meredith, they'd said, due to a restraining order against Meredith's first husband that was still in effect. The Santa Raquel police were extra protective of The Lemonade Stand residents and had wanted to make sure that Steve Smith had not violated his restraining order.

Jenna had asked how or why they'd known Steve was in town to begin with. Lila had wondered the same. She'd said that a friend of Max's, a cop from Las Sendas, had done some follow-up research on Max's behalf.

Chantel was still in the picture. That had been on Thursday afternoon, when Jenna had returned from visiting Yvonne in the hospital. Almost forty-eight hours ago.

Jenna knew because she was counting the hours.

She'd thanked Lila for the information, told her that she didn't need any protection and walked away.

"I wasn't surprised to hear Steve had been around," she told Lila now.

Lila had clearly already assumed as much.

"He's why you're here."

She nodded because it was the expected response.

"You're sure you don't need police intervention or protection? They tell me your ex was a police detective."

"He was, and I'm sure." The courts had done what they could—granted a restraining order. And that had done nothing at all.

Steve was smart. He knew how to keep himself out of trouble. Or knew who to contact to make certain that whatever evidence there might be against him would disappear. He was a master manipulator.

"What are your plans?"

"To figure out how to say no to him without feeling guilty." It was a lie but one that would ring true to the director of a domestic violence shelter. "And then to move on with my life."

"Has he violated the protection order?"

"No." The answer nearly choked her. It made her sick to her stomach.

But she had to do this on her own. She'd reported Steve in the past. She'd let the shelters help her. She'd even let a thug help her.

And Steve was still here.

"We can't all follow the same path, Meredith," Lila said quietly, but firmly. "We teach the same doctrine because it's the best that we've got. But it doesn't work for everyone. Not every time."

Standing there, listening to abused and battered women laughing with real joy, Jenna remembered that first night when Lila had come to her room.

She'd told her she recognized herself in Jenna. And for a second, she felt hope. Lila knew.

And she was there to help.

All Jenna had to do was confide in her.

But the second passed. And her hope died.

Because Jenna knew that the only way she was ever going to be free from the fear of being alone was to fight her demon. Alone.

ON SATURDAY, THE body of Melissa Anderson was raised from her grave. The judge had signed an order for an emergency autopsy. If a decorated former LVMPD detective was on the streets, possibly armed and dangerous, the state was obligated to take whatever measures possible to apprehend him.

Chantel had suggested taking Caleb to the beach.

"If Smith is out there, he'll see you with me and assume that you've moved on. That would put you and Caleb out of any possible danger."

Maybe. Or maybe Smith would think he was like him and having a little fun on the side. Maybe their presence on the beach would be an open invitation.

Or maybe he didn't want to go to the beach with anyone but his wife.

He spent the entire day in front of the television with his son, instead. They alternated between football and Disney movies and ate peanut butter sandwiches.

"THANK YOU SO much for my party." Maddie's thick-tongued words tripped out of her mouth with excitement a full four hours after her surprise as she stood, arms filled with presents, at the gated entrance to the pool area. Maddie and her sister-in-law, Lynn, were two of the last to leave, having insisted on helping clean up.

"You're very welcome," Jenna told the woman. "I'm just glad I've had a chance to get to know you and share in your most special time," she said.

"Well my most special time is in bed with Darin," the woman said, her expression completely serious. "We get to sleep with each other every night and I still can't believe it sometimes," she added.

Lynn smiled a knowing smile, and Jenna wished she'd gotten to know the nurse better in her time at the Stand.

"Well, I'm glad you liked the party," Jenna said.

"I did." Maddie juggled her presents and nodded her head. "I was *sooo* surprised, wasn't I, Lynn?"

"Yes, you were." The affection in Lynn's voice warmed Jenna at a time when she wasn't sure she'd ever feel warm again.

"And Darin will be *sooo* surprised, too, won't he?"

"Yep."

"But you didn't tell everyone that the party should have been for you, too."

Jenna looked to Lynn, not sure how to respond.

Didn't Maddie understand that this had been a *baby* shower?

"No, I didn't because we wanted you to have your own party," Lynn said. "You and your baby deserve a party all your own."

"Oh, so then next Saturday we can have another party for you and your baby all alone?"

The consternation on Lynn's face surprised Jenna almost as much as Maddie's comment.

"You're pregnant?" she asked.

Lynn glanced down and when she raised her head, her face was red. "Well, yes, but Grant and I weren't going to tell anyone yet. Not until I'm a little further along. We didn't know that Maddie knew."

"Darin told me," Maddie said, grinning from ear to ear. "He heard Grant whoop and holler in your bedroom and went to see why but you were talking in a funny voice and so Darin thought you might be naked and so he just listened and then he told me what he heard."

Jenna knew that Lynn and her husband lived together with his brother and Maddie—and Lynn's three-year-old daughter from her first marriage—in the big bungalow at the back of the property.

She'd wondered at the time how Lynn did it. Taking on a handicapped couple expecting a child.

But as she listened to Maddie, as she saw the warmth in Lynn's gaze, as she stood there with the

two of them she was more envious than she could
ever remember being.

This was family.

And a family of her own was all she'd ever
wanted.

It was something she was never going to have
if she didn't convince Steve Smith that he had to
let her go.

CHANTEL COOKED BREAKFAST Sunday morning. Max
awoke to the smell of bacon, climbed out of bed
alone, feeling more like himself than he had since
Meri left.

Meri was gone because she'd chosen to leave.
And as her husband who'd promised to love and
cherish, to honor and protect, he was going to see
that Steve Smith was no longer a threat to her. And
then he'd take his son and get on with his life.

The words sounded good in his head before his
feet hit the floor.

He wasn't as sure of them fifteen minutes later
when, Caleb in his arms, he walked into the kitchen
to see the sexy blonde in jeans and a braless tank
top, whisking scrambled eggs over his wife's stove.

"Diane called," she said. The words were accompanied by a look that had him doing a ninety
degree turn. Grabbing a toaster pastry from the
shelf, he sat Caleb on the living room floor, un-
wrapped the pastry, gave it to the toddler cold and

untoasted, turned on the television and was back in the kitchen in less than a minute.

"What'd she say?"

"Cause of death wasn't the car accident."

"What was it?"

"She had a brain bleed due to a severe blow to the head. She was dead before impact. And that was why she crashed. Not because of blood alcohol levels, which was what they blamed the accident on the first time around."

Forensic science at its best. And unless you were some type of celebrity, or the suspected victim of a decorated cop, there probably wouldn't be access to it.

"The coroner ruled it a homicide," Chantel said. How a woman could look so sexy making an announcement like that Max would never know.

And that was probably why he'd never been able to get as close to Jill in several years of marriage as he had with Mcri on their first date. Because, like Chantel, Jill had a certain hardness about hcr, a skin grown thick enough to shield her, the result of having to observe some of life's uglier moments.

She hadn't really needed him.

And Max needed to be needed.

"Does this mean there's a warrant out for Smith's arrest?"

"Yes."

"In Nevada only?"

"National law provides for an arrest in any state

if a perp is wanted on criminal charges. He'll have to be extradited to be tried, but that's not going to be a problem."

He couldn't believe it. The nightmare was finally going to be over.

Lightheaded, bemused and completely disoriented, Max picked up the gorgeous blonde in his kitchen and kissed her full on the lips.

After which he dropped her to her feet and wanted to die.

CHAPTER TWENTY-FIVE

JENNA LEFT The Lemonade Stand for the last time Sunday morning while Lila was off the property and her housemates and Renee were at the private, nondenominational church service held in the theater in the main building.

She signed out, so no one would think she'd been abducted. And left a note for Lila, thanking her for her hospitality and included a check for ten thousand dollars. It wouldn't go all that far at The Lemonade Stand, but it was as much as she had in her personal account. She wouldn't spend money she shared with Max without his permission.

When this was all over, she'd be dead. Or she'd have access to her joint account with Max.

There was another note for Carly and Latoya, with a personal message for each, and a third one for Renee.

She begged the older woman to have the strength to love her son with the tough love he needed. And told her that she considered her one of the only true friends she'd ever known.

As she sneaked out the gate, and slipped away,

taking only the purse she'd come in with, and the prepaid cell phone, she sent up a prayer that Yvonne would heal. And remain strong.

That Maddie would have a healthy baby.

That her young client who stuttered would overcome his speech disorder.

And that if anything bad happened to her, someone would find the diary she'd left hidden underneath her mattress—she didn't want it found too soon—and give it to Max to save for Caleb.

She'd left instructions to that effect on the first page of the diary.

If she made it through the next few days, she'd come back to The Lemonade Stand to thank everyone in person and collect the diary.

In tennis shoes, jeans and a black pullover, she walked for several miles in the morning coolness. Not hiding anymore. If Steve found her, all the better.

Ending up at the beach—not her and Max's beach, but another public beach with cliffs that jutted out into the ocean—hadn't been part of her plan, but it wasn't outside the plan either. She needed a place well away from The Lemonade Stand. Well away from Max and Caleb.

She picked a place in the sand and sat down. Pulled her cell phone out of her bra, and dialed a number she knew by heart. A private number that Steve gave out to very few people and had forwarded to whatever cell he carried.

"Meredith?" He answered on the first ring.

She'd known he would. And the familiar sound of his voice still sent cold chills down her spine and brought bile to her throat.

"Yeah, Stevie, it's me." Thanks to him she had the strength to play this through.

"I wasn't sure you got my message."

The note on her van. He'd told her to call. That was all. Nothing else. No overt threat.

But the note had been enough. She'd heard the threat inherent in it. Just as he'd known she would.

They'd been best friends. Lovers. They'd told each other all of their secrets. They'd known each other better than anyone else had ever known either of them.

And he'd betrayed her confidences. Used them against her in the most vile way possible. In the name of love, he'd taken every beautiful thing she had to give and turned it into a twisted mass of fear-based choices.

She wanted to do the same to him but was glad she couldn't. Glad that she wasn't a vile person, too, in spite of the hell he'd put her through.

"Are you still in Santa Raquel?"

"I can be. In an hour, tops. Where should I pick you up?"

She told him the name of the beach. Described her location. And then sat in the sand, watching the waves. And waited for him.

A WARRANT FOR a man's arrest was fine, but didn't do a whole lot of good if they didn't have the guy.

Max heard Chantel on the phone Sunday morning, and gathered that some kind of bulletin had gone out in both Nevada and California to alert law enforcement that an arrest warrant had been issued, that he was a former cop and a licensed private detective who would probably be armed, and to be on alert.

He was wanted for murder and was to be brought in, no questions asked.

He was considered dangerous.

Max figured he and Caleb would lie low for the day.

THE BEACH WASN'T CROWDED, but there were enough people around that Meredith blended in. Some were in suits, braving the cool temperature to swim in the water. And some, like her, were fully dressed, just enjoying the fresh ocean breeze.

Conversations floated in and out of earshot. An occasional squeal pierced the air. The waves created a white noise that might have relaxed her on another day. In another life.

Meredith took many deep breaths. Enjoying the salty tang of the ocean air. Gazing at the horizon and knowing that the possibilities were endless. Even today. Anything could happen.

And there was always someone stronger than the strongest human. Hope and faith and joy. Those weren't things man could control. Or take away. You had to give them away.

She wondered when she'd done that.

And still, the water, the endless, endless water comforted her.

She didn't hear him. But she felt his presence behind her long before he sat down and sidled up to her in the sand, his legs sliding along the outside of hers, his chest to her back, his arms around her ribs.

Did he remember breaking them?

"I feel your heart pounding, my dear, sweet Meredith." His voice was low, gravelly. And different, too.

Missing something.

"I'm excited to see you," she said, though she didn't know why. She wasn't. And his thinking so wasn't part of the plan.

"You've missed me."

"Of course." In the way you missed a deadly disease when you'd been cured. Always remembering that it had been there and fearing that it might come back.

"It took longer than I expected for you to call." He gave a squeeze to her midsection. Not so much that it hurt. But she remembered the pain. And drew breath from the part of her that knew not to feel anything.

That girl inside her who'd been born one day long ago, while she'd been standing, bleeding and

broken, but feeling nothing, at the side of the highway, desperately trying to get back inside mangled
steel.

"I had to take care of some things."

"The boy."

"He's been out of my life for weeks now."

"Two and a half to be exact."

"You've been watching me."

"Of course, my love. You knew I was."

"I saw you."

"A few times."

"You let me elude you." She understood that
now. She'd escaped Steve's clutches over the past
few weeks because he'd allowed her to.

So he could enjoy the hunt.

"I knew I had you," he said. "You've been mine
since the day I walked into my sweet sister's house
for your graduation party and saw you standing
there looking so beautiful and sexy and shy in
those black leggings and long shirt that looked
like a dress. They're back in style now, did you
know that?"

She did. But she didn't wear clothes like that
anymore. She didn't wear anything that would attract attention to that which was not available.

"I see women everywhere that remind me of
you. Sometimes, I have to admit, I help myself to
them. Just for a sip."

He'd been helping himself to women as long
as she'd known him. She just hadn't known that

about him back in the beginning. He was letting her know, now, right up front, that he wasn't going to stop seeing other women. Not even for her.

He covered her breast with one hand and she didn't push his hand away. He had to believe he was the one in control until they were someplace private. She'd known the plan wasn't going to be easy.

Or safe.

"You've always come back to me," she said now, cramming as much of her as she could into the persona she had to play.

"Just as you always come back to me, love."

"Not always, Steve." If she overplayed it too much he'd be on to her. "And I wouldn't be here now if you hadn't threatened me."

"My sweet Meredith, you do me a disservice. I don't threaten. And besides—" his head lowered until his lips were nuzzling her neck as he spoke, "—with you I don't have to threaten, do I, love? You need me just like I need you. Deep down. Where the secrets sleep but never go away."

"I don't need you, Steve." If she'd agreed, he'd get suspicious.

"You do or you wouldn't be here."

"I don't want to need you." She had to be enough of herself, enough of what he'd be expecting, to keep him calm. And she had to focus on the horizon, the waves, the same ocean that had welcomed her and Max and Caleb to her shores every Sunday.

That was her strength. The ocean. Those memories.

Her impetus and motivation for putting her life in the hands of the devil himself.

"Now that, I believe. You don't want to need me, but you do." He squeezed her breast, nipped her on the neck and pushed his groin up against her backside.

No way in hell, buddy. She'd die because of him, but she was not going to have sex with him. That was not part of her plan and was never going to be.

"Come on, let's get out of here," Steve said. "I want you all to myself. At least for now."

Meredith stood with him and when he laced his fingers through hers, she let him lead her up the beach.

She had no idea where he was taking her, but figured it didn't really matter.

As long as it was private.

CHANTEL CAME CHARGING in the front door just before noon on Sunday, her expression pinched and about as serious as he'd ever seen her. Including the day Jill was killed.

Moving Caleb from his lap to the couch beside him, he said, "Watch TV, son," and followed Chantel to the kitchen.

"What?" he asked, standing in front of her barefoot and in sweats. "Has he been arrested? Is it over?"

"Meredith is gone, Max."

He stared at the woman he'd kissed and then

run out on. He hadn't seen her again until she'd knocked on his door twenty minutes later and told him breakfast was ready.

Her actions indicated that she was willing to respect his privacy. To accept his need to pretend that nothing had happened between them. At least until Steve was caught and Meri was safe.

"She left where she'd been staying this morning. And you might as well know now, she was at a shelter for abused women."

Oh, God. Okay. Calm. Calm. Calm. "What about the unmarked cars watching the place?"

"They were watching for Steve, for someone trying to break in, not someone leaving. Or she somehow slipped by them. I don't know. At this point, we believe she was running from Smith all along...."

"Wait, who's we? And why? And how do you know she's gone? A shelter, Chantel? And you didn't tell me? Which shelter? I called the director of The Lighthouse. They hadn't heard from her."

"They wouldn't have told you at that point if they had."

"Sure they would. We all know each other. I help with the fund-raisers and..."

"And everything changes the second your wife becomes a resident," she said. She was leaning against the counter, her arms wrapped around her without a hint of softness anywhere.

"So that's where she's been all this time? At The Lighthouse?"

"No. She's been somewhere else. A unique, private place. But where she was doesn't really matter at this point. She's gone. She left notes indicating that she wasn't coming back."

"Notes?"

"For the director and some of the residents."

That was so Meri. To care for those around her. And to leave them?

"She's never run from a shelter before."

"We don't think she's running anymore."

Max needed to sit down. He was a strong man with healthy muscles. They just weren't holding him up well. He swayed a moment and found a counter with his backside, letting it bear his weight.

"The Santa Raquel police force put out a missing person's alert on her, though technically, she's still considered to have left on her own."

"The entire police force is looking for her? That's bad, isn't it? They think she's in danger. Serious danger."

"Don't you?"

He didn't want to think. He wanted to get in his car, go find his wife, bring her home and lock her inside with him and Caleb. For the rest of their lives.

"Maybe she's on her way home," he said. "Did anyone think of that? It's not like Smith could waltz in here and get her. You said police have been watching the place and if she was at a shelter there'd be security and cameras and every cop in two states is aware of an arrest warrant out for him." Why wasn't she thinking of all of these things?

"She left three hours ago. She'd have made it home by now. And if you want to know the truth, I'd been hoping, all the way here, that I'd walk in that door and find her sitting here with you two. I was going to give you hell for not calling to let me know she was home, and then enjoy your apology...."

The scenario was a good one. He wanted it.

She was telling him something else, too. She was ready to join him in welcoming Meredith back into his life if that was what he wanted. She wasn't holding him to whatever promises she might have hoped for in his kiss. "Maybe she stopped someplace. A store. To pick something up. Meri liked to plan moments, you know like themed dinners to celebrate little things. So, yeah, she's probably hard at work on some kind of homecoming thing. She'd do it up big, thinking she owed me an explanation or an apology...."

Or was it him thinking that?

Chantel's brown eyes softened for the briefest moment and his stomach started to churn in earnest. "There's more, isn't there?"

The woman in his kitchen nodded. "I just didn't want to have to consider it," she said. "A team is

processing her room now, Max, looking for anything that might help us understand what was going
on with her, where she might be and why, but we've
already got an idea."

"What?"

She watched him. And he could hear the clock
ticking down the seconds on Meri's life. "Tell me."

"An older woman…the note she left her said
something about the woman having become one
of her only true friends…her name's Renee…she
said that Meredith had been doing this research…
about the minds of abusers.…"

Chantel was struggling for words.

And Max understood that she was trying to prepare him for the fact that Meredith was probably
already dead.

CHAPTER TWENTY-SIX

STEVE WAS DRIVING an older green economy car. The same one she'd seen him in the day she'd left Max and Caleb. She couldn't make out the license plate number as they approached, and it wasn't as though it was going to matter in any case.

Either she'd succeed with her plan and the plate wouldn't matter. Or she wouldn't and wouldn't be able to tell anyone the plate number anyway.

"Where are we going?" she asked, playing her part.

"I have a house not far from here."

"You rented it, you mean?"

"No. I own it."

"You bought a house in Santa Raquel."

"Yes."

"When?" Talking helped pass the time and block out emotion.

"Four years ago."

"When I married Max."

"Just before, actually, and we're going to have to deal with that, you know," he said, sending her a sideways glance as he shifted and pulled out into traffic. As soon as they were in a steady line of traffic, Steve's hand slid from the gear shift to her knee.

Staking possession. Stating ownership. Whatever.

He might have her body. But he didn't and never would own her. That was the difference between then and now.

And why she might just pull this off.

When they stopped at a light, Meredith watched as a police car pulled up two lanes over. The officer was looking around him, but didn't glance their way. Which was fine. It wasn't as if she was going to ask for help. Or wanted it.

"So you've been living here?"

"No. I've got a place in Nevada. And one in Colorado, too, actually. I just come here when I need a Meredith fix."

When he was feeling like less than a man. And then what did he do? Spy on her?

She prayed to God that was all it was, not something involving unknown innocent women who'd be taken in by his dark good looks and lithe physique.

"So why contact me after all this time?"

"Believe it or not, because I love you."

His tone had changed and she glanced over once more, catching a glimpse of the man she'd once known in his eyes. The man who'd stolen her young heart and taught her what loving was all about.

Before he taught her what it wasn't.

"I don't understand."

"I've got enough money for us to do whatever we want to do," he said. And she wondered from whence it had come. Had wondered when he'd mentioned the home in Colorado. "You have to understand, Meredith...." His tone reminded her of long ago Steve.

She wondered if something had happened to change him. If maybe this really was just about moving on. About apologizing and letting go.

"You married a doctor. I knew I was going to have to up my ante if I was going to continue to have any hold on you...."

He was not changed enough.

"I've spent the past four years taking whatever job had the highest pay, doing some things I'd rather not have done. But I'm the best at what I do, a lot of people know that, and now I can offer you more than your doctor will ever be able to."

He couldn't. But she didn't bother trying to explain that it wasn't about the money. Or that he'd never have enough of anything else to suit her.

"So that's it? You think I'm just going to leave Max and our son and get back with you?"

She'd be flabbergasted if she hadn't done so much reading over the past couple of weeks.

"I know you will. Because you know what I will do if you don't. And you know I'll get away with it, too."

"You're pretty sure of yourself."

"You're here, aren't you?"

Not like he thought. Not at all like he thought. She had to keep reminding herself to stay one step ahead of his domineering personality.

"And you want me that way? Knowing that you had to threaten me to get me here?"

"I only have to threaten because you have your own issues, sweet Meredith. You needed the family that I wouldn't give you. I understand that now. So I'm prepared to give it to you."

"What does that mean?"

"I'm going to impregnate you," he said as though the answer was obvious. "Then your Max won't want you. You'll divorce him. And you'll have to marry me again. Because you want a family more than anything. And you can't stand to be alone."

He knew her so well.

And not well enough anymore.

A flash of Lynn Bishop's startled face when Maddie blurted out that she was pregnant sprang to her mind. Meredith would like to have told Steve that he couldn't impregnate her because she was already pregnant.

But even if she had been, she wouldn't have told him. He'd just do whatever it took to get rid of Max's baby inside of her and replace it with his own.

And if she was pregnant, she wouldn't be there. She'd have had to protect that baby. She'd probably be in another state. Another country. Still on the run.

And God knows, part of her wished she was.

As soon as Chantel left, Max called the woman he knew at The Lighthouse and arranged to bring Caleb to their day care. All of the staff knew and adored Meri and would keep Caleb safe for as long as it took to get Meri back home.

"We'll be praying for you, Max," they told him in triplicate as he dropped off his son and a diaper bag with, he hoped, anything Caleb might need, and raced out the door.

The police thought Meri had gone after Steve Smith. That she'd known he was there and that she'd gone to take him on, all by herself. That woman Meri had befriended at the shelter, Renee, certainly thought so. And Meri had confided in her more than she had in Max. Apparently she'd given Renee details about the day her family had been killed.

He'd always assumed Meri, a twelve-year-old girl at the time, hadn't remembered much from that day. He was a pediatrician. He knew how doctors took care of traumatized kids. And had imagined the normal kinds of injuries, physical and mental, that she'd probably suffered.

Never once had it occurred to him, or had she let on, that she'd been completely conscious and aware as she'd fought to get into the mangled car and save her family.

Sitting under a tree on the edge of the beach across the street from the little house that Smith owned, Max chomped on a blade of grass and tried to pretend that he was strong.

That he didn't feel like crying.

How he and Meri were going to get through this, he didn't know. They had a lot to work through. But first, he needed her safe. Home. In his bed. In his arms. Or even just…safe.

A car he didn't recognize pulled up and he sat up straighter.

"What in the hell are you doing here?" He identified Chantel's voice before he saw her get out of the passenger side of the car. Another woman, also dressed in jeans and a black leather vest was behind the wheel. He recognized the holster on her belt as a department issue.

"It's about time you showed up. Do you have any idea what he could be doing to my wife in there?" There'd been no sign of life. But that didn't mean anything. The shades were drawn.

"You shouldn't be here, Max."

"Did you get the search warrant?"

"Yes." She held up an envelope. "But Bailey and I go in without you."

"I didn't expect to go with you. But when you bring her out, I will be here."

Or they could arrest him. He stared her down.

"Fine, but you're staying over here, across the street."

He nodded, not wanting to waste another second arguing over a moot point. He'd stay put until he didn't.

Period.

"WHAT DO YOU want to name our kid?" Steve didn't seem to be in a hurry as he took side streets and then drove along the ocean, outside of Santa Raquel.

"I…Steve…you…we haven't seen each other in four years. Don't you think we should talk?"

"What's there to talk about? You had your fling to get back at me for having mine and now it's done. You pledged your life to me forever and I'm holding you to it. I already know your favorite color is purple, that you don't like squash, but love peas and that your lucky number is eight. What's there to talk about?"

She and Max never seemed to stop talking. They'd see a house and be off discussing something they liked or didn't like about it. Or drive by a family and discuss the pros and cons of their mode of transportation.

They talked about his work.

And hers.

Even hampered by having to preserve patient confidentiality privileges.

"I got my degree. I'm a speech pathologist now."
She couldn't just sit here. She'd go nuts. And ruin
her plan before she'd had a chance to fully imple-
ment it. She'd play right into his plan, get frightened
and give in, become his hunted possession again.

"So?" he said, not taking his eyes off the road.
"You won't have to work anymore. You always said
you wanted to be a stay-at-home mom and that's
just what you're going to be."

"Are you going to be working?" She was just
curious. He hadn't changed much in the four years
since she'd seen him. Still in his late thirties, he
wasn't going gray yet. Hadn't gained any weight.

Yet he looked...smaller.

Or maybe she'd just set her sights higher.

"I'll work as I please," he said easily enough.
"It's the beauty of going private. You don't answer
to anyone but yourself."

"And your clients." She was beginning to wonder what his client base looked like. There were a
lot of high-rolling hoodlums in Las Vegas. And
Steve had rubbed arms with a lot of them when
he'd been on the force.

"I take the jobs I want and leave the rest," he
said.

So maybe he *was* on the up and up. From what
she understood, when you worked for the big boys,
you did what they wanted when they wanted or you
didn't do anything for anybody ever again.

Not that she cared one way or the other.

She wasn't going to be having his baby. Or living his life.

It would be her life, or none.

That point was nonnegotiable.

Steve just didn't know it yet.

PACING THE SMALL grassy area between the beach and the road, Max had barely worked up a sweat on his first level of panic when Chantel reappeared.

Alone.

Oh, God. The blood drained from him and he braced himself.

They'd been too late. His throat closed up.

"She's not there," his friend called from the other side of the street and for a couple of seconds all Max could hear was the roaring of the waves in his ears. And then, from a distance, the faint sound of her boot heels clicking on pavement as she crossed toward him. "No one's there. But someone's been there recently, Max. There's fresh milk in the fridge."

"Do you think she's been there?"

"There's no sign that a woman's been there. And nothing that would identify the male. Just men's clothing, a disposable razor, a can of cheap shaving cream."

"Let me in there and I'll tell you if Meri's been there," he said. "I can smell her."

Animalistic, maybe. But also true.

Chantel must have believed him, or just took pity

on him, but she walked him through the house. And with a heart that felt like lead, and was thankful, too, he shook his head. "You're right, she hasn't been here."

The place was small, two rooms, plus a bath. Old wood floors that were splintered from lack of care. Cracked Formica cupboards. It seemed fitting for a detective turned private eye on the lam. But not for Meri.

Not at all for Meri.

He followed Chantel out and asked his friend, "So what now? If he didn't bring her here is it feasible to believe that he doesn't have her?"

"It's possible that he doesn't," she said. "Anything's possible." Her glance was pointed.

Meri could be dead in the woods, Max. He read the message in her eyes.

"He could be headed to Mexico with her," he said. Because it was preferable to the other vision he'd just had.

"He'll never get across the border."

Nodding, he stood, hands in the pockets of the jeans he'd thrown on before leaving the house.

The man was history. It was just a matter of time.

"So now what?" He repeated his earlier question.

"We'll have someone on this place and keep scouring the area. Mostly, we wait for him to turn up someplace. A bus station, a gas station, doesn't much matter, we've got the area covered."

And if he took Meri out of the area? The other

officer, Bailey, exited the house and climbed back into her car.

"It doesn't do any good to ask what-ifs," Chantel said gently, her face turned up to Max's. "You have to think positive and let us do our job."

"I am thinking positive. You're going to get him."

He just prayed to God Meri would be alive when they did.

"Good, now go home, and I'll call you when I hear something."

He was staying put.

"Someone needs to be at your house, Max. Meri might turn up there. She might be in trouble. Need help."

Okay, he'd go home. But he wasn't going to like it. Not one damned bit.

"Oh, and Max, when they went through Meredith's room they found a diary. It's been entered as evidence right now. A detective is reading it, to see if there are any clues there to Meredith's whereabouts. But from what I've heard, you're going to want it. She loves you, Max. She did it for you, just like you thought. She knew about Smith and she left so that he wouldn't get near you and Caleb."

Max nodded, too choked up to respond. And went to climb in his van and drive home as he'd been instructed.

CHAPTER TWENTY-SEVEN

THE HOUSE WAS...NICE. One floor, marble tile throughout, except for the bedrooms that had newish carpet, plush in a neutral tone.

The walls were soft beige with accents in appropriate places. A dark red wall in the living room alcove. One deep gold wall in the master.

There were two other bedrooms. One painted a light purple and one painted light green. Her favorite color and one of his.

Out back he'd put in a swimming pool, kidney shaped, with a Pebble Tec bottom and waterfall. There was also a built-in gas grill and kiva fireplace.

All of the things she loved.

"I told you I know you," Steve said, grinning like a kid as he followed her from room to room. "And wait until you get to the kitchen...."

He'd installed a double wall oven, glass top stove, and convection microwave. The countertops were granite and the island was big enough for a couple of bar stools.

"And look." He opened the cupboards. All of them. And she recognized everything in them.

Her pans. The dishes she'd chosen when they'd moved from the apartment to their house in a nice desert community outside of Las Vegas.

She stood there and stared. All thoughts of a plan, of abuse and life and even death...just stood still. "You kept it all."

"Of course I did!" Steve came into her peripheral vision. He opened a couple of drawers. "Here are your favorite black utensils," he said, "right next to the stove where you like them. And over here are all of the others." The drawer was twice the size of the drawer she'd had in Vegas.

He'd paid attention to the finest detail.

And knew her far better than she'd ever realized.

Or maybe she had known and hadn't been able to accept the disturbing ramifications, the fact that his intimate knowledge gave him power over her. "I did good, didn't I?" He was a little boy in a grown man's body.

"Yeah." The word was drawn out of her. "You did good."

"Now do you believe how much I love you?"

He came closer, walking that walk. The one where his hips swaggered a bit and he was going to grab her by the hips and press himself against her.

"I never doubted your love, Steve." Turning, she dug into the cupboards. Buying herself time. Doing her desperate best to keep control of her mind.

And take control of his at the same time.

The task was much harder than she'd imagined.

She wasn't even positive she'd be able to handle her own thoughts.

He was a bad man. A very bad man.

"Look, here's my baby cup!" Someone had given it to her when they'd cleaned out her folks' house. It was sterling and had her name on it.

She'd thought she'd lost it.

"And my set of Corelle." They'd quit making the pattern she'd liked best.

"I brought your clothes, too," he said. "Everything's in the closet and drawers just like you like it."

"You plan to have us live here?"

"It's where you want to be, isn't it? Since this is where you came. You love the ocean. I could tell when I saw you there all those Sundays."

Her stomach cramped again as an eerie sense of death washed over her. He'd been watching her with Max and Caleb.

For a long time.

Probably since before the baby was born. The whole time she'd been pregnant....

Oh, Max, I need you! The cry tore from her heart and reverberated through every pore in her body.

Please! Be here! Remind me that I belong to you, not him. That you are real.

But she didn't belong to him anymore.

She'd left him.

MAX PRACTICALLY BROKE the chair he'd been sitting in as he raced to grab his cell phone from the counter Sunday afternoon. Caleb was still at the shelter. They planned to keep him for the night because Max needed to be ready to leave the house on a second's notice.

"Have you found her?" he asked, as soon as he saw Chantel's number come up.

"No, Max. And it's not good news."

His chest caved. "What?"

"The house isn't Smith's, Max. The owner just got home. It's a guy from LA who got divorced a couple of years ago and comes up here to use his metal detector on the beach. The business, Pepper, Inc., was a venture he and his wife started together. They spent their weekends up here in that little house experimenting with making different foods out of peppers. Pepper jelly, etcetera. The business went under before it took off because of the divorce."

"So we have nothing?" He'd spoken louder than he'd intended. And knocked his hand against the counter. Over and over. What was he going to do? How was he going to find Meri now?

"We have an APB out for her, Max. And they're going to run his photo on the evening news. Hers, too, if you'll allow it."

He'd given a photo of Meri to Chantel, who'd given it to Wayne in the very beginning.

"Of course I'll allow it," he said. Meri needed all the help he could give her. And the evening news was an hour away. That gave him sixty minutes to call his folks and anyone else he could think of who would be traumatized to see the news on TV.

"In the meantime, we need you there, in case she shows up. Keep your phone charged. Your computer on. We don't know how she might try to contact you."

Or *if* she'd contact him. He could hear the doubt in Chantel's voice.

"And I'll be out with Bailey, canvasing every beach neighborhood we can find for any sign of a green car, or any other distinguishing characteristics. We're checking on more of the homes purchased in the last four years and have others on that task, as well. We're going to find her, Max. I promise you."

"We don't know for certain that she's with him." He had to put it out there. To remind everyone not to assume the worst. Not to write her off yet. "Meri's resourceful and damned good at keeping herself safe."

He wasn't sure if the reminder was for her or for him. But he took it to heart.

And kept it there while he made some very difficult phone calls.

MEREDITH HAD TO get Steve to talk to her. Had to take him back to the boy who'd wet his bed. She had to be methodical. Cruel.

A vision of Max came to her mind. His eyes

filled with that hint of moisture they took on whenever he was emotionally aroused. He'd be devastated by her death.

She couldn't kid herself into thinking otherwise.

And looking through the bottom cupboards of that kitchen, reconnecting with things she'd forgotten, things she'd loved, things she'd have gotten rid of given the chance, an old colander, a loaf pan that had made perfect bread, she had to be honest about something else.

This might be it. She might be reaching the end of her life. And she couldn't go lying to herself.

She'd left Max because when she'd received Steve's note, she'd known Max would go to his cop friends and put them all in danger. But she'd also secretly feared that he'd leave her. He'd been so adamant that he couldn't go through losing a second wife.

She'd had her issues. He'd had his.

A very weak part of her had feared that when he found out that Steve wasn't a thing of her past, but a very real threat in their present, he'd have lost it. Freaked out about losing her. About the dangers.

And he'd have left her.

So she'd left him first. To protect him from having to face the threat of Steve in his life. And to protect Caleb.

But in a sense, it was to protect her, too. She'd

known, as soon as she knew Steve was back, that she was going to lose Max one way or the other.

And somehow she'd known she'd never survive him leaving her. She had to be the one who left.

She hadn't expected it to be that day two and a half weeks ago after taking Caleb to day care. But she'd known she was living on borrowed time.

Subconsciously, she'd been ready.

She heard Steve behind her, going into the bathroom. Heard him relieving himself. With the door open.

He'd been a big one on spouses not closing doors between them. Ever. He'd said intimacy was important and shouldn't be given to anyone but a spouse. And at the same time, no intimacy should ever be withheld from a spouse....

Meredith hadn't agreed. Until the time he'd broken down the door that she'd locked behind herself.

She'd learned to hold her bodily functions until he was away from the house after that. Or use the spare bathroom when Steve was in the shower. Or out mowing the lawn. Or on the phone. Or asleep in his chair.

A woman living with a madman learned to be resourceful.

And the memory of that particular resourcefulness was the catalyst she needed.

When Steve came back into the room, she took his hand, led him to the table and sat down.

"Steve, we have to talk."

"THE CAR COMPANY pulled up all the files for the days that the agent who recognized Steve had worked the week he was in," Chantel told Max when she called after the story of Meredith's disappearance ran on the evening news. "In California, license plates stay with the cars, so we should be able to get a list of plates," she said. "Police are contacting all the people who bought those green vehicles. We should at least find out what name he's using through the process of elimination," she continued without letting him get a word in edgewise.

"You're getting worried," Max finally said, interrupting her.

"We need to stay positive, Max."

Sitting alone on his couch, seeing his wife's still image on the television screen, Max was beyond being even remotely capable of keeping the panic at bay. He was now one big mass of panic. Of grief and fear and anger and frustration. Of determination and hope. "Just find her," he said into the phone.

And tried to believe when Chantel's soft "I will," came back at him.

"YOU ARE NOT trying to disobey me, are you, Meredith?"

The words were new to Steve's repertoire. Meredith swallowed. Maybe the intimacy of sitting at the kitchen table hadn't been a good idea.

"Of course not," she said. "You know I know

better than that." Hearing the words, feeling them coming up from inside her, she recognized her return to playing it safe with him at the first sign that he was going to get aggressive with her. Attempting to placate him to avoid the pain.

She'd promised herself she wouldn't do that ever again.

He nodded, clearly appeased. "So what's all this nonsense about things being different from now on?"

She'd been telling him that she realized how much they needed each other. How being with Max, who hadn't known her when she was a vulnerable teenager, who didn't really know about her years in foster care, who'd grown up with two loving parents who were still alive, had been so different from being with Steve.

She hadn't mentioned how much better life had been with Max. The truth would defeat her purpose entirely.

The idea was to get him to a place where he was actually feeling their connection. Where he could feel how much *he* needed *her*.

She had to get him where he was vulnerable. Where his weaknesses hid.

She needed them in the open.

"I've grown up, Steve. And you're right. A part of me will always belong to you. Nothing is going to break that connection."

Her strength was born from the horrible things he'd done to her.

"I'm hoping that this time around we're going to be able to meet each other on more honest ground," she continued, surprised at how clear and confident she sounded. She was actually pulling this off.

"I'm hoping we'll be able to acknowledge what we need from each other. To trust each other as the only possessors of our deepest secrets."

"Did you tell your doctor that you were an outcast? Does he know how socially inept you were as a kid?" His need to point out her own fallibilities to take the spotlight off his, told her she'd hit home.

So far so good.

She'd learned about mental manipulation from the master.

The afternoon was still young enough. But the sun had gone behind some clouds, leaving the kitchen in an eerie gray light that she knew would fade to darkness as the day wore on.

Meredith gave herself over to it. Letting what would come, come.

"No, I didn't tell him any of our secrets," she said, looking Steve straight in the eye without blinking. By sheer force of will. He knew that she blinked when she lied if she had to look at the person she was lying to.

She hadn't told Max about the bedwetting. But it wouldn't have been a big deal to Max. A boy with urination issues was all in a day's work to him.

"I need things from you, Steve," she said. "And you need me. Because I know your secrets. And I love you. All of you. I've never thought any less of you because of those secrets. To the contrary, I love you more because of the way you rose above them."

She took a deep breath. Thought of Max and Caleb. And teared up. Just as she'd planned. "My heart breaks when I think of the boy you were and then I think of the man who grew out of that and I couldn't love you more," she said. "You shouldn't have had to struggle so hard to earn the respect you deserved."

He leaned forward, his elbows on his knees and took one of her hands in his, rubbing it gently. Adoringly.

"You've got a good heart, Steve."

A long time ago, she'd believed that about him.

"You're a caring, giving man who wants to right wrongs." He had been that man once, and in some ways, still was.

Head bowed, he nodded.

"It takes a very special man, a very strong man, to be sensitive," she said softly, instilling any hint of love she'd ever felt for him into her voice. "Your father didn't understand that. But I do."

He glanced up at her. "This is why you're mine, Meredith. You understand."

"I do. I always have."

Raising a hand to gently caress her face he said, "I love you so much, sweetie. And I am so, so sorry for all of the times I've hurt you. It's going to be different this time." His voice broke. A first.

And she knew it was now or never.

THE PHONES HAD started ringing as soon as the first image of Steve Smith had appeared on the news. And continued to come in when Meredith's image followed. She'd been sighted on the beach. He'd purchased a six-pack of beer the night before.

She'd been spotted on Canal Street. In another state.

He'd had fast food for breakfast.

She'd been seen at a bus station with three kids.

He'd sky dived that afternoon.

All in all, over a thousand calls came in during the first hour.

"We've got operators and police following up on every single one of the tips, Max." Chantel sounded breathless as she relayed the latest news. The sky had turned cloudy, hiding the sun. The house was growing dark, in spite of the fact that it was only midday.

As he took Chantel's call, Max turned on some lights. He'd been pacing in the near darkness without realizing it. Now he paced in soft light.

It didn't make much difference.

"Is it true that the longer she's gone the less chance we have of finding her alive?"

"Don't go there."

"The statistics about the first three hours being critical—"

"Those are for kidnapping victims, Max. This is different. Meredith left of her own accord. The cameras at The Lemonade Stand confirmed that."

He kept seeing a pool of blood on the street.

And knew that Meredith deserved better. He'd promised to be the calm in her cacophony.

"She's out there, Chantel. And she's alive. Bring her home."

Those were the words that rang true.

And he was going to keep believing them if it killed him.

CHAPTER TWENTY-EIGHT

"THERE...DOES THAT feel good?" Meredith sat on the floor at Steve's head, gently massaging his temples. She had no professional training as a masseuse, but he'd taught her, a long time ago, to know what he liked, what made him feel good and cared for.

She'd led him into the master bedroom by the hand. Had him lie down on the floor. He'd been as pliable as a child.

"You've always had trouble relaxing," she reminded him softly. "And I've always been able to help." Her voice was almost melodic, as she used every ounce of strength she had to touch the man with tenderness, to find love to transfer from her fingers to his heart.

"Mmmm." His eyelids relaxed and the muscles in his face softened. When his fingers lay flat on the carpeted floor of the bedroom, she said, "You go to other women, but you need me, Steve."

"That's right." The words were almost drugged-sounding. Drugged with drowsiness. Contentment.

For a quiet moment, Meredith worked her magic on him, as he'd taught her so long ago. And believed that she was with the real Steve Smith. The kind, sensitive boy who'd grown into a man who wanted to help people. Not the tortured child who grew into a man who had to hurt people to feel his own strength.

"That's why you always come back to me." She was merely repeating his words back to him. The ones he'd uttered in the weak moments. The ones that came in moments of contrition. When he'd been afraid he'd lost her love.

"Yesss."

Reaching down, she found the spots where his shoulders met his neck and gently pulled upward, to just behind his ears, and then ran her fingers through his hair to the top of his scalp.

"I'm sorry I ran away from you."

"It's okay, love, I wasn't the easiest guy to live with," he murmured, eyes still closed. "But I'm going to be better this time."

He believed those words. She understood that now. And knew that his own conviction was, in part, what had convinced her to believe. All those times. Which one of them had quit believing first?

Or forgotten the truth?

She had to stay calm. To do this. And somehow, from someplace deep within her, she found the ability to continue to touch him without shaking, to move forward with her plan.

She couldn't look back. Or question what she

was doing. She had to be willing to die for this, and she was.

"I won't ever run from you again, Steve," she said softly. "I promise you."

"You always kept your promises," he said, sounding more and more like a little boy.

She'd succeeded. She'd taken him back to the man he'd been. To the boy he'd been.

"And I'll keep this one, but I need something from you this time."

His eyes didn't open, but she saw the fingers lying on the floor stiffen. "You said this time would be different, and I've grown up," she told him, infusing her tone with as much goodness as she could find.

Which meant pretending she was talking to other people. Whoever flashed in her mind that would work. Olivia. Lila.

She focused on Lila. Anyone closer to her… she couldn't think of them right now. Couldn't let anything draw her away from the moment.

But Lila was there, in her mind. Not quite a mother figure, but almost. And Renee.

Steve's fingers relaxed again.

It wasn't her fault that her family had died, that Chad had died. She'd had things left to do here on earth. It hadn't been her time.

Reaching under Steve's shoulders, she scraped her knuckles on the carpet and pulled upward, from his shoulder blade to his neck and up to his scalp. Widening her range.

She didn't speak anymore. Relax, she sent the word silently. Relax. . . .

She'd lived because she'd disobeyed her father. She'd left her seat belt unbuckled.

And she'd done it because she'd listened to herself, to her own instincts. Probably to her child's inner voice. She'd trusted herself. And she'd lived.

Chills spread through her.

And she heard Lila's voice in her mind, telling her she wasn't to blame for Steve's violence. She'd chosen to marry a like soul for all the right reasons. And somewhere along the way, Steve had made some very bad choices. Choices that were prompted by bad things that had happened to him, yes, but still his choices.

Not hers.

I deserve to be happy.

The words were loud in Meredith's mind. Drowning out every other thought. Every impression, until all she saw was sunlight.

And Lila. An indefatigable spirit that floated in and out of people's lives without seemingly having one of her own. An angel with secrets she wouldn't share.

Just like Meredith had had secrets she didn't share.

"Steve?"

"Mmm-hmm?"

"I need you to do something for me."

"Sure, love, anything."

"I need you to let me go."

The muscles beneath her fingers bunched and Meredith slid back and away from the man she'd allowed to steal too many years of her life. Standing, as calm as she'd ever been, she moved as far away from him as she could get, keeping her arms behind her.

She was ready to die if it came to that.

"What on earth are you talking about?" He was sitting up, eyes open, looking confused.

"I need you to let me walk away."

It was an impossible order. She recognized that even as she issued it. And pressed forward because there was no other course.

"You promised never to leave me again."

"I promised not to run from you. I need you to let me go, instead."

"Are you crazy?" The tone in his voice warned of building anger. Of violence to come. And she stood her ground unafraid.

"You have a problem, Steve. Created by your father, but driven by something inside you. And I can't live with the constant threat of your violence." Meredith's tone faltered as the woman she'd been surfaced. The young, vulnerable woman who'd had her heart, her trust and her body broken.

On her journey to find and return the younger

Steve to the room, she'd connected to her younger self, too.

A complication she hadn't planned on.

He was standing, hands on his hips. "You know I can't do what you're asking, Meredith. And I'm not the one with the problem. Anything that happens to you, you bring on yourself."

Meredith was proud of herself. She didn't back up. Or back down. "No, Steve, your inability to control your temper or your fists is not my fault."

"You've grown a sassy mouth, Meredith." He took a step closer. She took a step back. If he got any closer it would be time. "I don't like it."

"I'm not backing down on this, Steve."

He took a step toward her. "Oh, yeah? Well, get this, little girl. You are mine. You married me for better or worse until death do us part. I am not letting you go. And there's nothing you can do about it."

She'd been prepared for this moment. And when it came, she wasn't afraid at all.

"I think there is," she said. She backed up as far as she could go. To give him as much chance as possible to think. "Because I can't live another minute on this earth with you as you are," she said. He'd used her deepest insecurities, her fears and needs, to control her. It might work the other way around. "If you let me go, I promise to keep in touch with you, to be a part of your life." She didn't know how she'd work that out. But she would. To buy her freedom.

"I've got you, Meredith. You're already part of my life. So why would I let you go?"

"Because if you don't I'm going to tell the world about your issues. I'm going to tell them how you wet the bed until you were ten. About how your father was embarrassed by you. I'm going to tell the world about your constant need to prove your manhood through affairs, and beating your wife. I'll go to the news, if I have to, you know. Decorated Vegas detective exposed. I'll write a book and publish it myself...."

As Steve's face turned beet-red, his big brown shoe came one step closer. And then another. "I'll deny every word. I'll tell the truth about you. Your lack of social skills. Your jealous threats. I've got connections, Meredith, a lot of them. You have none, because you're so antisocial. I'll drag your reputation through the dirt and no one will believe a word you say about me." The facial features that were relaxed mere moments before were twisting into a sneer she knew well.

"You know how the human race works, Steve. Once I place doubts some will believe, others will start looking for proof. And I have a feeling that if they look hard enough they'll find something. You've had a lot of people cover your ass who might not be so willing to do it anymore. Are you willing to take that chance?"

One more move forward. Her back was against the wall. "Are you?"

"I've got nothing left to lose, Steve. You do."

The menacing forward movement stopped.

"I won't live another day with the threat of you and your stalking and your violence. I can't do it anymore, Steve. Either you let me go or kill me. Because if I'm alive after today, and not free from you, I will expose every dirty secret you ever had. Any way you look at it, you lose me. But if you let me go, I'll be the friend who keeps your secrets safe."

Her words carried all of the weight of any threat he'd ever made. Because she meant every single word.

And her truth rang in that pretty bedroom with the ocean so close, the horizon filled with possibilities only yards away.

"You bitch!" With lightning fast reflexes, Steve lunged at her. He grabbed her wrist and wrenched her arm out of its socket. She could hear the cracking noise, just as she felt the sting to her hand as he broke her fingers.

"You actually think you're going to blackmail me?" he said. "You think you're going to rob me of my wife?"

She'd had to be free from the fear. And maybe she'd succeeded. Because she didn't feel afraid. Or did she?

She didn't think so.

A slap to the face, the spinning in her head, was making it hard to think. Steve's heavy leather shoe swooped in, kicked her feet out from underneath her. The carpet wasn't nearly so soft under her hip as she landed. She was going to have a bruise.

The hard leather toe in her back hurt.

One to her left shoulder, one to her ribs and she thought she was going to throw up.

Curling into a ball, Meredith thought of her mother. Couldn't picture her face. Lila's was there. She was a fetus and the other woman would nurture her.

"Get up, woman. Don't you dare think you're going to start this and not finish it."

Steve's hands pulled her up, set her on her feet, and then dug into her arms as she swayed.

Why didn't he just do it and get it done?

But she knew. He didn't want to kill her. He just wanted to hurt her so bad he'd break her spirit, and then he'd be happy again.

Nice again.

For a while.

She knew how this went.

She started to laugh. Funny, he was going to half kill her because he was enraged over the fact that she'd told him he'd have to kill her.

"What are you laughing at, bitch?" he asked. And she laughed again. She couldn't help it. Life was funny.

And she wasn't afraid.

She wasn't afraid.

"Shut up!" He slapped her mouth, and her lip split. Blood pooled in her mouth.

She was glad Caleb would never see her like this. Such a good little boy. Who was going to grow up to be a man just like his daddy. A good man. There were so many of them out there....

One more slap to the side of the head and Meredith swooned. Too dizzy to think, she just knew stars and ringing...and pain, too. A lot of it. Everywhere.

She didn't care. She was free of him.

With a rough thrust, Steve let go of her.

He always did when it got to this point. When there was no challenge left in her.

"You disgust me," he said.

"No, Steve, *you* are disgusting." How she got the words out, she didn't know. And wasn't sure he could understand them, but she didn't care. They were for her.

And for Max. And Caleb.

"Either kill me or let me go," she said. "Because I'm not playing your game anymore, Steve. I don't care what you do to me. I'm not afraid. Don't you see? You've lost your power over me."

She was standing up to him. Finally.

She'd come here to finish this. To be free of the fear.

"You're kidding, right?" His sneer was nasty.

And her head hurt so badly she was going to

puke. Meredith tried to move, to stand. She got up on all fours, and started to gag.

"You stupid bitch." Arms grabbed her midsection, dragged her the few feet to the adjoining bathroom and hung her over the toilet.

"You got to do something you do it there," he said. "And don't even think about turning this on me."

He stood in the doorway. She could see him out of the corner of her eye.

Steve never touched her face above her mouth. And she'd always known why. He needed to be able to see her life shining out from her eyes.

He'd never managed to snuff out that life. Another funny.

Something sharp touched her hand, the blade of a knife. He wrapped her fingers around the handle and then it was gone.

"You tried to kill me, Meredith. I have a knife here and when they find it, it will have only your fingerprints on it. So just remember this, my love, if you ever, ever think about disobeying me again, or turning me in, or telling any more of your ugly little lies about me, I *will* turn you in. I will tell everyone how you tried to kill me. It will be your word against mine and I know what to say and to whom and don't you doubt for one second that I will do it."

He knew the police commissioner. Had saved

his daughter. Steve had saved a lot of good people. And caught a lot of bad guys.

He risked his life without thought of cost to himself, just to make the world a better place....

Could she just go to sleep with her head on the toilet seat? For just a little while? Or did she have to puke first?

Blood cleaned up off of toilet seats.

And they weren't that expensive....

"I'm going to give you some time to think about what you've done." Steve still stood in the doorway, so tall and strong. "And when I come back, I'll expect an apology."

She always apologized. Why didn't he ever have to apologize? Well, she wasn't going to. Not until he did.

"And you can expect more punishment. You've been a very, very bad girl...."

The door closed. She heard a lock click.

He'd installed a key lock from the outside. She hadn't even noticed. Probably because it was just like the one on the bathroom at home.

No, her home wasn't in Las Vegas. And it didn't have bathroom locks. It had child safety locks....

That thought brought up the bile. And Meredith retched, splitting her ribs with burning pain every time a muscle moved.

When she was done, she wiped her mouth with the back of her hand, lay down on the cool tile floor with her head on the plush rug in front of the sink and closed her eyes.

Her day hadn't gone quite as planned. She wasn't dead and she wasn't free.

Steve was a highly skilled and trained detective. He'd won their little skirmish.

But she'd won her war.

She wasn't afraid of him anymore.

CHAPTER TWENTY-NINE

MAX HAD BEEN on the internet. And around the yard. He'd checked every baseboard in the house for nicks and made a list of those he really should putty and dab with some touch-up paint. He put the list on his desk.

And then went back and checked the walls for nicks.

Made a similar list.

Put it next to the one already on his desk.

He looked at the insides of the toilet tanks, making sure the plastic fittings were in good working order. And lay on his back underneath each sink. He wasn't a plumber, but a guy could tell if fittings were old and giving way. He could turn the shut-off valves and make certain they still worked.

He looked at the tile grout. Made a list of places that needed a little help. Put the list on his desk.

He emptied the trash.

And looked over the furniture, making a list of pieces and parts that could do with a spot of the furniture varnish he kept out in the shed.

The shed.

Meri had been in there. Presumably the same day she'd cleaned. He'd have known if she'd been home twice since she'd left.

Meri? Oh...please...Meri.

He didn't know what to ask. Didn't know what she wanted. To come home to him?

To be free?

Dropping to the floor, pen and furniture list in one of the hands linked behind his head, he did a sit-up. And then another.

He lost count somewhere in the fifties.

But he didn't stop doing sit-ups.

Nope, he wasn't going to stop sitting up.

MERI. MERI. MEERRRIII....

She heard the voice. It was an angel. A man? A woman? Just an angel. She was being called home.

Meredith wanted to go home. She was ready, wasn't she?

She couldn't have Max, not with Steve still claiming ownership of her. And Steve wasn't going to let her go. She was no longer afraid.

Not afraid to die.

Home.

Bed.

A big bed. With soft sheets.

She liked the way it looked.

So she floated some more and let herself go....

MAX WAS STILL doing sit-ups when the phone rang. Grabbing it out of the breast pocket of the purple scrub shirt he'd pulled on after getting home, he pushed the answer button without breaking his rhythm.

Down. Up. He could do it one-handed.

"We've got something, Max."

Down up. Down up.

"One of the cars...they found the only one sold that didn't match a name and address on the release forms. The company definitely has shady business practices, but they came through in the end. We have the VIN number and license plate."

Down up. Down up.

"He paid cash, with the agreement that there'd be no paperwork other than the mandatory release form, which only requires an odometer reading. Fortunately for us, the other green car sales over the past months were legitimate, so..."

"Address?" He pushed the word out as he sat up.

"It's bogus, unfortunately, but he bragged to that old buddy of his that he had a place on the beach, right? We've had someone watching months of tape of cams on the public beaches...."

Up. "You know where he is?"

"We have the vicinity. He's been caught on camera several times at The Santa Raquel public beach. But there are hundreds of homes in the area...."

"Then you need hundreds of people knocking on doors. I'm in."

Jumping up, he pulled on the jeans he'd exchanged for old sweat shorts sometime during the day. If she thought he was going to stay home when Meri needed him and there was something he could actually do....

"I know you are, hon," Chantel said, her tone laced with friendly affection. "I'm just around the corner from you. Bailey's going to stay at your place and you're coming with me."

"Okay. Good. I'm ready."

He said the words. He was tying up his purple high-tops—because purple was Meri's favorite color—as they spoke.

But he wasn't sure if he was ready.

Ready for what?

To find Meri? Bring her home?

Or to find another pool of blood?

Either way, he had to go.

MAX'S HAND SMOOTHED its way up her side, over a scar, lingering there to kiss the silken line.

"No," she murmured sleepily, wanting so much more than a simple touch from him. "It represents pain," she told him her secret. "It reminds me."

"Which scar is it, Meri?" His whisper covered the scar and it vanished.

"You are so hot," he said. "And I can't get enough...."

She knew the feeling. Oh, God she knew the feeling. Arching her back, Meredith met him, body to

*body, strength to strength, partner to partner, as
his naked body entered hers.*

She took him into her.

"And the two become one," he said.

*The words were beautiful. But it was the catch
in his voice that stole her heart....*

Oh...God...her heart....

*She hurt so much and didn't want to hurt any-
more. The elephant was back. He was big and mad.
He'd been on the table but now he was on the floor.*

And so was she.

He was going to trample her.

FOUR DIFFERENT, LARGE neighborhoods were located directly across Highway One from the Santa
Raquel beach. The two-lane highway that ran up
and down the entire coast of California was the
access point to some of the nicest homes in that
part of the state.

Max was out of Chantel's car and off up the
street before she'd pulled to a stop at the entrance
of the first neighborhood. Going door to door with
others who were searching and asking neighbors
to help with the search. He ran into her again when
she hunted him down at the end of the next street.

"Max!" She was on foot, running toward him
at full speed, like a linebacker, grabbing at him as
she reached him.

"What?" He pulled his arm out of her grasp. She
wasn't slowing him down.

"Max." She touched his arm again, getting his attention. And when he looked at her, she said, "They've got him, Max. Wayne just called. They've got him." She was panting as she spoke. Out of breath. "He walked over to a cop guarding the entrance to the neighborhood and turned himself in."

He understood every glorious word. He just couldn't believe it.

"So Meri's okay?" She'd said they had *him*. She hadn't said anything about Meri.

"We don't know." She was catching her breath. "Now listen," she said when he was about to head off up the road, continuing knocking on doors, searching yards....

"They were together," she said. "We know that much. He had some crazy story about Meredith trying to kill him, but he was crying and just kept saying he was sorry. Over and over. He had blood on his hands, Max."

The word that spewed out of his mouth wasn't one he'd ever heard growing up.

"Max...hold on. We have to stay calm," Chantel said, giving his arm another squeeze. "We have to find her, Max."

"Doesn't he know where she is?"

"He isn't saying, Max. Says that if he can't have her then he sure as hell isn't serving her up to you. He said that his life is over, and it's fitting that hers is, too. He said she wanted to die, and now she'll get her wish. She needs us, Max. But it's pretty clear we don't have much time. We've got extra patrols out. And the volunteer group that is already forming. We're going to find her."

He heard the words. All of them. But his head was roaring. Like he was at the ocean. With Meri. Just the two of them.

"We have to assume she's hurt pretty bad." Chantel didn't spare him. "There's an ambulance on the way." Whatever else Chantel had been about to say was lost as Max ran up to the next house. And the next.

He already knew the plan. Had his orders.

Knock on doors. Ask the appropriate questions and apologize for the intrusion.

Somewhere along the way, he forgot about the apology.

His wife needed a doctor. And he was one.

He just had to get to her.

"No! No! No! No!"

"Get up Meri! Get up! You are not going to die. Not going to die. Not going to die...."

"Not going to die. Not going to die...."

Meredith choked as her dry, clogged throat worked its way around the words. "Not going to die."

She heard a voice. Didn't recognize it as her own. But knew that it was. Repeating what the white figure in her dream had been telling her. "No. No. No. Get up. You are not going to die."

Trying to move, to figure out where she was, all she knew was that she had to get up. Something was telling her to get up.

She opened her eyes, and cringed as the light brought flashing pain to the top of her head. She was in a small room. Alone.

The pain was familiar. One she knew.

She had to get up.

And it all came flooding back to her. Steve. Her ultimatum. The beating.

She had to get up.

She was supposed to be free or dead.

Instead she was on the bathroom floor of the home Steve had bought for them. The home he'd been coming to for four years, spying on her and her family. Stalking her.

She had to get up.

He'd locked her in. He always locked her in. There was a window. Up high. Could she get to it?

She had to get up.

Meredith tried to move her tongue. Touched the tip of it to her lips. Her neck hurt. She tasted blood. And salt.

But didn't think she'd cried.

She had to get up.

There was moisture on her face. And her neck. Beneath her, everywhere. A pool of her own blood.

She had to get up.

And so she did.

All at once. Moving her arms and legs at the

same time, she almost vomited again as the agonizing pain took over her entire body.

She wasn't going to last long. She knew that. Wasn't going to get far.

But she could not die in a pool of her own blood.

Didn't want to die in a bathroom.

On her hands and knees she almost crumbled. Sweat poured from her body. She was so hot. Dying.

No.

She wasn't supposed to die. Had her father told her that?

With one hand she grasped for the edge of the sink. Pulled herself up and lunged for the doorknob to hold herself up on the other side while she tried to climb on the garden tub and get to the window. She could break it by putting her fist through it.

One more cut wasn't going to matter.

Her sticky, wet—was that blood—hand got to the knob. But it didn't hold her steady as she'd thought it would.

As it should have.

As she'd expected.

It moved. Turned as her weight fell against it. And the door.

They moved in unison, she and that hard wooden door.

He hadn't locked it.

MAX HAD NO idea how many people cased those four neighborhoods. Dozens. Maybe more.

He didn't slow down enough to make eye contact or exchange words with anyone. He was going to find Meri.

House after house received his thundering footsteps, his brusque knock, his hurried questions and piercing gaze, and then he was gone. Off to the next.

For every house where someone didn't answer the door, he called over an officer to investigate. And then he moved on.

I will find you, Meri. The mantra was all he knew. He remembered making the promise to her once before, in person, when she'd been having a particularly hard day.

She'd been pregnant, as he remembered it. And scared to death that Steve was close by. That he was going to come steal her away from Max.

He'd held her in his arms. Loving her for all he was worth. So certain that all they were dealing with was post-traumatic stress. A medical issue, really. Right up his alley.

He'd whispered a lot of words to her that afternoon.

She'd ask what-if and he'd have an answer.

I will find you, Meri.

He finished one street and moved to the next. And the next.

I will find you.

What he found, as he turned a corner, was a mass of people rushing down the street.

Panic consumed him. He'd seen this scene before. A street. People rushing to the scene. A pool of blood. He couldn't move. Couldn't breathe.

And then he could. He was a doctor. If anyone was in trouble he could help. Because life was about everyone helping everyone else.

He'd heard the words from his cradle, from a mother who was older than all the other mothers, and so much wiser.

A mother who'd imparted her wisdom to her baby before he'd been old enough to form the words that would let her know that he was taking it all in. Every single word.

Into his mind and his heart. Into his soul.

With more strength than any one man could possibly have, Max tore up the street and pushed through the moving crowd to the front of the pack. He had to assess the situation to know how to help.

Breaking through the front edge of rushing people, he was only a couple of yards away from their target when he saw her.

A stumbling, bruised and bleeding woman. Arms outstretched.

Calling his name.

The sky was black as night as Max paced outside the private exam room where they'd taken Meri as soon as they'd reached the hospital.

He'd done what he could for her on the ride over in the ambulance, started an IV, ordered blood, patched up the worst of her wounds, splinted fingers that were obviously broken. But he'd had no way of knowing what other bones were broken, or what internal damage had been done.

And she couldn't tell him.

The second she'd run into his arms out on the street two hours before, she'd passed out and hadn't regained consciousness.

"Her pulse was good."

Coming up behind him, Chantel offered the cup of coffee she'd gone to collect.

"That's right."

"She's young and she's got good reason to live."

He'd told her that, too. And he nodded.

"She's not going to die, Max, you know that," Chantel said now, giving him a sideways look as she joined him as he paced the hallway. To and fro. To and fro. "She got herself to you, though after seeing the scene, God knows how. But she did. She came to find you. You were calling to her. She has plenty to live for."

Chantel was a beautiful woman. And a good friend. "You do, too, Chantel. What you did for me. You're... I... *We* owe you."

"Is that an invitation to Thanksgiving dinner?" she asked him with a smile that wasn't at all sad.

"I think it was."

"Then I accept. I'm looking forward to getting to know this woman who inspired such faith in you."

He didn't know what to say to that.

"It amazes me, you know? How much you believed in her. You just knew...."

Shrugging, he said the only thing that came to his mind. "I guess that's what love does to you."

"Yeah, well, watching you...I think that I never knew what love was before. I've never felt like that...so sure...."

"Your time will come. If you let it...."

She started to say something, but didn't get a chance.

"Max?"

Turning on his heel, Max spun around. "Yeah, Ben...."

The doctor was pulling off his surgical gloves. "She's going to be fine," he said. "I wanted you to know immediately."

"She is?" There were a million medical questions he should be asking, but he couldn't think of anything but Meri's sweet smile.

"She's a very lucky woman."

He'd said those same words himself, about a child who'd been in an accident and survived in spite of the odds, one who'd come through a surgery better than expected....

"She'll be sore for a while, of course. She's got a broken rib, which I've taped, but I could see from the X-rays that it wasn't the first one or even the first time for that one. Someone said the man who did this to her is in custody."

Ben asked to be called to testify. He rattled off specific medical diagnoses for each of Meri's seventeen specific injuries. And then he said, "But there was no internal damage. I don't see how...."

He paused. And the grin on the other doctor's face seemed to be mixed with a bit of emotion, too, when he said, "We were able to save the baby, Max. She'll need extra bed rest for the rest of the first trimester. And maybe throughout the pregnancy. The placenta was damaged. But not alarmingly so...."

"B-b..." Max shook his head, foggy headed, a bit unsteady—all things he recognized as symptoms of shock. "Did you say baby?"

"You didn't know she was pregnant?"

"As far as I'm aware, Meri didn't even know. We've been trying for a second child for a while, but it was taking longer than it did with Caleb...."

He was blubbering. Just like any other husband or father. And he grinned. "Is she awake? Can I see her?"

"She's asking for you."

"Did you tell her about the baby?"

"I thought she knew. I wanted to assure her that all was well."

"What did she say?"

"I just told you, she asked for you."

"Go to her, Max. I'll see you at home later,"

Chantel said. Bailey was picking her up and Chantel was leaving her car for Max.

Chantel's and Ben's grins followed him into the rest of life.

MEREDITH DIDN'T REMEMBER much about the day she'd faced her demon and won. Not even the part before she'd been beaten.

It was all a hazy nightmare that ended when Max was there with open arms, catching her as she fell.

And she knew, over the next few days in the hospital, and then at home, with Caleb so careful and sweet as he climbed up next to her in the recliner, with Max never more than a foot away from her, that she'd finally, for the first time since she'd been a twelve-year-old kid standing on the side of the highway, completely and fully woken up from her nightmare.

"You guys ready?" she asked, standing up slowly as she slid from the van and supervised as Max unbuckled Caleb from his car seat and helped him down.

They were both dressed in black suits—Caleb an exact replica of his father—with light purple shirts, dark purple ties, and deep purple high-top tennis shoes.

"You promised you'd tell me the second you start to feel tired," Max said, one hand holding on to their son's and the other arm around her waist as they started slowly moving forward.

"The doctor said I'm fine, Max," she reminded him. "I've even been cleared to go back to work."

"Part time. And only as long as I drive you."

"Only for another week. Six weeks he said. And it's been five."

"Are you forgetting that I'm a doctor, too?"

"No." That was all she said. Because she trusted that it was all she'd have to say.

"I'm doing it again, huh?"

"Yes."

"I'll get better, Meri, I swear. I will not smother you with my overprotectiveness. It's just…when I thought I'd lost you…."

"Sshhh." Stopping in the private parking lot, she put a finger to his lips. "Don't ever, ever apologize for loving me, Max. Or for taking care of me. Because I can promise you, I'm going to spend the rest of my life protecting, loving and caring for you and Caleb, and whoever our new little one turns out to be."

"Ma…sit…." Caleb pulled at Meredith's hand.

"Mama doesn't have to sit, Caleb," she said, wishing she could bend down to him like she used to be able to. And would be able to do again. She'd pick him up and hold him on her hip. She'd carry him.

For now, she was content to change his diaper one-handed. For another week, until the cast on her hand came off.

They had to go in. Lila was expecting them. And

she hoped, Renee, too. She'd asked Lila to see if Renee was free that Sunday evening to meet Max and Caleb.

They'd just come from having a family photo done because while she'd been away for those weeks it had dawned on her that they'd never had a professional family photo taken and she'd been afraid that had been a sign that Max and Caleb weren't meant to be her family.

She'd taken care of that one. As soon as Max had asked her what she wanted to do on her first day out and about.

And bringing the two of them here, on this very special visit to The Lemonade Stand had been the second.

It wasn't often that husbands were welcome inside the shelter's walls.

But Max was a very special husband. A very special man. And Meredith wanted her friends to know that men like Max really did exist.

"Ma...ady." Ady? Caleb had so many new words that Meredith was having a hard time keeping up with them. But he was pointing. And she understood. Lila was there, standing in the open gate.

"Yes, Caleb, that is very much a true lady," she said, and with slow steps and her husband's support at her back, she moved her small family forward.

"Surprise!"

One voice, one body, jumped out at them. A very pregnant Maddie Bishop, all dressed up in a pretty blue maternity dress and matching shoes, with a bow in her blond hair.

Beyond that, Meredith didn't have time to assess everyone as they came up to the gate and a chorus of voices, more voices than she could determine or count called, "Surprise!"

She caught a glimpse of the immaculate, flower-filled grounds just beyond the gate and stopped. Pink and blue ribbons floated from trees. At least twenty tables, each with about ten chairs arranged around them were set up in rows and each one was decorated with a white tablecloth and a pink-and-blue flower arrangement. The chairs all had balloons tied to them.

Turning, she looked up at Max, and said, "You knew about this." Just as Lila bent down to Caleb, "You must be Caleb," she said. "Would you like to come with me?"

The little boy didn't answer immediately. His hesitation obvious, he looked up at his parents, who looked at each other.

Lila waited patiently for his answer, a serene, comforting look on her face.

"Go ahead, buddy," Max said.

"I'll bet Lila has some fun games for you to play, Caleb," Meredith added. "Go ahead, sweetie. Mommy and Daddy will be right here."

Caleb grinned and seemed to be strutting as he walked away with Lila.

"So, this is Max." Renee appeared in the opening of the gate then. And Maddie said, "Would you like me to help Lila with Caleb, Jenna?"

Jenna.

She felt the small touch as Max reacted to Maddie's words. "Yes, Maddie, I would love that," she said, and turned to introduce her husband to Renee—and then to Carly and Latoya. And many of the other women she'd had the pleasure of getting to know during one of the absolute worst times of her life.

It wasn't easy, living with the aftermath of domestic abuse. There were parts of Meredith that would never be what they once were. She was wiser. Less naive. Her innocence was gone.

She was aware of a depth of pain, mental, emotional and physical, that many people would never understand.

"I love you, sweetheart," Max whispered in her ear as she sat with him at the head table and listened while one after another of the residents stopped by and told her that they'd been praying for her, that it was so good to see her, and that she was an inspiration to them.

"I love you, too," she told Max. And stood up.

Lila had used a microphone earlier, and now Meredith picked it up.

"Excuse me," she said and waited until she had everyone's attention. "First off, I want to thank you...." She stopped, started to cry, got herself under control, and then continued, looking at Max,

"*We* want to thank you." His smile was warm. Tender. Imbued with an emotion she fully understood, a very private message to her that would be with her forever, in this life and beyond. And for her alone.

Someone coughed.

"Sorry," Meredith said, trying to smile, but not doing such a great job of it. What she had to say was extremely important.

"Ladies, apparently I am the guest of honor at this party because I'm having a baby…." She broke off as the yard filled with cheers and applause. "But!" She held up a hand. "But…" she said again. "I am not the heroine of anyone's story. I made a very, very serious mistake, my sisters. I almost paid with my life."

She searched the crowd. Looking for one face. Not knowing if it was out there or not.

"I was offered help," she said, still searching. "I had the chance to trust. And I didn't do it. I thought I could handle my situation on my own. I was certain I had to. Because…." She paused again. Swallowed back the tears. "Because I was so certain I'd done all of my work, that I was cured and my only problem was the fact that my abuser wouldn't leave me alone. I felt like the system had let me down. Counseling and shelters had let me down. And I was so, so wrong. I wasn't healed. I was as much a victim of Steve Smith's abuse while I was here among you, as I was during all those years he hunted me. Because he made me believe that I was all alone. He had me so deeply manipulated that I felt like I was alone when I was sleeping next to the man I love with all my heart." She looked at Max, whose expression was filled with an emotion and strength she would never forget. "I felt alone no matter where I was. Even when I was here with you all, especially when I was here with you all, I felt alone."

She broke off and searched the crowd again.

"But I wasn't alone. And one woman showed me that. Without counseling. Without knowing my story or giving me any advice, she somehow managed to show me, with the help of each and every one of you, that I wasn't alone at all.

"And when I lay on that bathroom floor... dying...." She stopped. Waited until she could speak again, and focused on the trees in the distance, the ones that lined the Garden of Renewal. "That one face was there," she continued. "And the voice. It was in my head. I can't tell you what it said. It was drowned out by my husband's," she said with complete honesty and a grin toward Max, and the entire crowd laughed through their tears. "What I'm trying to say is you aren't alone. Please, please, if I am to be any kind of example, let it be an example of what not to do. Don't ever think you have to face your abuser alone."

She glanced at Max, and snippets from every

one of the late night talks they'd shared over the past five weeks floated in and out of her mind.

"You can't have Max, he's mine," she said, pausing while everyone laughed again. "But there is always someone. Someone who's been there. Someone who understands. Who knows exactly how the pain feels, whether it be mental, emotional or physical. Find that someone, my sisters, each and every time you are struggling, anytime you feel alone, most certainly anytime you think you have to handle something on your own, find that someone. I guarantee you, she's there."

As she said the last words, a movement by the Garden caught her eye. And she saw the woman she'd been seeking. She was coming out of the Garden, but as her face turned toward her, Meredith knew that Lila had heard every word she'd said.

And knew she'd been talking about her.

"WOULD IT BE crass to say that I miss having sex with my wife?" Max half groaned the words as he lay next to Meredith in their bed that Sunday night. He was admittedly a little full of himself.

He had the most amazing wife in the world. He'd arranged that evening to volunteer at The Lemonade Stand, and to be a part of a growing list of financial donors to the facility, as well. He'd married a victim of domestic violence. The truth wasn't going to go away.

And while Steve Smith was being held without

bail on charges of kidnapping, abuse and first degree murder, he knew that there was a chance the man would be free again someday. He also knew that nothing that could happen on earth was going to take Meredith out of his heart or away from him.

"It wouldn't be crass," she said. And then, when he did no more than nudge his nose against her neck, said, "So are you saying it?"

Was there doubt in that voice? He reared up, looking down at her perfect features in the glow of the night-light plugged into the wall. "You're kidding, right?"

She wasn't kidding.

"Hell, Meri, it's about killing me not to make love to you. I wake up with a hard-on at least twice a night…." He probably hadn't needed to be that crude, but if she thought…

"I… You haven't even French kissed me once since…"

Up on one elbow now, he smoothed the hair away from her forehead, careful not to touch the soft spot on her skull where her ex had hit her. "You're recovering from a very brutal beating, Meredith," he said in his best doctor's voice. "And your mouth needed time to heal."

"It's been healed for weeks."

The doctor voice wasn't doing it. "I didn't want to…"

"You don't have to be afraid of me, Max." Her soft words fell into the night air. "I won't break."

"You were…" He couldn't repeat what that bastard had done to her. "By a man you trusted. I can understand completely that having a man touch you might be traumatic."

"Max Bennet, are you trying to think for me again?"

Shit. "Maybe."

"Well, don't. And for your information, you want to know what I was doing on that bathroom floor after Steve beat the living crap out of me?"

He knew. She'd been bleeding to death. He got sick to his stomach every time he thought about it.

But he did think about it. Because he wasn't ever going to make light of anything in their lives. His head was out of the sand and it was staying that way.

"I was dreaming about this," she said, grabbing a hold of his penis and holding on.

He shifted, growing hard in her grasp, afraid he was going to explode in her hand. "You were inside me," she said, "and doing this…."

Her hand moved up and down along the entire length of him. Yep, he was definitely going to explode.

"You said, 'and two become one,'" she told him.

"I said that on our wedding night."

"I know."

Was she trying to drive him crazy? If so, she was succeeding.

He moved against her hand, beyond caring if he embarrassed himself all over her.

"Your words were there, Max," she said, licking his nipple as she continued to ride him with her unbroken hand. "In my head and in my heart. You…." She squeezed his shaft and he was right there. "This."

And then she kissed him, full on the lips, tongue to tongue, before lowering her mouth to kiss the head of his penis.

Max could have died a thousand deaths that night, but he didn't. He was too busy finding inventive ways to make love with his wife that didn't hurt her or their baby.

Because Max was going to spend the rest of his life making certain that his wife, Meredith Jenna Bennet, as he now thought of her, was never going to know pain from a man's hand again.

* * * * *

LARGER-PRINT BOOKS!

HARLEQUIN *Presents*

PASSION GUARANTEED SEDUCTION

GET 2 FREE LARGER-PRINT NOVELS PLUS 2 FREE GIFTS!

YES! Please send me 2 FREE LARGER-PRINT Harlequin Presents® novels and my 2 FREE gifts (gifts are worth about $10). After receiving them, if I don't wish to receive any more books, I can return the shipping statement marked "cancel." If I don't cancel, I will receive 6 brand-new novels every month and be billed just $5.05 per book in the U.S. or $5.49 per book in Canada. That's a saving of at least 16% off the cover price! It's quite a bargain! Shipping and handling is just 50¢ per book in the U.S. and 75¢ per book in Canada.* I understand that accepting the 2 free books and gifts places me under no obligation to buy anything. I can always return a shipment and cancel at any time. Even if I never buy another book, the two free books and gifts are mine to keep forever.

176/376 HDN F43N

Name	(PLEASE PRINT)	
Address		Apt. #
City	State/Prov.	Zip/Postal Code

Signature (if under 18, a parent or guardian must sign)

Mail to the **Harlequin® Reader Service:**
IN U.S.A.: P.O. Box 1867, Buffalo, NY 14240-1867
IN CANADA: P.O. Box 609, Fort Erie, Ontario L2A 5X3

**Are you a subscriber to Harlequin Presents books
and want to receive the larger-print edition?
Call 1-800-873-8635 today or visit us at www.ReaderService.com.**

* Terms and prices subject to change without notice. Prices do not include applicable taxes. Sales tax applicable in N.Y. Canadian residents will be charged applicable taxes. Offer not valid in Québec. This offer is limited to one order per household. Not valid for current subscribers to Harlequin Presents Larger-Print books. All orders subject to credit approval. Credit or debit balances in a customer's account(s) may be offset by any other outstanding balance owed by or to the customer. Please allow 4 to 6 weeks for delivery. Offer available while quantities last.

Your Privacy—The Harlequin® Reader Service is committed to protecting your privacy. Our Privacy Policy is available online at www.ReaderService.com or upon request from the Harlequin Reader Service.

We make a portion of our mailing list available to reputable third parties that offer products we believe may interest you. If you prefer that we not exchange your name with third parties, or if you wish to clarify or modify your communication preferences, please visit us at www.ReaderService.com/consumerschoice or write to us at Harlequin Reader Service Preference Service, P.O. Box 9062, Buffalo, NY 14269. Include your complete name and address.

HPLP13R

LARGER-PRINT BOOKS!

GET 2 FREE LARGER-PRINT NOVELS PLUS
2 FREE GIFTS!

⬧ **HARLEQUIN**®

Romance

From the Heart, For the Heart

YES! Please send me 2 FREE LARGER-PRINT Harlequin® Romance novels and my 2 FREE gifts (gifts are worth about $10). After receiving them, if I don't wish to receive any more books, I can return the shipping statement marked "cancel." If I don't cancel, I will receive 4 brand-new novels every month and be billed just $4.84 per book in the U.S. or $5.24 per book in Canada. That's a savings of at least 19% off the cover price! It's quite a bargain! Shipping and handling is just 50¢ per book in the U.S. and 75¢ per book in Canada.* I understand that accepting the 2 free books and gifts places me under no obligation to buy anything. I can always return a shipment and cancel at any time. Even if I never buy another book, the two free books and gifts are mine to keep forever.

119/319 HDN F43Y

Name _____ (PLEASE PRINT) _____

Address _____ Apt. # _____

City _____ State/Prov. _____ Zip/Postal Code _____

Signature (if under 18, a parent or guardian must sign)

Mail to the **Harlequin® Reader Service:**
IN U.S.A.: P.O. Box 1867, Buffalo, NY 14240-1867
IN CANADA: P.O. Box 609, Fort Erie, Ontario L2A 5X3
Want to try two free books from another line?
Call 1-800-873-8635 or visit www.ReaderService.com.

* Terms and prices subject to change without notice. Prices do not include applicable taxes. Sales tax applicable in N.Y. Canadian residents will be charged applicable taxes. Offer not valid in Quebec. This offer is limited to one order per household. Not valid for current subscribers to Harlequin Romance Larger-Print books. All orders subject to credit approval. Credit or debit balances in a customer's account(s) may be offset by any other outstanding balance owed by or to the customer. Please allow 4 to 6 weeks for delivery. Offer available while quantities last.

Your Privacy—The Harlequin® Reader Service is committed to protecting your privacy. Our Privacy Policy is available online at www.ReaderService.com or upon request from the Harlequin Reader Service.

We make a portion of our mailing list available to reputable third parties that offer products we believe may interest you. If you prefer that we not exchange your name with third parties, or if you wish to clarify or modify your communication preferences, please visit us at www.ReaderService.com/consumerchoice or write to us at Harlequin Reader Service Preference Service, P.O. Box 9062, Buffalo, NY 14269. Include your complete name and address.

HRLP13R